Blind Faith

Sagarika Ghose

HARPER  PERENNIAL

NEW YORK • LONDON • TORONTO • SYDNEY • NEW DELHI • AUCKLAND

HARPER ● PERENNIAL

Originally published in India in 2006 by HarperCollins Publishers India in a joint venture with The India Today Group

HarperCollins books may be purchased for educational, business, or sales promotional use. For information please write: Special Markets Department, HarperCollins Publishers, 10 East 53rd Street, New York, NY 10022.

First U.S. Edition

Library of Congress Cataloging-in-Publication Data is available upon request.

ISBN: 978-0-06-135026-9

08 09 10 11 12   ID/RRD   10 9 8 7 6 5 4 3 2 1

Blind Faith

For IS and TS
And all those willing to make a leap of faith

1

January 2001

ALQUERIA, GOA

When the plane from Delhi to Goa exploded in mid-air and plummeted into the Arabian Sea, the sky wavered momentarily like a computer screen ribbed by static.

Below the falling airliner, the sea curved into a bay. Smooth ocean's forehead against a springy hairline of palm. The waters of the bay were calm, ploughed occasionally by barges carrying manganese ore to big ships parked on the horizon. When the plane plunged in, the bay became a painting in which the colours had dissolved.

At this very time, a fire raged on the seashore. In the seaside village of Alqueria, Sharkey's Hotel burnt as strongly as the aircraft had before it hit the water. Fire engines along the beach sent blue flashes into the coconut trees. A lone figure sat upright on the beach, tense with accomplishment. Villagers gathered at the seafront, staring at the sky, at Sharkey's, at the shards of plane sticking out from the water.

We are constantly reminded, noted Father Rudy, priest of the Church of Santa Ana, that even after centuries of evolution, the human remains as wild as any animal.

Alqueria. Tiny fishing village in north Goa.

That night Alqueria was surrounded by fire. In the water, a burning plane. On land, a beach hotel in flames.

The papers carried the news next morning:

South Wind Airways flight SW 448 from Delhi to Goa, crashed into the Alqueria bay in north Goa last night. There are no reported survivors and navy divers are continuing their search for bodies. The black box has been found. Eyewitnesses say they heard a thunderclap and an explosion that looked like a fireworks display.

The international conspirators who claimed responsibility for the bomb were the outer splinter of a cell gearing up to collaborate with more complicated international organizers elsewhere in the world. This explosion was only a small local rehearsal. A case study. A test of patterns of airport and aircraft infiltration.

The year was 2001 and it was January.

Eight months later, other aircrafts would cut through tall buildings on the opposite side of the world to herald a new century.

But in Goa the bombers had unknowingly interfered in another plan.

A plan that went unreported in the newspapers.

2

January 2000

LONDON

Mia saw him for the first time in London and at once realized the truth of the phrase, 'not being able to believe one's eyes'. He reminded her eerily of her father's painting. He was a replica. A colour facsimile. A 3D projection of the man from the painting. A painting that had hung in her room for as long as she could remember. She frowned and looked again. Yes, unmistakably him. The man from the painting had leapt out of the canvas and walked into her life and the impossible had occurred as easily and as ordinarily as taking a train to work.

She stared around and upwards. Boundless city, once on the frontlines of the Luftwaffe, now swarming with nations, religions, sexualities. And miracles. Yet for her the city had become remote. She felt excluded from it, as if the drunks sleeping in hotel doorways along the Strand were trying to trip her up as she passed. Bankers, lunchtime joggers, newly arrived Serbs, blues guitarists and students from the Czech Republic shouldered past. She felt far removed, sitting alone on a high wall from which she couldn't climb down. She was at once over-excited and bored, liable to burst into tears even at advertising jingles, sometimes wanting to fade out from the world, other times wanting to courageously lead it.

'A rapidly alternating state of sorrow and elation is often believed to be one of the first symptoms of hyperactive psychosis.' *The Drama of Depression* by T. Rosenthal and M.O. Silver, M.D., a book she had been reading on the advice of a colleague.

She had recently moved back into her parents' nineteenth century, white, stucco-fronted flat in Belsize Park from her own apartment in Putney. She worked for a satellite television channel called SkyVision where the purple and pink studio sofas reminded her how unhappy reunited families could be.

She tried to find the sun but it was only a vague outline through the clouds. Every evening she watched the faces on the Northern Line and wondered why everyone wasn't protesting aloud that the sun should be more responsive to consumer demand; that by not providing adequate amounts of sunshine it was artificially driving up its own price.

Her parents' apartment looked out onto a cherry tree and it was only a five-minute walk to the Eagle And Flag. After her father's recent suicide, damp faces had begun to grimace through the wallpaper. His ghost lived on in the odour of oil-paint-and-turpentine that hung about the rooms.

But now, as if to compensate for his death, her father's painting had come alive in front of her eyes.

The painting had appeared in Hyde Park. Clothed in white, mystic, wonderful. Ebony skin rose out of his white clothes like granite crags in a landscape of snow. Under a thick beard and bushy, shoulder-length hair she sensed a careless slant of cheekbone and a thin line of jaw. He wore small round glasses. Windswept. Windblown. Someone who looked as if had recently touched down on earth. Perhaps he wasn't real and she was hallucinating. Her brain had registered something other than the physical reality – the way she had recently mistaken a stranger for a neighbour who, she had known, was long dead.

Yet, there he was, standing in a crowd of people in Speaker's Corner in Hyde Park, holding a demonstration of some kind, which she had been sent to cover for SkyVision. A group of men, in white shirts and trousers and no warm clothing despite the cold, held up banners. 'Purification Journey', the banners read. 'Join the Movement to Purify Humanity'. 'Your Water Is Pure, But Is Your Love?'

A red-haired man was making a speech: 'This is the time for the Inner War! A war between the positive and the negative self! Don't turn your back on this war! Look around you! We have returned to a world of lust and obscenity. What is our solution? Come and find out in the Purification Journey. Learn breathing exercises, the joy of being human, the Pure Love of the Mother Woman. Learn about the Inner War.'

He stood a little apart from the group. The odd man out. She noticed that strapped to his back was a childish toy: a wooden bow and arrow. A hilarious, fancy-dress party accessory. His eyes were intense and watchful, a novitiate, recently inducted into a monastery, looking around and thinking: Ah-so-this-is-my-life-now, this-is-my-life.

Except for the bow and arrow, he was frighteningly, incredibly, similar to her man from the painting.

She couldn't work any more today. She had to go home and look at the painting again. She folded up her notebook, waved to the cameraman and called: 'Hey!'

'Yah?' he yelled into his camera.

'I'm not feeling too well. I'll call in and take the day off, okay? I'll be back tomorrow. These guys are going to be here for a while.'

'Bet they are.' His voice came round his denim-jacketed back. 'They're pulling crowds. Jesus. Fucking Halloween!'

'You carry on with some shots if you like' – she pointed towards the bow and arrow exception – 'and take some of Robin Hood. I'll see you tomorrow.'

'Yeah, Robin Hood,' he zoomed in. 'Must be freezing their asses off.'

She turned on her heel and almost ran to the tube station.

⁂

It was January and freezing. Rivulets of dirty snow ran along the pavements. The streetlights looked wan in the gloomy afternoon. Cold rampaged through the city, curling into a dragon tongue of ice that licked at every footstep. At home, icy rain slanted down on the cherry tree outside her window.

'What happened, Goldie?' shouted Mithu as Mia walked in. 'No work today?'

Goldie was Mithu's name for her. It was a translation of the Bengali *shona*. It was a concession to England. It was an acknowledgement of the displacement of the family from India to Britain. It was an allusion to the cultural difference between mother and daughter. Only at the very bottom of this hierarchy of references, was it a grudging endearment.

She raised sheepish eyes to her mother. Mithu was a graceful, excitable Bengali from Kolkata who had met and married her father Anand on a trip to the tea gardens of Darjeeling. Mithu's family was now scattered over Canada and the United States; she despised Kolkata almost as much as she loved and missed it.

'Not feeling too well.'

'Skipping work?'

'Only for today. It's such an awful day.'

'Every day is awful,' sighed Mithu, getting up from the sofa and throwing her magazine to the floor. 'Have some cha.'

'Okay, thanks.'

'At your age you shouldn't be coming home to a mother,' Mithu slammed the kettle on the stove. 'You should be coming home to a husband.'

'Ma,' Mia replied at once. 'Listen, I'll move back to Putney if you like. Don't want to cramp your style. Besides,' she looked around, 'this place is a bit strange to me now.'

'I didn't mean it like that, Goldie!' Mithu cried. 'You *always* misunderstand everything I say. You *twist* everything.'

Mother and daughter looked away from each other in mutual exasperation. Without her father they were like a theatre company without an audience and had no reason to stay together in the same repertory.

Then Mithu fluffed her newly trimmed hair and said: 'I've decided to get married again. And move to America.'

The man from the painting had stunned her. But normally marooned on her high wall of grief there was little that could touch Mia. Day-to-day life had been vital only in her father's gaze. Without him, numbness came easily; a brain-dead state of robotic responses. 'Great, Ma!' she replied automatically. 'Good news. Go for it. Is it Tiger?'

'Who else? Tiger's a very nice person. He's easy-going and he doesn't drink like your father used to. He always comes straight to the point. He's being transferred to New York. He wants to take me with him. Lovely, no? The Statue of Liberty... It's always so cold in London these days and see how dark it is outside.'

'This is very good news, Ma, very good news,' Mia said in the singsong that she and her mother sometimes spoke. 'Everyone will be happy for you. Everyone will. No one will say, "Oh no she shouldn't have, oh no she shouldn't have." No one will say that. Papa wouldn't say it either. He'd say, "Go! Go on and make a life for yourself."'

'I don't care about what your father would or wouldn't say,' snapped Mithu, shaking the teapot with menacing jerks. 'I care about you. I can't make a life for myself just like that. How can I make a life for myself when you are still unmarried?'

There was another silence.

'In India,' declared Mithu, 'at your age, you would have been a mother-in-law by now. Understand? A mother-in-law!'

'A mother-in-law at twenty-eight? That sounds like a criminal offence.'

'Why not? It used to happen in Bengal. If you married at seven, had your first child at ten, then you would have a twenty-year-old son who could be married by the time you're thirty, which is almost your age!' calculated Mithu.

'A bit competitive,' Mia said, draining the last of the tea. 'Everyone fighting around in the same generation.'

'Not at all,' returned Mithu sharply. 'There would be *no* generation gap.'

She stared at her daughter. Not strictly beautiful but appealing. Definitely appealing with her crown of soft curls and her petite frame. Dark eyes and long eyelashes that blinked constantly with an excess of thought. The shy yet reaching-out quality of the only child in spite of her attempts at self reliance. Something sweet in the curve of her cheek. She spoke in an unusual and droll way and when she wept her whole being crumpled in silent sorrow. When she laughed (which, these days, was hardly ever) she looked as if she had never been happier in her life. Every emotion played out fully on her face, which looked fierce from some angles but innocent from others. She had her mother's natural grace and her father's black hair. If she dressed right, if she grew her nails or styled her hair, she might be quite attractive. But she was a discontent. As much of a grouch as Mithu was a blithe spirit.

And nowadays, Mithu suspected, Mia had lost her mind.

Mia had always been her father's daughter. The dead Anand: Marxist-turned-Mystic. A radical in his student days at Delhi University, Anand had enrolled in Naxalism as an undergraduate, slinking through mountain villages in the dead of night with a couple of police packs sniggering about rich-kid revolutionaries, on his tail. On one of his trips to the north Bengal hills, to try and convince tea-garden workers to overthrow their masters, memorize the teachings of Lenin and strive for the workers' and peasants' Utopia, Anand had met Mithu, who had come to Darjeeling on holiday with her parents.

Mithu didn't have any knowledge of Marxism, but she did have a lopsided grin and fawn-like limbs; Anand's nascent artist's eye was captivated.

Subsequently, all the Naxal uprisings were stamped out, the leaders were lodged in jail, and others were made to squat on burning stoves to get them to confess. Anand was tempted back to the bourgeois life in the nick of time by his businessman father. He completed his studies, published his thesis on farmers' agitations in the north Indian hills, married Mithu, and moved to England to teach History of South Asia at London University.

In London, for many good reasons, he became convinced that Communism was stifling the religious genius of India. And turned to a spiritual quest. He began to paint and became a far better painter than an academic, revealing how much more excited he was by god than by Marx. His oils on canvas were technicolour and realistic and although there was always some confusion among critics about why a Leftist historian like Anand only explored godly themes, yet lots of people bought his paintings and the family moved to Belsize Park on his combined earnings as rational academic and mystic painter.

Mia was born in England. Anand and Mithu never went back to India except for fleeting trips to Delhi to visit Anand's widowed mother, who died a few months after he became a British citizen. Anand had insisted that Mia understand well who she was and where she came from. He had pitched a wigwam for Mia in the back garden with a banner announcing, 'I'm not a *Red* Indian!'

He painted the Sistine Chapel with Jesus' shadow falling over the dome like a raincloud. He created Mount Kailash reflected in Lake Manasarovar like an upside-down pyramid in a pebbled sky. He painted the qawwals of Nizamuddin's shrine in Delhi with whirling sufis reflected in their eyes. The Kashi Vishvanath temple at Benares with a demon-faced priest shrieking in a typhoon of incense. He even painted the church St. Martin-in-the-Fields in black and white strokes with only the plasterwork in colour.

Last year, Anand had gone to the Eagle And Flag, then for a walk by the river, fallen into it, and drowned. The police report said there was a massive amount of alcohol in his blood. Alcohol-induced suicide.

Mithu said it was just like him to go off and commit suicide when the daughter was still unmarried. He had become so English in his ways, so English and disconnected. Not tied up like Indians were, tied by this life and the next, tied up in an elemental, fire-and-water sort of way.

Father – efficiently incinerated in a crematorium. Nothing whatsoever left of him anywhere in the world. How foolish were those who believed in ghosts and spirits. Papa was gone, vaporized into the odour of oil-paint-and-turpentine, no other shred, no remnant of him, anywhere at all.

Even greater than her sorrow was Mia's puzzlement at his desertion. If he had died of illness or accident he would have simply and gracefully transmuted into an ancestor whom she would have missed and mourned for. But to throw himself into a drunken death by water – just as they were getting to be such good friends and setting up their debate along such promising lines, just as their conversation was beginning – was so unexpected, so shockingly uncharacteristic, that she couldn't but see it as a terrible rejection of herself.

He had often said that she had been his favourite painting. But without him, she was only half-finished, the brush strokes dry but incomplete...

The undimmed focus on the good, the trekker's upturned face towards the sun of new delights – all of that was gone forever. Poor old gentle Pop. Hope he wasn't too disappointed if heaven turned out to be full of Marxists.

Now the oil-painting man had appeared. He had walked out of the painting and into her life and transformed Hyde Park corner into a festival.

❦

'Your father did a terrible thing,' grumbled Mithu clattering the teacups into the sink. 'But there's no point missing him

all the time. You'll wander around all your life, trying to find
a father here, trying to find a father there and never being
able to find a husband. That's what will happen to you.'

Mia stared apologetically at her mother. She had never
been a companion to her. She, with her gloomy silences,
could never be a companion to a childlike virago like Mithu,
who needed pampering and cosy moments. Anand had been
the unifier of mother and daughter. He had been mother to
them both. He had spread his apron and let them pull in
different directions.

Anand's death had had a very different effect on Mithu.
Mithu, after a few days of robust weeping, had rapidly gone
global. She became re-sexualized. She cast off her dowdy,
professor's-wife clothes and mutated into a sari-clad Boy
George with plucked eyebrows and powdered cheeks. She
became lively and democratic in her friendships and dumbed
down from novels to glossy magazines in relief that she no
longer had to please Anand by pretending to be highbrow.
She sprinkled gold dust on her forehead and streaked her
hair with Natural Auburn 5.1. She painted her fingernails a
rich red and dangled gypsy earrings from her ears.

Mithu's survival skills were admirable, thought Mia. Lost
in the Amazon rain forest she would speedily contract a
marriage with the king of apes so he would take her into his
protection. Abandoned in the Sahara she would jump on
the back of the passing captain of the Bedouin and take
over the best tent. Mithu's need for marriage was equivalent
to the immigrant's need for an air ticket. Marry with steely
determination and give birth to a range of new passports.

'Don't worry about me, Ma,' Mia climbed the wooden
steps to her room. 'You deserve all the happiness in the
world. I'll meet someone, there's no hurry. You go ahead.
Get married. Go to America. I'll stay here with SkyVision
and move back to Putney.'

Since this morning, between the time I left for work and came back, I've made an extraordinary discovery. A false discovery perhaps, but for me, a discovery nonetheless. What would Rosenthal and Silver say? They would say that the man was nothing but a delusion, a mirage caused by the drunkenness of grief.

'No hurry?' shouted Mithu. 'What do you mean, no hurry? Of course, there's a hurry. You might get prolapse of the rectum! Mejo Mashi had it and nobody would stay with her because of the smell. Only her husband cared for her. Until his dying day. Even though they were staying in a leaking place overlooking the basti because they had no money left. Oh god,' Mithu shuddered at the memory. 'Thank god, I never have to go back to that horrible country.'

'No point thinking of rectums and all, Ma, and you don't ever have to go back,' Mia called down from her room. 'You're on your way to America.'

'Only if you help me, Goldie!' Mithu called up the stairs. 'I can't get married before you. I can't. First you. *Then* me. If you don't, I won't. You have my life in your hands. Remember that. You must get married. Married! Married! Married!'

The silence of death was the most annoying thing of all. The hushed wipe-out, the impossibility of further contact, the irritatingly vacant space. Quiet runways stretching towards other quiet runways. Everything as it was, yet everything in mourning. Why had he not stormed into death more grandly? Drowning was such a weak surrender, such a slothful fall. *Do not go gentle into that good night*, Papa, *Rage, rage against the dying of the light*...

The streets, the billboards, the trees would remain, but she would be gone one day too.

Gone where?

Perhaps to some Hollywood-created studio where there were layers of shining clouds or an oily pit crawling with spindly arms.

Rain whispered in the cherry tree outside. In her room – where Mithu had often burst in smelling of chicken essence demanding explanations about men and music; where Anand had knocked softly when she had a fever and laid his palm on her hot forehead – was the painting that contained him. She kicked off her shoes, sat cross-legged on her bed and peered at it on the wall. Yes, the face in Anand's painting was exactly like that of the man at the Purification Rally. She could see no difference.

She had seen him every day for the last seven years. She had watched him looming above her Raggedy Anne. She had studied him in the evenings, glowing in the light of her bedside lamp. Her father's gift to her on her twenty-first birthday had been his painting of the Kumbh Mela, the largest religious festival in the world.

'What an experience, Maya,' Anand had exulted. 'How can I describe it so you will understand? Imagine a huge Hindu Woodstock … a spiritual Glastonbury… crowds of people! Thousands! Hundred thousands! The water with the sun overhead, mist along the banks, sadhus and nuns, tourists, yoga teachers, a giant celebration of being a nobody.'

'A nobody?' she had asked.

'Sure, a nobody. That's what we are. Non-entities next to a river that is millions of years old. One of India's greatest contributions to world civilizations is the idea of the naked body. The naked body not as a pornographic product, but as a civilizational ideal, the most pristine surrender to being a nobody, a non-individual, nothing but a technological member of the Milky Way.'

Anand had bought her a dog-eared copy of GS Ghurye's *Indian Sadhus* written half a century ago. The sadhus and their ascetic reformist spirit was unique to India, Mia read. But while some are beautiful lotuses, the vast majority have become unhealthy scum. Only when the water begins to flow again and the people are awakened to life, then, and only then, will the scum be carried away. Until life returns to that long dead spirit of rebellion and renunciation, sadhus will remain monstrous distortions of the ascetic ideal.

Sadly, no one was interested enough in the ascetic spirit to re-ignite the flame of philosophical protest that once burned so brightly. The relegation of almost the entire tradition of sadhus to hippies and dharma bums, to comic book depictions by India's scornful elite, Anand said, was no less a tragedy than the intellectual conquest of India by the British. Indian historians write of workers, peasants and kings, but they never write of sadhus or the Kumbh Mela because their minds are imprisoned in scorn – scorn for themselves and a squeamishness about their own traditions.

None of Anand's paintings had been as talked about, as written about or as appreciated as this particular painting. It had been displayed at the Tate Modern. At the back of the painting, Anand had written in black paint: *To my dearest little Maya, love from Papa.* 'Maya' was an improvement on 'Mia' Anand had said. Mia was as pretty as a Hollywood heroine, but Maya meant god's dream.

The Kumbh Mela or the Festival of the Pitcher. Every four years, on the banks of the Ganga, thousands gathered to take a dip in the river in the conviction that the cleansing bath would wash away their sins. If they didn't gain peace in the after-life or everlasting union with the almighty, at

least there might be a raise in salary or favourable rates of
interest in a new bank loan. In Anand's depiction, a ghostly
white river arched across the painting like a sky. Below the
river sky, pilgrims, ascetics, elephants and cattle-drawn carts
were drawn in painstaking detail. In the foreground was a
face in magnified close-up, of a young bespectacled priest
with black hair down to his shoulders and a thick beard
down to his collarbones.

And under the hair and beard, a careless slant of
cheekbone and a thin line of jaw.

⁂

'All well?' Her SkyVision producer asked the next morning.
'How are you feeling today?'

'Fine. Sorry. Just a headache suddenly. Bit strange living
with my mother after all these years...'

'Get them today, won't you?'

'Definitely.'

'Not yoga instructors...not Kashmiri protestors. So what
is this Purification Journey all about? Should make a cute
tailpiece.'

'Yes.' She felt his hand on her arm, 'Never heard of
them before, I must confess.'

'Mia,' He gripped her elbow. 'We're a little worried about
you, darling. You've not been yourself lately. You need to get
back into the swing of things. Your mind is all over the place;
you're simply not being able to concentrate. You forget
something almost every day. Is there something wrong?'

'I'm fine,' she shook herself free. 'I'm absolutely fine.'

'If you carry on like this, you'll need some help,' he said
firmly. 'We all think so.'

'Oh rubbish!' she tossed over her shoulder. 'Just been
a bit preoccupied, that's all.'

'It's your dad, isn't it?'

'Come on, it's been a whole year.'

'Then stop acting as if you're going mad.'

'Fuck off!' she laughed. *Mad!* That tired term used by men to dismiss women, as the sisterhood says. Maybe Rochester locked his wife away because she was a real big cheese.

'You're losing it, child,' his voice echoed after her as she ran through sparklingly empty corridors. 'You need a break.'

＊

She confronted him again.

He was standing among the group, standing very still, as if concentrating hard. The red-haired man was shouting, 'We are in the process of getting ready for a new Inner War! The war to save our values! The war to save our ability to love! A war to save our families! To save ourselves from ourselves!'

The men were all young. They were tall, spare, a ramp-row of trendy faith-healers in their white clothes; a chorus-line of groovy godmen.

She walked up to him. When lightning waits behind a thundercloud, the cloud looks perfectly calm. Only when the lightning bursts out suddenly from behind, does the cloud shine jaggedly. The traffic that rumbled around Marble Arch was as loud as always. But when his voice sounded in her ear, for a moment, everything jangled louder than a fairground.

'Yes?'

Through his glasses, his eyes on her were sharp and interested. She felt angry that he looked only interested instead of instantly passionate. She felt the atmosphere between them grow charged with memories.

'Yes,' he said again. 'Can I help you?' His voice sounded hoarse, as if he was speaking from the back of his throat.

'Hello,' she replied. 'I'm a journalist. You know, a reporter? Television? SkyVision channel. I've come to interview you. There's' – she pointed to the bulky denim jacket – 'the cameraman.'

'Me? Interview me?'

'Yes. Can we chat?'

'So I'm your freak show for the day? The mad man with the bow and arrow?'

'Not at all!' she lied loudly.

'Instead of interviewing me,' he said wearily, 'maybe you should interview yourself. Ask yourself a few questions.'

'I do that all the time,' she smiled. 'But I'd like to know a little more about you.'

'Well, I'd like to know a little more about you.' He spread his hands in a gesture of incomprehension, 'I'd like to know why you think I'm worthy of being interviewed. We have been touring all over England, Europe, United States and Japan and I've met many people whom I would like to interview. I would ask them why they are all running to buy gold. Running to buy things. Why they are happy to serve the empire controlled from New York and London. I want to ask them, must everyone be a banker or an accountant? Just run after money? How much money do you want, Ma'am? How much money does everybody want? Is there no such thing as just a celebration of being human? To be remembered not for making money but for taking being human as far as possible?'

'Lovely idea,' she grinned. 'Wish I didn't have to work. Come on,' she said. 'Let's take being human a little further into the park. Let's sit down somewhere. Please come.'

They settled down on a bench, watching the buses circle around the trees down towards Oxford Circus.

What was his name, she asked. Karna, he replied. K-A-R-N-A. And why the bow and arrow? Just part of the costume of a novice. He wore the bow and arrow because he was a novice. Once he had completed his first mission, he would wear the same white uniform as the others. And could he please tell her a little bit more about the Purification Journey? He thrust a black-and-white printed pamphlet into her hands. It read:

Rebirth of Pure Love: The Need for a New Inner War

The 21st Century has dawned. But we have strayed from the true path.
The true path towards Pure Love is the rebirth of simple life patterns.
Let us recreate the peace of the past.
Let us work towards the Rebirth of the Mother Woman.
Let us wage the war with ourselves so we may set free our best selves.
Come to PAVITRA ASHRAM, NEW DELHI, INDIA for a 15-day Purification Retreat.
In unpolluted lakeside air, learn about the martyrdom of past heroes, eat nutritious food; live a simple life.
Learn to purify being human.
Learn to serve in the new struggle and the war of our century: the war within.

'This particular instruction,' Mia said, 'interests me. The Rebirth of the Mother Woman.'

'Well,' he leant forward. 'If it was up to me, I would put that right at the top. But the Brothers thought otherwise.'

'The Rebirth of the Mother Woman? What does that mean exactly?'

'Exactly what it says.' His stare was so sharp that she thought his glasses might crack. 'Fight the female ego! Make the woman return to her natural habitat, her home, and accept her role as mother. Not aspire to become a computer-tapping sexual slave who wears less and less clothes.' He shrugged, 'Lots of people are saying it. We are also saying it.'

'So what's your solution?' She scribbled, 'Purdah? Burqa? Segregation?'

'You are trying,' he laughed, 'to sensationalize it. Give it funny names. Make it sound old-fashioned and silly because you are so convinced of the rightness of your ways. You can accept no challenge, you can tolerate no disagreement because you only want affirmations of what you think you already know. All I said is that the human mother is becoming an object of lust. In fact, she is the object of her own lust, her own vanity. In the guise of freedom and equality, women are being degraded, encouraged to pursue their worse rather than their better selves. A mean selfish woman is apparently an ideal woman in today's times. To paraphrase Rousseau, woman is born free but everywhere she is in chains.'

Mithu, for example, Mia confirmed to herself, was definitely not capable of the Pure Love of the Mother Woman. In fact, Mithu was an excellent candidate for the Purification Retreat. Perhaps she should be sent off with this sporty brotherhood to their ashram and return, purified, dressed in white, and raging about the Inner War.

She frowned into her notepad. Yet another eccentric whose life made an excellent alliterative tagline. How easily a clever sentence might leapfrog out of the paper. 'Male Mystic Meets Modern Mom'. 'Furious Forecaster Fights

Feminism'. 'Demagogue Demands Domestic Duty'. Just another clank of metal in her prison of 20-second summaries of events, her armoury of one-liners and text messages, a deluxe steel prison set back comfortably from the flabby rough heartbeat of the day-to-day business of evolution.

Her father had analysed her predicament on many occasions. He would say:

An excess of instant-knowledge has made you too easily pessimistic. Too many pictures have finished off your capacity to see and too many words have robbed you of the ability to speak. You've ceased to grow. Unless you free your mind to the possibility of faith, you'll never understand the world.

She had protested: But you don't need to believe in order to grow! You just need to travel and read.

Aha, but what is travel after all but a kind of pilgrimage, basically a journey seeking unknowable truths? One of the world's greatest travellers, Ibn Battutah, wrote of how a nameless fakir carried him through a parched landscape when he was too exhausted to walk any further...

Nameless fakir, who?

Exactly. Just a stranger who carried Battutah to safety and then disappeared...

You mean it was god?

Maybe. Maybe not. The important thing is he never could find out.

So the tourists on the Costa Del Sol are on a pilgrimage...?

Of course they are! They don't know it but they too are pilgrims, they've gone there to pray for love and happiness in the future. And they're naked, just like the naked sadhus at the Kumbh, perhaps there's some unconscious link between the search and nakedness.

❧

Perhaps Karna was searching too, trying to reconstruct a bruised world in the way he could. His words were meaningless. Yet he wasn't just playing a part. He was struggling to believe his own clichés. He hadn't said the right things. He hadn't tried to reassure her by affirming that he was a mere anecdote. Instead his words had come tumbling out, amateur and raw. He had no polite skills. He was only a bespectacled monk from a river bank who had rushed out of his ashram to teach people how to love each other. For his pains, Scotland Yard might drag him away, strapped to a stretcher, and slam him in a cell for daring to be so corny.

Her father's painting was even more attractive in the flesh. The hare-brained speech and crazy costume made her want to hug him hard and never let go. Anand had deserted her, but she would hold on tight to Karna. She imagined him injured, beaten by the police or stoned by Neo-Nazis, a battered Jesus, a suffering diviner. She felt awakened to fantasy. He would create a new body for her with his hands – a moonlit, newly voluptuous body. His skin would be darkly luminous, and when he threw his hair behind him, she would catch a glimpse of his long throat. In the rain, he would be a bedraggled rock star on stage, wet with sweat and dripping hair.

His formal manner infuriated her, so did his talk of this stupid Purification Journey. She wondered if she should tell him about the painting. Had her father seen him somewhere and captured his exact likeness? Maybe Anand had caught a glimpse of him on one of his many trips to India. She wanted to tell him that she knew him very well. That he was more muscular and tall than she had hoped for. That to see him now was a message from the dead, that her father hadn't even seen his subject's best angles. Perhaps most people in the world are waiting to be carried away by strangers on the street, or searching out fervent religious preachers to fall in love with because the software sector was turning out to be far too unromantic and their camouflage of office jokes was wearing thin.

She bent into her notepad, but instead of taking notes, drew a face that was an ideal version of her own, with every feature stretched to perfection. 'Interesting,' she said after a pause. 'Tell me, d'you ever watch TV?'

ALQUERIA, GOA

The road to Alqueria ran along the sea. It was a zigzag of a road. A road with a split personality. A slam of sunlit sea on one side, quiet palm and mango forests on the other. The forests sloped upwards to a red dust hill where the old Portuguese fort stared out across the water. Next to the fort was the church of Santa Ana (presided over by Father Rudy) with its whitewashed walls and blue curlicues.

Tiny seaside Alqueria: one of the world's forgotten ancestors. Where the spirits were ancient and powerful.

Wayside shrines dotted the zigzag road. There was a white crucifix planted under a cashew bush with a marigold at its base. Next to Sharkey's Hotel, under the big banyan tree, villagers lit clay lamps every evening. Under the rocky steps that led off the zigzag to the beach were scattered hibiscus petals and stalks of rice. In Alqueria, Father Rudy told his congregation, all kinds of gods pranced in the shadow of humans. When a smiling arc of palm leaf drifted to the ground, you knew it wasn't just another leaf.

In the evenings, music from the church choir accompanied the fishermen to the taverna. Family homes with pillared patios, red-tiled roofs and icons on their walls came alive with lights and buntings. Bougainvillea, jackfruit trees and abolim flowers grew in the back gardens of the houses that lined the zigzag.

Sloping down from the zigzag was Capuchine Beach and its crescent of sand. On one of the bends of the zigzag was the popular Sharkey's Hotel. Its whitewashed walls were painted with palm trees and beer bottles. Red paper lamps hung from the ceiling. The rooms on the first floor were comfortable enough though the sheets were faded and the floors were sandy. The best thing about Sharkey's was its stunning location, with the bay in front and Alqueria stretching behind. Ad executives, chief financial officers and models with bandannas streaming from their hair and cellphones tucked into their sarongs, came to stay during the New Year holiday and arranged all-night parties. There were techno, rock 'n' roll and Bollywood remixes on offer and an *a la carte* of Goan sausages, fish curry and beer, as well as first-aid when the parties became violent or when the Goa police exploded in on their motorbikes on the suspicion that someone was selling drugs.

Indi, who owned Sharkey's Hotel, lived in a white-painted house on the far side of Capuchine Beach. The house overlooked the rocky part of the beach and a clear lagoon set back from the sea by an undulating bank of sand.

In the evenings, when Indi sat in her veranda, her face towards the lagoon, all movement on the beach stopped. The financial consultants and models who tripped past in their Speedo suits came to a standstill. And the fishermen who pushed their motorized crafts into the water whispered that when Indi was nearby, the poor prawns and pomfrets in the sea seemed to stop swimming and give themselves up distractedly to the fishing nets.

Indi was brutally beautiful. Her beauty had always been as formidable as a conquering army. At five feet ten, she was the tallest Indian woman Alqueria had ever seen. Her skin was the colour of freshly churned butter and she had eyes that stretched from the bridge of her nose to her temples. Her eyes were unlike any other. They were the colour of the ocean in the monsoon, azure streaked with grey, eyes that thundered and stormed under black brows. The straight nose and cheekbones that angled out of her skin were chiselled to knife-edge sharpness but there was nothing pure about Indi. Everything about the voluptuous figure and defiant expression, was brazenly sensual. Her clothes seemed to want to constantly fall off her body, as if in apology for covering up what should be displayed to the world. Her grey-streaked black hair flew around her face and when she smiled she looked wickedly unpredictable. She was a master-craftsman's gift to himself. A prima ballerina's swan song.

She was blind. Her stormy ocean eyes were dead. She hadn't been born blind. She had been born with retinitis pigmentosa, an incurable progressive degeneration of the retina. She had been night-blind as a teenager, lost her peripheral vision in her thirties, developed tubular vision in her fifties, until one afternoon, one hot afternoon, something snapped and her vision went completely.

All her seeing life she had felt two thick black arms crowding into her eyes from the sides in a deathly embrace. Indi called these two arms her prison bars. Prison bars that were marching in towards the centre of her eyes from the sides bringing the blackess of solitary confinement. For many years she had seen the world as a distant planet, a circle of existence framed by a galaxy of pure darkness. Perhaps this was the way god saw us, she thought – as a far-away aberrant circle in a surface of uniform black.

The diagnosis was delivered to her parents when, as a fourteen-year-old, she began bumping into too many doorways at night. There was no known cure for retinitis pigmentosa. The retina could not be rescued. She must start learning Braille, the ophthalmologist suggested, to equip herself mentally and try and enjoy her life as much as she could, because inevitable darkness awaited her in old age.

She had tried not to notice the prison bars when she was younger because they started as faint threads. But as she grew older they began to thicken, getting broader and fatter until finally, one hot afternoon, when a dry wind came beating against the windows, they swelled and blocked out the sun forever.

Indi had learnt to feel her way along walls. She could tell if a wall had been recently touched by sunlight and if it led into a doorfront, or if a wall was damp and smelt of a bedroom. Bedrooms smelt of underwear, living rooms of shoes, cigarettes and farts. Footsteps were eloquent on character: angrily stomping or shuffling or suspicious. She felt the sun on different parts of the body like the touch of a friend or the push of an uncaring bystander. She could smell the starch on a napkin and judge whether it had been recently washed or not. She had never been able to properly distinguish colours, and sometimes dressed in wildly clashing clothes. She had never properly been able to see the power of her own beauty, but sensed it in the startled intake of breath she heard when someone saw her for the first time.

Sometimes she would smell and count her way to the lagoon and turn her face to the sky and bend her head this way and that to ease some sliver of sunlight into any remaining crack in the undulating dark.

But all she came away with was the mossy smell of the lagoon and remembered souvenirs of the sun on her skin.

🦂

She was extremely difficult to deal with. Frightening Indi – with the fresh-butter complexion who shouted at the top of her voice. Night-blind by her early teens, the family shuddered everytime they heard the thud of Indi against a bathroom door or an unladylike grunt when she stubbed her toe. During the day, although she was losing her ability to cross roads, her frontal vision was still strong and she would run out of the house, in taxis or in the family Ambassador, manically filling her days with a panorama of sights and feverish reading; committing it all to memory, building a restless visual bank for her future poverty. She was always impatient, her mind fixed on the coming apocalypse, always enraged that all those millions of rod and cone cells were giving up on her, noisily enclosed in a self-centred world of her relationship with the sometimes steady, sometimes wavering prison bars.

'Don't you get tired,' Indi blinked scornfully at her mother, 'of using only small small words? Why don't you ever use a really big word?'

Shiela Devi had been confused by this question and had run off to Indi's father, Ashish Kumar, quivering in fear. They had tried to dress her up in the conventional way. In fresh pink saris and white linen blouses, with ribbons in her hair. But however pretty and sweet they tried to make her, however kind and gentle they convinced each other she could become if they tried hard enough, they knew that, at any moment, Indi could throw off her pink clothes and emerge hissing and sensual, her speech as arch as her body, as boastful and as blind as only she could be.

The family lived in a house called Victoria Villa, in the Civil Lines area of Delhi, the genteel enclave where Indian collaborators with empires had been allotted spacious bungalows for their loyalty. Victoria Villa was a single-storeyed house built in the British style and named after the Queen Empress. A wide veranda ran around it, leading through triangular arches into a flat lawn. In the lawn were two splendid old trees. A jamun with its leaves hanging shyly to the ground. And a tall semal covered in the early part of the year with brash red blossom.

Victoria Villa was the property of the Ray family, who had owned it after the British left. The Rays were one of India's most energetic clans, successful soldiers, businessmen and doctors, but fatally cursed. Cursed, it was said, by the the Four-Armed-One.

A century ago, the patriarch of the Ray clan had been a poor fisherman in West Bengal. One morning, out on a catch, his boat sprung a leak and began to sink rapidly into the sea. But, suddenly, miraculously, a beautiful woman with eyes the colour of the ocean came rising up from the deep, black hair streaming behind her, fitted – so the legend went – with four arms. The Four-Armed-One was as strong as she was beautiful and quickly ferried the patriarch and his boat to safety. He immediately fell in love with his supernatural lifeguard and together they founded a huge family.

The Four-Armed-One brought luck to the patriarch and he soon grew rich. But as it turned out, she was as evil as she was beautiful and one night when the children were asleep, she stole into his bed and devoured him. Hair, bones, tongue and all. Then she walked back to the ocean from where she had come, fell into it and never returned, leaving her children orphaned and confused about what exactly had happened to their folks overnight. However, since they were all of semi-divine (although slightly macabre) lineage, they all grew up well enough, developed vigorous brains and healthy appetites, escaped the village and became civil servants and businessmen in the city.

The Four-Armed-One left the family an enduring legacy. When any of the family were near death, wherever they might be, they always saw her standing stockstill at the foot of their bed with her four arms crossed.

Great-aunt Pola had had a heart attack when the spirit of her long dead cook (so she claimed) came flying out of the refrigerator, still apparently agitated about the cut in wages, and tried to suffocate her with a cauliflower. Great-aunt Pola never recovered from the attack and came to live in Victoria Villa where she uttered a dire premonition before she died: 'Be warned,' said Great-aunt Pola to Ashish Kumar as she lay on her deathbed. 'One day a girl will come, who will be like *her* who now stands by my bed. She will devour all those close to her.'

'It's Indi,' Shiela Devi whispered to Ashish Kumar after Great-aunt Pola died. 'The Four-Armed-One has been reborn as Indi. I'm sure of it.'

❧

Indi was sent to Holy Mary Convent School where the nuns tried to teach her not to shake her legs while sitting in a chair and to button up her shirt, which she always left a little undone. She worked little, read voraciously in spite of her eyes, and streaked effortlessly to the top of the class, much to the disbelief of her parents.

After an impressive career in college where, because she couldn't play tennis or go to the cinema, she spent most of her time fiercely reading in the library, she began to prepare for the civil service exam, as her father had.

If she passed, she would become a civil servant, like her father.

Ashish Kumar, six feet two and dashing in his youth, was a man of immense personality. When he was in a rage, government clerks whispered that the fire in his eyes could ignite piles of files and send official notices up in smoke. He liked his yoghurt thick and perfectly set. During meals, he would turn the bowl of yoghurt upside down to see if it was runny. If it ran water even a little, he would hurl it across the table at Shiela Devi's face.

One night, as Indi watched her mother stand on the frontlines of her father's airborne yoghurt, she had a bad idea.

A few days later, Sister Cyril, principal of All Saints College for Women where the girls from Holy Mary Convent went, rang Ashish Kumar saying that she was sorry to hear of his son's death in a car accident.

'Death of my son?' exclaimed Ashish Kumar. 'But, Sister, I have no sons!'

There was a silence at the other end of the line.

'That's what I thought, Mr Ray. But your daughter told us that you also have an older boy. Or you had one.'

'No, Sister, I am blessed with only two daughters. The elder has graduated recently, thank god, and is now studying to join the civil service. Indira. As you know. The other remains in your college.'

'Yes, of course I know your daughters, Mr Ray,' said Sister Cyril briskly. 'Indira was one of our best, if not the best. How proud we were of her and what she achieved in spite of her suffering. Paromita, your younger, unfortunately has none of her gifts... In fact Indira was the one who told us about your son. She rang the college and told us. It was very kind of her. We've just had a memorial service for him. A fine young man by Indira's account.'

'A fine young man…' said Ashish Kumar carefully.

'We are so proud,' said Sister Cyril.

'Of who, Sister?' inquired Ashish Kumar politely.

'Your son, Mr Ray,' said Sister Cyril after a pause. 'Apparently he was a fighter pilot.'

'Ah,' mused Ashish Kumar. 'My son. The fighter pilot.'

There was another silence. The rituals of sorrow are indeed extraordinary, Sister Cyril sighed. Perhaps bereaved parents cultivate a certain forgetfulness that shelters them against the empty days. 'God bless you, Mr Ray.'

He thundered for her to present herself before him in his study. The study was a semi-circular room with casement windows set with dusty window seats. Outside the windows, swayed the jamun tree. Ashish Kumar often lay here on the white hospital bed, bought for dying Great-aunt Pola, reading *The Last of the Mohicans.*

'What son? What car accident?' he roared. 'Are you mad or what?'

She hung her head, but he could see that beneath the lowered eyelashes she was barely listening to him. Naturally, he had been extremely disappointed when she was born. She had been such a big healthy baby that she could easily have been a male child. But she was not. As she grew older, he had begun to get even angrier because she seemed to succeed at everything in spite of being a disappointment… She grew unacceptably beautiful and embarrassingly curvaceous. She understood more mathematics than he ever could and on top of everything else, she was blind, blind to the horrors she was wreaking on those around her. She was freed by blindness, strengthened by blindness, made wanton by blindness. Blindness made her wild, a creature of the wilderness.

He was powerless to rein her in, helpless against her success, impotent against her unseeing dominance and powerless in the face of her scorn. Since she couldn't see properly, he was easy for her to ignore. Easy for her to regard as negligible while he chafed and fretted about his own smallness, six feet two and still maddeningly small in his daughter's disrespectfully absent eyes.

'You told a lie? Why?'

'Lie?' she asked. 'What lie?'

'You told Sister Cyril that you have a brother. That he was killed in an accident. Why?'

'I felt like saying it. I wish I had a brother. Instead of—' she jerked her head at the cowering Pom – 'that idiot.'

'Don't you think it's wrong to lie?' His face was red with fury and triumph. 'You're not young. You're going to become an officer in the civil service. And you act like a child.'

'I felt sorry for you,' said Indi calmly. 'You don't have a live son so you may as well have a dead one. A man without sons is not a man.'

'Get out!' shrieked Ashish Kumar. 'Get out of my sight!'

'Indira,' Shiela Devi wept. 'Was it you who sat in my poor womb for nine whole months?'

She sneaked out into the lawn that night, treading barefoot so she could recognize the path, to smoke her cigarettes which she stored in a test-tube buried under the semal. As she lit up and inhaled, Ashish Kumar came up behind her and whispered softly, 'So, my dear. You are smoking?'

She started and exhaled hurriedly into his face. 'Once,' she held up her head, 'in a while.'

She ran her feet over the triangular edges of the bricks that lined the flowerbeds. Tiny upturned bricks formed a neat mountain range enclosing the nodding pansies.

He stepped in front of her and snatched her wrist in a hard grip. His mouth was twisted in a sneer but his eyes were frightened. 'Your lie about my son was a shameful matter. A very serious, disgraceful matter.'

She struggled to free her hand, the cigarette still burning between her fingers. 'I was teasing you,' she said, trying to laugh.

'You must not do all this.' He looked at the cigarette, 'Telling lies to your college principal. Lying to a nun. Asking them to hold a full scale mass for someone who doesn't exist... Now you are smoking. What will you do next? Sell your body to anyone who wants it?' All of a sudden her father shifted his grip to her fingers and twisted the burning cigarette into her palm. The heat burned into her skin. Tears sprang to her aching eyes but she didn't make a sound.

They stood under the semal, the father crushing the lit cigarette into the daughter's palm, smelling the singed skin and watching her hand thrash involuntarily like a wounded bird. Then the cigarette fell to the ground and Ashish Kumar turned away red-faced.

Indi hopped around in pain. 'You gave me a third degree burn!' she shouted. 'You burnt me!'

'Go into the house,' Ashish Kumar hissed over his shoulder as he walked away. 'Your mother will make you better.

'You fraud!' she screamed after him. 'Pretending you don't lust for a boy!'

Loud prayers from the shanties surrounding Victoria Villa ran up the trees.

Indi sank to her knees and cooled her palm on the wet grass.

The world became her adversary. Her blind and blinding beauty brought out the worst in everyone around her and made it impossible for her to find love. All she met – even from her parents – was jealousy, suspicion and fear. She began to detest her over-the-top womanliness. She thought of herself as a grotesque creature who drove everybody away, a ravishing half-blind Amazon to whom nobody could bear to get close. She became convinced that no one, not even an infant, was capable of goodness towards her, that nobody would ever sympathize.

Whoever this god is, who gave me this ridiculous body and face, then snatched away my eyesight, deserves to be impaled on a cross or drowned by the flood. A woman hated for her beauty, yet unable to defend herself against the world. Blind like Helen Keller. Brilliant like Sappho. Voluptous as Juno. No revenge, no ill temper, no immorality is enough to make up for this injustice, this burden of unseeing womanly exceptionality.

She read and wrote furiously, with half-a-dozen reading lights turned on the books, and became an intellectual and a patriot with no-nonsense views. The country as an abstract entity was the focus of her love, not the people who made it up. She wanted to work for India, to give her life for India, not because of the Indians she knew but because she sensed comfort in the idea of a presence greater than all the pettiness she felt surrounded by.

She turned to her nation-state for ideals and protection. She disagreed with Gandhi's romantic notion of India's ideal villages. Villages must be transformed, not worshipped. She wanted progress, cities, industrialization, modern hospitals, modern roads, and modern education. She fought against the return-to-antiquity line and the return-to-tradition argument. Whose tradition? she raged. Tradition that burns widows and forces the poor to clean the shit of the rich? Onward, she roared, onward in a great forward movement. She had no time for god or flabby spirituality or silly prayers and ritual, threads and powders, what she called the weeds and grains of cowardice. She took her civil service exam and vowed to work towards the social good, towards forgetting the black bars that leapt at her every morning when she opened her eyes, towards creating a larger world for herself where the black bars were irrelevancies. She would toil, offer her services to the community. Once the school or the hospital was built, they would forget to mistrust her.

※

Ashish Kumar's loathing of Indi was encased in love and fatherly pride. She looked like a whore but thought like a statesman. She was going to be totally blind one day but already she had read far more than he had. She was a prostitute-scholar with the waist and bosom of a dancing girl, yet sailed through difficult exams with frightening ease. She painted her lips red and coloured her eyelids blue but her mind turned over with critiques of Gandhi and Nehru's Five-Year Plans. She was a mythic figure. She was good. She was wicked. She was the personification of moral purpose without fuss or sentimentality. She was a daughter who would be far greater than her father, he predicted silently to himself, and unconsciously, in a far corner of his brain of which he was quite unaware, Ashish Kumar began to plot her destruction. He became subconsciously aware – rather like Neanderthal man may have become aware of lurking danger in the forest but found no words to articulate it – that Indi's shadow threatened not only his survival as a human being but also his survival as a species.

Yet he would be shocked and outraged if anyone confronted him with his plot. She was his treasure, his pride, he told his friends and relatives. Beautiful, brilliant Indi who would take the family name to great heights. He would do everything in his power to help her, he would get her the best medical advice, he would throw parties in her honour and celebrate her every milestone.

And he would wait patiently for the time to strike the blow before she killed him with her magnificent presence.

The burn mark on Indi's palm never faded. A reddish stain on her line of fate.

❦

In Alqueria, Indi reached for her Braille novel and ran her fingers along the pages. Alqueria-on-the-bay. Here the forests are havens and the homes are plump matrons who forgive me for everything I've done …. I'm a gatecrasher in this old silence. A sinner who has slipped, unnoticed, into heaven.

She turned her face towards the space where she sensed the ocean. Was he there again? No, he hadn't been here for a few days now. Where had he gone? Perhaps he had lost interest in her and found some other person to haunt.

She called him the Phantom Listener because he reminded her of Walter de la Mare's poem. The Phantom Listener who watched her and heard her, but whom she couldn't see. For almost two months now she had felt that there was someone standing silently outside her house near the lagoon. The presence sometimes vanished, then it was there again. Sometimes she felt a hot stare on her skin. Sometimes a quick breath next to her arm. She smelt something, something damp, something chemical, like a dye or glue. The presence of someone walking behind her when she went for her evening walk to Sharkey's.

The Phantom Listener lay on her roof, peering at her with an upside down face as she sat in her veranda.

She knew the scraping sounds on her roof weren't the monkeys that always swung between the trees and occasionally jumped down on roofs, because the monkeys made jumping sounds. This was a rhythmic scraping; human hands clawing for a grasp.

One night, she had heard what sounded like a human yawn, a yawn so close that she had felt the exhalation ruffle her hair. She had lifted her cane and slashed it through the air and heard an ever-so-faint gasp.

She had heard the Phantom Listener step back. She had smelt the stale chemical smell again. She knew all the smells in Alqueria. But there was this new smell suddenly. A stink of decay and neglect.

She turned her face towards the lagoon… He was playing a cat and mouse game with her. He was mocking her sightlessness, testing her sense of hearing and smell, trying to confuse her with his arrivals and departures. She shook her head. No, he wasn't there now. But she felt certain he would be back.

When he came back she would be waiting for him because she had never been scared in her life and didn't intend to start now.

3

LONDON

'Never,' said Karna. 'I never watch CNN, BBC, Fox etcetera.'

'Of course not. So you won't get to see this interview?'

'No.'

'Right. Okay, could you look into the camera for a second?'

As the cameraman filmed, the sun scampered out of the clouds like a child running out from behind his mother suddenly wanting to play, twinkling briefly down through the trees, forming leaf patterns against Karna's white shirt, before being engulfed again by a dark, mother cloud. He sat at a comic distance from her on the bench, refusing to risk even the slightest touch, looking like a visitor from another century trapped against his will in 21st century London.

'Good idea not to watch the big networks,' she smiled, waving at the cameraman as he gestured that he had enough shots of the mad guru. 'But you should tune in to us. We're much smaller.'

'All you media people do is make fun of us. Make fun of things you can't understand. In fact, you are programmed to make fun of us. There may be many among us who are frauds. But, there may be a few of us who have some value. And all you do is look at me and think about yogic sex, tantric orgasms and snake tricks.' He seemed edgy, ill-at ease, someone buffeted about by the world, forced to grow up fast and develop all sorts of philosophies to make the world more bearable for himself.

'There is that temptation,' she agreed.

'I also can make fun of you. I can make fun of you as someone chained to big companies, wearing foolish clothes, having all forms of base physical relationships, leading a second-rate life.'

'Absolutely right,' she smiled again. 'Mine is exactly a second-rate life. In fact, it's a third-rate life. But I'm trying to make an improvement. That's why I'm interviewing you. We interview people from all parts of the world. Politicians. Movie stars. An international range of guests.'

'I don't want to be your international guest,' he exclaimed. 'I'm a sadhu. A priest. I wasn't earlier. But I became one because of the way the world treated me. You know,' he pointed his finger at her, 'it's not a coincidence that people who question the world are consigned to the corners. If they didn't consign us to corners, they would all go mad themselves.'

They talked all afternoon and into the rainy darkness of six o'clock. The cold began to close in around them as crowds hurried home and tourists melted away towards the pubs. Across the path, she noticed the Purification Journey Brothers were dispersing quietly through the freezing mist.

She wished she could see his face more clearly under the Castro beard. If Anand had painted him in such perfect detail, could it be possible that she too might have seen him before? Perhaps Karna was famous, perhaps his face had appeared in magazines or newspapers and inspired Anand.

Perhaps they had all seen him on their trips to Delhi to visit Anand's mother. Seen him in a puja pandal in Kolkata, among the people gathered to watch as the women danced during sindoor khela. Or in Varanasi, on Assi Ghat, huddled in a blanket of hash smoke on the steps leading down to the river. He had existed all this time in some distant city. She might even have heard his voice on the phone in a cross connection. Seen the arch of his neck in a crowd.

The Purification Journey didn't matter. It was only a joke he was playing on the world. A marketable formula to lead the gullible to his ashram. She could process it into a headline and dump it in the daily trash can of journalism to be taken away by paper recyclers and made into grainy sheets scribbled on by children and crumpled into waste. That would be the public arrangement. But in private, alone, he would be the idealist riding in to rescue her from the luxuries of cynicism.

'You talk about the Mother Woman,' she waved the pamphlet. 'Where's your own mother? Your father?'

'Oh,' he laughed. 'I have no mother or father.'

He was an orphan, he said, one of the thousands abandoned on a footpath in India. The only mother he had known was a billboard with the picture of a cow above his head, saying 'Drink More Milk'. He had lived under that billboard for the first three or four years of his life, sheltered by it, fed by charitable folk on festival days, sleeping in temple verandas, at the mercy of the beggar syndicates. Then, on one Independence Day, when the prime minister in a speech from Red Fort exhorted citizens to help the poor, the Purification Journey Brothers had adopted him and a few others as part of their new Hope-on-the-Road street children project, taken him to their Pavitra Ashram, and put him in school. When he was old enough, the Brothers even sent him to college where he got a degree.

His childhood had been happy enough. During festivals, the Brothers would dress him up like Krishna, paint him navy blue and stick a peacock feather in his hair so that wonderstruck passers-by would give him money. Sometimes they would take him to the slums through puddles of water into tin-roofed huts with shit curling in at the front door, so he could entertain factory workers and street vendors with his natural gift for story-telling. He said he had grown up close to the ground and in times of trouble, the ground would protect him. He was a renunciant who had vowed never to marry.

'A renunciant?'

'Sure,' he smiled. 'All pray and no work.'

'You say you want to purify love,' she searched her mind for a suitable query. 'But isn't all love pure?'

'No, not all love. When god created love it was pure. But love is being ruined. Ruined by lust. Ruined by jealousy. The love of man and woman is being ruined by competitiveness. We have taken our message all over the world. To New York. To Paris. Asking people to purify their love.'

His voice was defiant. He was inviting her to tease him because his outfit and conversation were tailor-made for ridicule; he was setting himself up to be laughed at, to have water dumped on his head, or for his hair to be pulled. He was ridiculous yet in need of protection; as if he was upholding the last of a dying world.

'And what religious denomination are you?' she asked.

'We have no religion as you understand it,' he said smoothly. 'We worship the Pure Love of the Mother Woman. To us she is the ideal.'

'And finally,' she asked before she switched her tape off, 'you said the bow and arrow was the dress of a novitiate. But why the bow and arrow, exactly?'

'Bow and arrow,' he shrugged, 'is for Cupid. To create love where there is none. For aiming at those who have a heart of stone and making them love. Just an ornament. Just part of my dress. Look,' he drew out an arrow and pushed it at her. 'Completely blunt. Once I finish my apprenticeship I'll take it off. I don't think it's stupid. No more stupid than a shiny tie. You don't' – he shrugged again – 'have to believe me. You can forget me. You can do your interview and walk away with me as your crank of the day. Everybody who is different is a crank. Only those who keep on buying ...what is it?...Dior and Nike... are not cranks. They are normal.'

'They too,' Mia agreed heartily, 'are cranks.'

Anand used to paint at dawn. Dawn, he said, was the time of insight. Dawn was the time of vision. One's own vision, not someone else's, bottled and tinned to acquire at a price in the shopping mall of vision. After Anand had died, she had woken early to try and hear if he was calling to her through the first watery rays of the morning but all she heard was the jangle of Mithu's new jewellery.

Irrationally, she brought him a slew of expectations. He would fill the emptiness. He would help her down from her high wall of grief. The intimacy of childhood would return, he would always watch out for her and care about what happened to her.

'Sometimes,' he smiled self-deprecatingly, 'I think I'm a genius, far ahead of my times. Other times, I think I'm nothing but an idiot. And you,' he pointed at her, 'think I'm a crazy guy from India who eats snakes and drinks human blood.'

'Karna,' Mia's voice was quiet. 'I don't know how to say this. Sounds silly. I've been a bit off lately. A bit loopy. My life's been a bit... here and there. My dad suddenly committed suicide, I moved back in with my mother, but it's not really working out. I need to make a new beginning. With my life. For some reason – and there's a good reason – for this good reason I feel as if I know you very well. As if I've known you all my life. No, no,' she said hurriedly as she saw him stiffen and sit up straighter, 'please relax. Nothing to be scared of. I know you are a – as you said – a renunciant, and I'm not making a move on you. What I mean is, I can't stop here. I can't just stop my interview and walk away and never see you again. I'd like to be friends and I'd like to get to know you better.'

'Of course,' he said excitedly. 'There is a connection between us. There is definitely a very deep connection. I have sensed it too, from the start, even though I did not want to mention it for fear of scaring you. We are going to be here all week for our publicity campaign. Please come again. And please come and visit us in India.'

'And can I meet you here?'

'I will be here,' he said after a pause. 'But then I leave on my mission.'

'Your "mission"?'

He smiled. 'Yes, my mission. There is a mission that I need to finish before I'm accepted as one of the Brothers. I can take off the bow and arrow once I have taught someone a lesson in love. But we will meet again. Let's meet every afternoon from now on. I'll be right here.'

'Great,' she said. 'I'd like that.'

'There are so many things I'd like to tell you. To convince you that there is no meaning in colour photos and magazines. Only a lot of stupid money chasing more stupid money.'

It's precisely because I'm so jaded, he sounds to me like a quack shrink. But there's an invitation here to let go of the weighty shit, to drop the posturing and rejoice in miraculous coincidences. Papa had no time for overeducated fault-finders and I could never bring myself to be corny. Papa wasn't afraid to sound foolish but I'm petrified of even a tiny concession to foolishness, to irrationality, to any kind of attention to that shopworn entity, the soul. *The Drama of Depression* is my bible. Rational thought is my shrine. Reason is my guide; I'm not driven by fleshy unreliable instinct or Zen intuitiveness or transcendental cravings. For my father, words were an obstacle; for me, they are everything.

Perhaps Papa married Ma precisely because she didn't have so many words at her disposal, while I've always searched for men who knew more words than me. Perhaps Papa jumped into the river so I would wake up to the seriousness of his way, to jolt me awake from my word-filled hauteur. Perhaps that's why he secretly turned his back on Marxist reasoning and opted for the other way. He said that I didn't think about salvation, never bothered about my soul or its journey, that I relied on my mind and not the wisdom of the heart, that I was too dependent on authors like Rosenthal and Silver.

But how is one to grow old and face death without the unknown audience?

⁂

'This is a completely loony cult!' she raged loudly at the SkyVision office. 'Some weird, all-male sect. Purification Journey, how to purify your love, purify your desire, reject the market, Pure Love of the Mother Woman. Extremely right wing on women and family values and all that. Fundamentalists. The guy's a nut.'

'Well, apparently you got on rather well with him. Careful, darling, next it'll be Pure Sex with a Python.'

The night streaked past on her way home. The music from the pubs made her wonder why she had let her social life become extinct.

ALQUERIA, GOA

Regrets, Indi thought, never come in a neat package marked 'regrets'. They hang about in bits and pieces like shreds of ash.

She turned a page of her Braille novel. Her house had been burgled recently. And the thief had taken away most of her Braille novels, as if he had known how dear they were to her. Thankfully *Pride and Prejudice* still remained. Along with the novels, all Sharkey's account books, some of them painstakingly transferred into Braille, had been stolen. The Phantom Listener had identified her belongings well.

Before the theft there had been three other incidents. A bag of dead rats had been thrown into the kitchen and the place had had to be treated with disinfectant for almost a week. No one had been allowed to use the kitchens, work had stopped and the food thrown away. Guests had been provided food from a hotel in nearby Fontainhas; costs had rocketed.

Then there had even been a short circuit in the central fuse-box; the switches had tripped and the electricity supply had been cut. The fuse-box had become a disembowelled gut with wires spilling out in different directions. Francis Xavier, Sharkey's animating spirit, guard, chef and lead guitar, had examined the box and pronounced that someone had opened it and set the fuses on fire.

And there were the blank calls. Sometimes, when Indi picked up her cordless, she heard the same quick breath she had sensed on her arm.

She was not as worried about herself as she was about Sharkey's Hotel because there had apparently been similar incidents all along the coast and in one particular case, it turned out that it was a property dispute and a sister had been harassing a brother simply to get his restaurant off her land. But the Phantom Listener couldn't be the disgruntled descendent of a past owner. All Sharkey's deeds were in order and had been scrutinized by lawyers. She had bought the land years ago on Justin's advice. Years ago, she had stood here, under the Alqueria zigzag and smelt serenity in the sea breeze.

A voice floated up under the roar of water.

'Indi!'

A voice in which she could hear the smile or sense the embarrassment; a voice which she knew stayed focused on her; a voice in which she could remember every expression. She knew the slow grin, the frown, the unexpected anger, the energy in the shoulders. She could hear attention wander, then turn back to her like a boomerang, doomed always to return.

She knew she enhanced his world every minute he saw her, she could feel his gaze touch her face and knew that it had remained unchanged for decades.

Justin.

For almost forty years, she had pranced in and out of Justin's life daring him to surrender. And he had conquered her by refusing to be rejected. For four decades they had tried to see who would break first. In a sigh or a question or an unguarded glance, they had looked for signs of victory.

She had never seen him old, never seen the grey hair he had told her about, nor the wrinkles or the hanging skin on his neck. She had only seen him properly when he was young. She had only seen herself young, she had been spared the sight of her own old age, even though she could feel the dryness of her skin and the ridges of stretch marks under her arms. In Indi's blindness, Indi and Justin were perpetually, irresponsibly, youthful.

They had met over three decades ago in Connaught Place in Delhi.

⁂

He was trying in vain to wave down a rickshaw. Buses and tempos hurtled past sending him teetering back to the concrete kerb of the circular road and he flagged her down asking desperately for directions as she drove by. She had stopped, fascinated somehow.

Justin had travelled many continents by now. He'd inhaled the spirit of the Sixties and become a textbook rebel. He felt stifled by his life in the luxurious east coast where he had worked as an intern, and felt drawn, instead, to the Third World.

While in America, he had felt as if bones and open mouths were rattling at him as he walked past the gentle greens towards his classes. He saw blood pouring from his food. He saw grimy baby feet running in distant plantations to provide him coffee. He saw long rows of brown bodies with asthmatic breath sitting in airless ateliers and cutting the diamonds which glittered in his mother's ears. He saw debt-ridden quarry workers with malnourished children working under a merciless sun to break stones that were used for the mansions of the far-away rich. He saw tiny infant fingers sewing gold thread onto garments sold to bored billionaires. His eyes acquired an unblinking stare, broken only when he laughed his slow laugh.

He had once been a glossy child with yellow curls dancing around his ears. But as he grew older he became shabby and unkempt. Shabbiness didn't suit him because Justin's sharp features were designed to be polished up for view. But he abused his appearance almost as much as he abused his heart.

A stubbornness began to grow inside him. He felt as if it was his responsibility to see things that other people could not. He felt impelled to ruin every dinner party that his parents forced him to attend by making statements that revealed how dysfunctional he was. After he had acquired his prized medical degree, instead of embarking on his parents' chosen course for him as a healer of the rich, he found himself making plans to travel to India. He began work in a government hospital in Delhi where the rusty machinery was speckled with newborn blood.

He knew only one way of penitence. He yearned only for one thing. To be able to love deeply and unconditionally. To love in spite of being rejected, to love in spite of being abused and humiliated. Only such love would assuage his guilt about the international injustices and the unfair world order, of which he was deeply, consummately, aware.

अ

At twenty-three, Indi's beauty and figure strained against her clothes. Every time she appeared among the family, relatives drew their breaths in and whispered to Ashish Kumar that they better get her married at once. Aunts became witty with jealousy at the sight of her.

Uncles looked away because she reminded them of their favourite whore.

When Justin saw her – a cerulean-eyed Juno sitting behind the wheel of an ancient Ambassador – an anxious conviction came over him. He saw creation at its most perfect. He saw his life easily elevated to the extraordinary even as filth pulled at his feet. He became unmindful of everything except his single great mission to love and thus bring a measure of balance to an exploitative world. He realized that the reason why fate had brought him to this country was only so that he could devote his life to this woman.

And when Indi first saw Justin, she felt as if there was a kindness shining out from him that she had never seen before. An honest yet somehow defeated kindness that made her stop her car and get out to meet him.

'You're American?'

'Afraid so.'

She laughed her throaty laugh. 'You're the enemy. We're with the Soviets here.'

'And you?'

'Me?'

'Who are you with?'

'I'm not with anybody.'

'Good,' he said because he couldn't think of anything else to say.

'What's your name?'

'Justin. Justin Reylander. And you are?'

'Indira. Indira Ray. Come. Come to my house. Come and meet my parents.'

She felt inexplicably in charge of this blond American, this man whose hair colour shone with a kindness she didn't believe in any more. As if he, of all the people who set eyes on her, was the only one who was brave enough to risk the blinding light of her dying eyes. And as if for his bravery he deserved her protection.

'Hey, no, that's crazy,' he protested like an old lover. 'I can't just show up at your home!'

'Of course, you can!' she cried. 'My parents are very happy today. They won't mind. They're having a party because I've just passed an important exam.'

Justin and Indi sat in silence in her room in Victoria Villa, while the party giggled in the lawn. They listened to the silence between them grow older. They wondered what life would be like if the other suddenly died. She felt as if her days would be broken in half, she would be an amputated limb if he were to now suddenly disappear. He comforted her by dispensing with the rituals of introduction, by acting as if he had always known he would find her.

'What are you doing here?' she asked, walking into his gaze. 'Are you CIA? Do you have a recorder hidden in your teeth?'

What am I doing here? I'm looking at the patterned landscape in a tumour that blossoms from a man's stomach. The stab wounds on a child that look like the edges of a hibiscus flower. The whorls of scabies on an old man left for dead.

He laughed. 'I'm a doctor. I've come to work here at the Medical Institute for a few months. I'm doing nights in Emergency.'

'I'm a civil servant. I'm in the IAS. That's the exam I passed. The Indian civil service exam.'

He leaned back in his chair and studied her. 'You don't look' – her pale blue sari was tied low on her waist and her blouse was a tiny slip of cloth, tight across her breasts, her hair swung down to her hips and there were rough daubs of blue shadow above her eyes – 'anything like a civil servant.'

'I'm trying not to. Why always dress the part? Why be what is expected? I have a license not to, anyway. You see, I'm half blind. Soon I'll be sightless.'

She told him about the retinitis pigmentosa. Her retina was dying at such speed that no force on earth could stop its death. She almost couldn't see anything at night and during the day two black prison bars stood to attention in the corners of each eye. She had lost her peripheral vision. She still had her central vision though, which tunnelled forward and beat against the prison bars. Sometime, in the next twenty or thirty years, she would be 'legally' blind.

'Yes,' he whispered. 'RP affects rod cells and cone cells. You might sometimes get white-out glares.'

'I do,' she nodded.

I'm going blind, I'm going blind was the refrain she woke up to, the song she went to sleep with and the chorus in her ears. It was her liberator and her dictator, the looming threat, almost a sexual charge, a beast forcing her to writhe against the light and dark to accommodate its appetite for her eyes. Over the last few months, while preparing for her examinations, she had fought against herself. She had locked herself in her room while her forehead became vermilion with pain and blood pounded behind her eyes. She had walked to the window to let draughts of air touch her eyelids. The jamun had rustled comfortingly during her shivering headaches. Unmindful of the doctor's warnings, she had stayed up all night studying and been ranked in the first ten among thousands.

'Unbelievable,' said Justin. 'An unbelievable feat for someone with RP.'

'Yes,' Indi turned her face towards her palm and held it at an angle where she could see the reddish stain of the cigarette burn across her line of fate. 'It is unbelievable. Thank god for my country and for what I can do for it.'

When the results were announced, she had thrown herself into celebration. She had lain naked on the floor of her room

and kicked up her heels in glee. She had bought herself a
bottle of rum and drunk a toast to herself. She had stood in
front of the mirror and let her hair cascade down to her
buttocks and stared at her disembodied appearance, far away
in a tube of light. She knew this was a vengeance on her
father. And she knew she had succeeded in fighting off her
helplessness at least for the duration of her professional life.

Justin felt his senses run into each other. He felt as if
he too was blind. Like an LSD crossover, he smelt her
beauty and heard her perfume. He was bewildered at himself.
His life in America was a universe away where she wouldn't
matter at all. He was bewildered at how willingly he became
her slave. He felt as if he was dying. As if his life had been
taken out of his hands and set on the slippery course to
some sort of abyss from which there was no escape.

There was a complaining knock on her door. 'They're
calling you,' Pom had whined. 'They're calling you outside.'

'Oh maaa!' Indi groaned. 'I have to go. I have to go and
smile and say yes and no like a programmed parrot and
cross my legs and not show my teeth. There's a pig out
there waiting to "see" me. Waiting for his mother to get
him married to me. Waiting for me to lead him like a fat
sow into the temple. If I marry him, I'll be the owner of a
pig. The owner, actually,' she winked at him, 'of a *rich* pig.'

'And will you?' he asked. 'Will you get married?'

'Come,' she whirled around. 'Come with me. I'll
introduce you as my American boyfriend. Then I won't
have to get married. They will all guess that I'm not a virgin
and that will be the end of the proposal.'

'No!' he cried aghast at this disrespect to local customs.
'No way!'

'Coward,' she spun in front of the mirror. 'You're
scared.'

He nodded, sitting on her bed with his head in his hands, surprised at how easy it was to throw one's life away.

When she appeared in the garden before her family, the gathering couldn't take their eyes off her.

'Congratulations, my dear!'

'Indi is an IAS officer! Such good fortune!'

'Indi, the pride of the family.'

'Come, Indi-ma,' Shiela Devi called. 'Come and have some of this tomato juice. A Virgin Mary for my new government officer!' Shiela Devi giggled and looked proprietorially towards the plump suitor who stood waiting in a starched white shirt.

As they crowded around, Indi dropped one of her bombshells, fortified by Justin's blue-eyed adoration.

'Why should I have a Virgin Mary, Ma?' shouted Indi so everyone could hear. 'You know I haven't been a virgin since the age of sixteen. One. Six. I told you about that affair of mine. I told you.'

After the party ended Justin waited in her room, feeling Victoria Villa vibrate with Ashish Kumar's bellows and Shiela Devi's screams. 'How dare you humiliate me in public?' Ashish Kumar's voice was so loud that the jamun tree in the garden shook with fright. '*How dare you?* You live in my house, you eat my food, and you treat me like dirt?'

'It was just' – Indi turned her green tempests on her father – 'a joke.'

'Joke? It's not for you to make jokes! Who are you to make jokes about these things?'

'The prime minister also has a great sense of humour,' said Indi brightly.

'Don't compare yourself with the prime minister, for god's sake!' screamed Ashish Kumar. 'Don't try to elevate yourself to standards you can't even dream of! For god's sake, you have a responsible job now. You have a position in society! You are an IAS officer. You will control government money!'

'He was such a good boy,' wailed Shiela Devi. 'Such a decent family. Now they will never even look at us again. Soon you'll be blind and nobody will marry you! You will ruin us. You were born to finish us.'

'And look at the way you're dressed up!' Ashish Kumar bellowed again. 'Just look at it. It's so cheap. Like an extra from Hindi films. No decent man will look at you. Is this how someone in the government dresses? Like a bazaar girl!'

He was tremblingly proud of her. He knew everyone regarded her as exceptional. He knew she would take the family name to far greater heights than he could. But why did she persist in letting him down? Could she not see how much he depended on her, how successfully he had fought against his disappointment when she was born?

She felt like a painted clown. A painted, unseeing clown, sitting in front of her parents, in her scanty blouse and her made-up face with her breath smelling of rum. She was a hideous caricature of a daughter. She was a drag queen, rushing out of her lair, feathered and perfumed, the butt of everyone's outrage. She could have easily told him what the roots of her anger were and why she felt so compelled to impersonate a volcano. But she didn't. Only Justin, waiting in her room at the back of the house, comforted her with his hidden presence.

Justin buried his head in his hands. He felt his spirit fall into a crater and then rise up again towards the moon.

When she stumbled back into her bedroom, stained with insults, shaking with rage, jumbled words and sentences pouring out of her mouth like vomit, he stared at her reflection in the mirror and sat with her until she fell asleep. He placed his fingertips at her temples to feel the thudding veins.

Then he went back to his room in the hospital and killed the running cockroaches absent-mindedly with his hands, counting the time he had left with her and the time he had left to live.

❦

'Indi!' he shouted standing on the beach in front of her cottage.

'What, Justin?'

'More trouble.'

'Trouble?'

'Computer trouble.'

'Computer trouble?'

An email virus had snarled the hotel reservation system. The engineers were working on it but they didn't think they would be able to fix it in a hurry. Meanwhile all the bookings had been deleted. Newly arrived guests were wandering aimlessly around on the beach. Some of them had taken the bus to other hotels. 'Oh god, where are you?'

'Here. Down at the beach. Come.'

'Come,' she muttered. 'I better come. Any sympathy for an old blind bitch like me? No, none at all. Hang on. I'll be there in a minute.'

She reached for her cane and began to feel her way down the wooden stairs. She knew the steps well enough. Hard footsteps down the stairs, soft and sandy on the beach. Down to where the beach began to smell sharp, touch the rocks surrounding the lagoon, then turn up and left towards the zigzagging road, with the wind sluicing her at right angles.

On the curve of the zigzag, under the gigantic hum of a banyan tree, Sharkey's Hotel.

'So,' she said. 'The Phantom Listener strikes again.'

'You think it's the same person?'

'Of course, it is. It's the Phantom Listener. The person or persons making the blank calls. Who stole my accounts. The rats. The person who smells of sulphur or whatever... I can feel him. I know when he comes. I can feel it when he goes.'

He put his arm around her. 'Move in with me at the hospital. Don't live on your own any more. Please.'

'Rubbish,' she scolded. 'I have my cane.'

'Indi,' grunted Justin, staring into her face. 'Please. I don't have a good feeling about this.'

She walked along the zigzag with Justin, listening. The quick breath, the glare on her face, she felt it clearly. She screwed up her eyes, willing her brain to transmit an image.

'Justin,' she asked, 'is there someone here?'

'Here?' his voice was hurried. 'Right here? Nobody I can see for the moment. No,' he looked around, 'there's nobody here. No Phantom Listener.'

'He's near me. Standing near me. And looking.'

'It's only me,' said Justin becoming increasingly troubled. 'The only one who's always standing near you is me...'

The scraping on the roof. The chemical odour. That long breathy yawn. *Gliding, wrapt in a brown mantle, hooded...But who is that on the other side of you?*

'We've waited long enough,' said Justin after a pause. 'We should tell the police. This may not be just a prank. Probably someone trying to push us out. I'll go down to the Fontainhas station.'

'I don't like you at all,' said Indi playfully, talking musically to the Phantom Listener. 'You are a foul spirit of some kind. I can sense you. I don't like you,' she sang.

'Indi!' Justin shook her shoulders. 'Knock it off!'

'You smell,' sang Indi again. 'Of nail-polish remover or gum. I can't quite make out. But you smell.'

'Jesus,' said Justin. 'I have to tell the cops.'

4

LONDON

Tiger, Mithu's astrologer-fiancé, worked in ABN Amro by day and charted the stars by night. Tiger's parents were from Leeds, his grandparents from Punjab and he was an amateur astrologer. After Anand's death, Mithu had visited him so persistently to ask if there was a second marriage in her stars, that he himself proposed.

His nickname was Tiger because of the two tiger skins he possessed, proudly displayed in his Marylebone Road flat. Tiger was in a hurry to marry the newly luscious Mithu and whisk her away to New York because an ascendant Jupiter had foretold that she would bring him luck in his new job. But he also knew that Mithu had vowed not to marry him unless Mia married first. So he found a prospective husband for Mia as fast as the horoscopes would permit.

The next morning, as Mia gulped her coffee with Mithu gazing at her in resigned bewilderment, the telephone rang.

'Mithu?' It was Tiger.

'Yes, it is I.' Mithu's father had been a member of the Kolkata Shakespeare Club and she had been brought up to always say, 'It is I' instead of 'It's me'.

'A boy.'

'A boy?' Mithu touched her forehead in grudging thanks to a hitherto aloof pantheon.

'Yes,' cried Tiger.

'For Mia?'

'Then for who, you?'

'But will she agree?' Detachment was the best principle in such times. Because the greatest of joys existed cheek by jowl with the severest of catastrophes and it was best not to get carried away by momentary happinesses. 'She hasn't agreed before.'

On previous occasions Mia had failed to turn up for meetings, devising arguments against arranged marriages and citing various cases where Indian brides had been abandoned or murdered by British Asian men.

'Talk to her,' urged Tiger. 'Talk to her.'

'How did you find the boy?' Mithu asked. 'How did you find the boy so suddenly?'

'I got his reference,' chuckled Tiger, 'from Mars. Mars. Which is at the moment in transit to Venus. It told me that he is in London in connection with his business. He's in business. Moksha Herbals. Selling herbal make-up to film studios as well as to top-notch places. He sells to all the major Mumbai film studios. Also to Body Shop, Selfridges – all stock his stuff. About fifteen outlets all over the world. Starting a retail at Heathrow as well. He's been here for a whole year. I've been talking to him. He's perfect, believe me. Perfect. Doing very well. Giving stiff competition to Kama Sutra and Lush. What a line he has. Nirvana massage oil, Ahimsa paint, Vedic eyeliner.'

'Sounds niche,' said Mithu in a moment of marketing doubt.

'Niche?' exclaimed Tiger. 'What do you mean niche? Totally mainstream. How d'you think Max Factor built the business in the Twenties? By supplying to film studios only then to the general public. High returns. And,' Tiger paused dramatically, 'only thiry-five.'

'And is he agreeable to this? Does he know?'

'He knows everything,' chuckled Tiger again, mysteriously this time. 'Knows how sad she is after Anand's ... passing. That moving back with you isn't working... knows that she mopes around all day. He knows.'

'He knows? What do you mean he knows? How does he know?'

'Simple,' Tiger chuckled again, even more mysteriously. 'The stars told him. He saw it. The stars are good, Mithu, the time is good.'

When Anand had been alive Tiger had crept about meekly with his digests, tarot cards and charts locked in his briefcase, intimidated by Anand's philosophical paintings. Now he was unabashed about planetary explanations for everything – from sour milk to delayed trains.

'He's not like the normal types, darling,' said Tiger. 'He's not going to lock her up in the house and make her cook for his mother all day. College education, fully from America. Wharton School. A-me-ri-ca. No hitting, beating, no dowry,' Tiger repeated. 'And best of all, no clothes. No problem with clothes. Any clothes. Jeans. Strap tops. Only thing is' – Tiger paused – 'India-based. She'll have to' – Tiger coughed – 'go there.'

'Oh no!' lamented Mithu. 'Why India? Why not Singapore or Hong Kong?'

'Hey, Mithu memsahib,' cried Tiger. 'Don't do *chik chik* like a fool. He has to live in India because that's where the suppliers are, that's where the laboratories are and the biggest buyers are. All the big film production companies. Raw materials. Herbs, aloe vera, eucalyptus oil, all that wonderful stuff. Hey, d'you know the fortune there is these days in aloe vera? Aloe vera is the new gold, lady. Aloe vera is the one stock I want to buy. And think of it. Going out: no problem. Working and having a career: no problem. Parties: no problem. Dowry: no problem. If all this is no problem, then what's the problem with India?'

'But why has he not found a girl for so long?' demanded Mithu. 'If parties are no problem?'

'Busy,' reasoned Tiger. 'Even his mother doesn't live with him. She lives in Goa where she owns a hotel. Beach hotel. Mother owns a big beach hotel. Really top-end stuff. It's called Sharkey's. Very sort of old-world classy, know what I mean? Shabby sophistication. I've seen the pictures.'

'Hotel?' Mithu frowned suspiciously. 'In Goa? There's a lot of drug taking in those places.'

'Mithu, Mithu,' Tiger moaned. 'You people are all getting left behind. They are more upper class than your entire family put together. Mother was a civil servant, understand? IAS officer! Even his grandfather was an IAS officer and his dad was in the army. What more d'you want? He got happy when I said Mia's dad was also dead. He said they'd have dead dads in common.'

Mithu put the phone down and stared accusingly at Mia.

'There is a chance,' said Mia, placing her coffee cup on the table, 'that the Indian Max Factor, may not like me. I may not be pretty enough. My skin may not be polished enough. Or I may not like him. It may not work out.'

'Work out?' cried Mithu. 'What do you mean, work out? What is there to marriage but more and more workout?'

'What if he kills me in a fit of rage? Face down in a village well?'

'What nonsense!' yelled Mithu. 'What sort of animals d'you think Indian men are? Don't make up these fancy stories about India just to make yourself feel good. That Indians are abnormal and only the British are normal. That Indians kill wives. Don't be an Orientalist!'

The great Edward Said, author of that heartfelt manifesto *Orientalism*, had been Mithu's ally in many a household battle with Anand. Her understanding of the book was rough but passionate and the word always shut Anand up and made him introspective about his paintings.

'Kills you!' she shouted again, triumphant at Mia's silence. 'Isn't that at least better than moping about and staring at me all day?'

'I'm not staring at you!' Mia cried.

'Then stop making faces at me. Always looking and judging and god knows what else. Boka mey. He may be very nice. And still you keep staring at me. Punishing me with your aging face!' Not even her worst enemy would say my daughter had an aging face, thought Mithu, the instant she had said it but people said funny things when they sensed they were on the threshold of a breakthrough.

'Fine, Ma,' snapped Mia. 'If that's how you feel, I'll meet him. I'll meet him and marry him and go away to India so you can be rid of me forever.'

'Good!'

'I'll do it. I don't care. You won't have to see my aging face again!'

'I'll fix it for the evening, Goldie,' Mithu's voice trumpeted after her as Mia ran out of the flat, 'This time it'll work out. I'm getting the feeling. Aamar chotto Shona!'

※

She felt light on her feet on her way to the tube. She had jumped off her high wall of grief and entered a charmed zone where astonishing things were happening. Her father had sent her his dream, she had met his muse who had turned out to be a renunciant monk. Now her mother was pulling her into her own dreams of a wedding and she was walking in, as if she too wanted to enter the charmed circle where the unexpected took place, and anticipation took flight.

Drs Rosenthal and Silver wouldn't approve. They would diagnose that she was experiencing a euphoric high which was only a prelude to a dark low; that her mind was racing ahead hyperactively and she was seeing connections where there were none. She was too light-headed to care, absurdly thrilled at this forthcoming proposal of marriage.

She spent the morning losing things, forgetting her mobile phone and drifting away from conversations. At lunchtime, she went down to Speaker's Corner to see Karna. A largish crowd had gathered and was listening with shifting attention to the red-haired leader's speech. Tourist cameras flashed and a policeman strolled around. Karna smiled and waved at her.

'Hello,' he said.

'Hello.'

'I'm glad to see you again.'

'Yes,' she smiled. 'I'm very happy to see you again, too.'

'I've been thinking,' he said, as they walked to their familiar bench, 'about your name.'

'My name?'

'Yes, what is it? You haven't yet told me.'

'Oh, I'm sorry, I should have told you. My name is Mia. Mia Bhagat. My parents are both from India. I was born and raised here in London.'

'Mia?'

'Yes.'

'Don't say Mia. Say *Maya*. Maya. Mia is a pretty Hollywood heroine. But Maya is much more profound. Maya is god's dream.'

'*Maya is god's dream?*'

'Yes,' he smiled. 'Maya is god's dream.'

To my dearest little Maya, love from Papa. Mia was a Hollywood heroine, but Maya? Maya was god's dream.

How could Karna know Anand's name for her? His black eyes were sharp but without clues. Something her father and he had perhaps planned when they had met in secret somewhere? Anand had painted the festival painting when he had visited the last Kumbh Mela in '89, over a decade ago. She had been sixteen at the time and vividly recalled his excitement. Karna looked as if he was in his mid to late thirties, he would have been in his early twenties, perhaps, when he met Anand. Or perhaps Anand had seen one of the Brothers from the Purification Journey. But how would he know about her name?

'And Karna? What does Karna mean?'

'Don't you know the story of Karna from the Mahabharat?'

Mia shook her head.

'Karna,' he said again, 'never got a chance to take his revenge.'

'Revenge? Against whom?'

He grinned at her. 'The mythological Karna didn't get his revenge, but I will. Read the story, Maya.'

She remembered visiting the Angkor temples in Cambodia, pedalling after her father down the lily-lined streets of Siem Reap, thinking how big and full of goodness was his multi-religious world, his world of Jesus, Kashi Vishwanath and Mecca. Goodness sustained by booze but bursting with high spirits and the belief that everyone could be a character in a painting.

That evening, when Vik appeared at the door, she felt her legs near her ears and her arms in the air in a silent cartwheel. Vik looked like a visiting sultan. Emperor Jehangir, beautifully dressed, with a wide smile. He was tall and athletic with pale skin, wavy brown hair and brown eyes. He bounced on his feet as he walked in, pumped her hand hard and said hello in an energetic voice. She had been expecting to be crushingly disappointed by her arranged match. She was expecting the businessman of Moksha Herbals to be shrewd and pot-bellied. Instead, she found herself looking at someone who must, judging from what she had seen of them, be one of India's handsomest men. Tiger and Mithu hadn't shoved her into the arms of a potential wife-killer. Instead they had rustled up an emperor.

A tide of tears began in her stomach. Ashamed and guilty tears. Poor Mithu. Poor Ma with her orange hair, standing, standing for many hopeful years, behind a counter with a sign saying 'Daughter for Sale'. Mithu wasn't mean. She was frail and human and out of her ineffectual embrace she had produced a Mughal prince for her only daughter. The tide of tears came crashing out of her eyes and flattened itself against her cheeks.

Tears came pouring out of Mithu's eyes too. She stood behind the rosy sofa, framed by the grimacing wall, humiliated all her life, by her own daughter, who had always misjudged her, always cast her as cruel, never believed she was capable of caring. Mithu and Mia wept in silent unison for a few seconds, while Vik politely looked away, until mother and daughter wiped their eyes embarrassedly and rushed to fetch him tea, asking about how he was enjoying his visit to London. Mia began a flustered harangue on the

Kargil war and how, in spite of all the hope generated after the Indian prime minister's bus journey to Lahore, India and Pakistan had still gone to war for a fourth time.

Termination before commencement, she thought. He thinks Ma and I are pathetic ladies eking out a desolate existence in a corner of London with him as the only ray of hope from the outside world. He'll get it over quickly and be gone forever.

But as they walked to the Eagle And Flag she felt his eyes on her in intimate appraisal. As if he had liked her transition from babyish blubbering to outrage at the India–Pakistan deadlock. Winter lights bloomed behind every bush as they walked. Elms rustled with a welcoming breeze and formed a leafy cathedral above their heads, enticing them to enter and walk far.

'I'm very sorry,' she sniffed. 'It's just that my mother and I were in the middle of one of our arguments. She can be the typical Indian mother sometimes. And I realize that you've been dragged here to see me. It's just pathetic, this whole arranged...thing.'

Vik laughed. 'Didn't expect my presence to bring on so many tears, I must confess.'

'I'm really sorry.' She could have hugged him for his generosity. 'You must think we're a weird pair. God, I'm so sorry.'

'Not a worry in the world,' he smiled. 'I don't think you're weird at all. I think you're lovely. But, hey, I'd like to make you feel better. I'm not so bad.'

How easily he had said it. How easily he had forgiven her and said that she was lovely. He was Jehangir, a prince of forgiveness.

'No, but it was awful the way we both started whimpering when you came in...I mean, you must've been gobsmacked by the way we just fell apart.'

Vik held her shoulders and turned her towards him. 'Stop apologizing. It doesn't matter. Now,' he smiled again, 'aren't you going to show me your city? I love it. Beautiful but also a little sleazy. Like Marlene Dietrich.'

She considered the parallel between city and movie star, concluded that it was apt and literary, and rushed into a tremulous confession: 'It's so very nice of you to come. So very very nice of you.'

'Very nice of you too,' he said mock-formally. He spoke with American-educated care. His sentences were measured and clearly enunciated. By contrast, her voice had become breathless. Her sentences broke off before they were completed, because these days she had become anxious to concentrate on the vibes that existed beyond spoken words.

'Anyway, you don't have to feel as if you're under any obligation,' she found herself insisting. 'I apologize. I'm really sorry. We could just grab a quick pint and be done with it. Tiger must have said that you have to meet me, because of their own plans, and forced you to see me. *They* want to get married and go off to New York, that's why *they*...'

'Relax, Mia.' His voice was soft. 'Don't worry. I love being here. It's a pleasure. Quick pint? No way. I mean, not just a beer. Now that we're here, let's, you know, hang out.'

'I've almost given up on marriage, you know,' Mia explained. 'One of my friends from university recently saved enough money to visit the Serengeti National Park after an email alert that the park wardens there were single and good looking. But then my friend returned after a few days with the news that the email had been a hoax and even the Serengeti National Park wardens were all married.'

He laughed, putting his arms around her shoulders and giving her a squeeze. 'You know, I have to say that's the funniest thing I've heard in a long time.'

The week slid into calm schizophrenia.

The absorption of unnatural circumstances is achieved easily by the depressed imagination noted Rosenthal and Silver.

At lunchtime she would go to the Purification Journey rally to talk to Karna. They would walk to their bench and she would listen bemusedly about a life away from money, the rewards of simple living and his belief in the Mother Woman. In the evening, she would go out with Vik and listen to his business plans and how well Moksha Herbals was doing, what an inspired idea it had been, how all the big studios in Mumbai were turning to organic make-up, how grinders of leaves and crushers of spices from the interiors of Bengal and Kerala had been given access to markets. He told her how inspired he had been by the story of Max Factor's invention of pancake which had transformed screen make-up and taken women all over the world by storm. He hoped for a similar discovery in his labs sometime and then there would be no limits on Moksha Herbals.

Karna sloped along, Vik walked purposefully, almost clicking his heels. Karna rarely smiled. Vik laughed often. He said he had decided early in life that a sense of humour was the best way forward. A sense of humour made the world safe for business. And now, after Moksha Herbals had stormed across many mountains and seas, he always had lots of parties where everyone could enjoy each others' company, do business and tell jokes. He said he loved luxury, good art and people. He always made sure his surroundings were the best in the world. She imagined his home, Jehangir's palace, where he, in a silk turban, wandered under flaming chandeliers and heavy gilt curlicues laced with spider-filled cobwebs.

He wore sharply ironed shirts and bright ties. His nails were neatly filed and his shoes were well polished. His clean-shaven face looked gym-fresh. Karna's polar opposite, she thought. They would jeer at each other.

He had a point to prove, he said. His MBA from Wharton had not only given him a good education but had also provided him a list of important phone numbers which had helped him create a product that had great appeal in the domestic film world and great international potential – both among wealthy immigrant South Asians as well as among certain kinds of buyers in Europe and the US. He wanted to prove to his international customers that they could do business with him. That they could buy his cosmetics, display them on the counters of expensive shops and be guaranteed satisfied customers.

He said, after many years of hiding behind high walls, India was rushing out towards the world. Rushing out with her ancient wares and newly acquired bodies and faces, clamouring to be heard; trying to sharpen up a slow creaky machine that was weighed under too many totems and lucky charms from the past. It was his destiny to prove that there was a new country behind the Himalayas.

A country crammed not only with lepers and snake charmers; a country in which he too strode among the crowds.

Things were changing. Fortunes were being built from mud. Hondas and Mitsubishis now negotiated dirt tracks. A young graduate might set up a computer centre in a mustard field and begin a lucrative outsourcing business to an American firm headquartered in Memphis. Today's cooks are tomorrow's motel owners in Dubai, and day-after's international tycoons. Fathers may push carts of fresh fruit down the street but they'll do their damnedest to make sure their sons become Members of Parliament. The old businesses in steel and coal were lumbering along, but there was another quicker, lighter economy offering its services to a new generation. Moksha Herbals had supply centres all over India. The freshest cream, the purest neem and young banana, the juiciest apricots and vanilla sticks were paid for and manufactured so that the sellers got the best possible price. A restless country had replaced a soporific one and he was a part of that action.

She was impressed. Clearly not all Indian businessmen were shallow smarties. As a mark of her newfound respect, she tried to make him laugh. The other morning, when she had stepped briskly off the tube in an effort to be the hotshot journalist on the move, she had landed chin first in front of Wimpy's with her hair under somebody else's shoe and her leg tangled in somebody else's briefcase. The gods had obviously been irritated by her stab at dynamism and tripped her up. And didn't he think that when Tiger gazed at Mithu, his hair positively frizzed with virile static? He laughed, throwing his head back and covering his eyes, and she was gratified.

They went to Tate Modern. She told him that Anand's paintings had been displayed here and she showed him her father's painting of the Kumbh Mela at home because she didn't know how to tell him about Karna. He said it was cool. He said the Kumbh Mela needed to be marketed far better than it was. They went to Covent Garden and to the Portobello Road market, ate in Greek and Indian restaurants and went for walks on Hampstead Heath. He bought her a lithograph of New York and she gave him a wool jumper.

The city had suddenly become generous and every building welcomed them with open arms.

One evening, he crossed his arms across his lanky chest and sized her up as a hairdresser sizes up a customer. 'Hey, you know what you look like?' he said. 'You look like a wild flower, a wild berry. Something growing freely in the grass. Not manicured and cut and twisted into a vase. Your eyes are not painted with my Vedic eyeliner. You're not wearing my Karmic lip balm. You're a hopeless consumer. My mother would call you a harum-scarum. But I think you're a love-in-a-mist. A love-in-a-mist. You know, the flower surrounded by green threads, like a mist?'

'I am in a mist most of the time,' she confessed. 'But Vedic eyeliner sounds great. I must remember to buy it.'

'No, don't!' he laughed. 'You don't have to. You're different. Most of the women I meet are just looking to hook any guy with lots of dough in any currency. But you don't give much of a damn, right? You're not fussed about money or how you look. You cry when you see a stranger. You cry about your father's painting. You want to get married so your mother can be free to marry her fiancé. Isn't that right? You're happy to throw your life away with a greaseball like me.'

'Hey!' she protested. 'Don't make me sound hopeless and when did I say I want to spend my life with you? And are you confessing you're a greaseball?'

'You're a tragic clown,' he smiled at her. 'Quirky, clever, aware of so many interpersonal dynamics. Let's do it, love-in-a-mist.'

'Do what?'

'Marriage, shmarriage, the whole fucking thing. Let's get the thing off the ground. Would you like to?'

Vik's face was long and regular. All over the world he would satisfy the definition, 'normal' and 'regular'. He was an advertisement for a universal corporate gene. He was the textbook definition of the word 'eligible'. Karna would look lost in an airport. They would look at him askance in a hotel lobby. He would be turned away from clubs. Tourists would take pictures of him.

'Yeah, I think so.'

She told Vik about her university boyfriend. She had clung to Sudden for three years and had tried different techniques to make him adore her. When she grew her hair, he had said she looked like a Greek prophetess and had taken her to meet his parents. But when she had pierced her eyebrow and entered the transparent dress phase, Sudden had suddenly left her. His devotion to her was dependent on the look of the day.

Vik laughed again. She confessed that she loved his laughter more than any other gift.

'You'll love my mother, love-in-a-mist. She's a great lady. She lives in a place called Alqueria. In Goa. She runs a motel there. She'll love you.'

She smiled at him in gratitude. He had known of Mithu and Tiger's plans. He knew that he had been set up to fall in love with her and marry her. Yet he hadn't run away from the trap. He hadn't wondered if she was seeing someone else. He had given her and her situation a chance and been generous enough to like her, in spite of her scheming mother and her planet-obsessed fiancé. He hadn't despised her, instead he had acted as if they had met by chance and had fallen in love by destiny. It was an act but it was an act of kindness.

She felt blessed.

They went to a SkyVision party. Steamers and balloons came flying through the air and bottles of wine popped in corners.

I'm swept off my feet by you, Mia. Do you have any feelings for me?

'Come on,' someone shouted. 'Let's dance!'

I think you're great.

'What's up? Is this your new boyfriend?'

Well, that's a start.

'God the music's awful. Let's have something else!'

It's the best start.

'Shit! Somebody spilled the juice!'

You won't regret it.

'Fuck, what's he done to his hair?'

I know I won't. Something about this feels right. There is a reason why this is right. You see, I met someone. An old friend of my father's. I met him recently. And somehow meeting you feels like a good sign. Although, I'm not superstitious.

You won't regret coming to my home.

'Karmakarmakarmachameleon you come and go you come and go …'

No, no. Definitely not. My father would have been delighted.

'A little bit of Monica in the sun, a little bit of Jessica all night long…'

I travel a great deal, London, Germany. They can't get enough of my stuff. But I'm not an old fashioned, traditional-husband type.

I'm not an old fashioned, traditional-wife type.

She wondered if this would be a good time to tell him about Karna. To give some hint of her fantasies about the sadhu who had been reincarnated out of her father's painting. To admit that she had recognized him after seeing him all her life and now dreamt more often of him than of Vik. That, somehow, it was precisely the appearance of Karna that had made her so happily accepting of Vik. It was Karna who made her want to jump off the deep end into the unknown, buoyed by an inexplicable optimism.

Reflected love. Attraction to one, so that in an ordinary reflex action, there is the readiness to meet and fall in love with another. So seduced by one that you become disposed to falling in love with many others almost immediately.

Mia was more imaginative than she was moral. She would much rather preserve a secret world than ruin the romance by being pedestrian and straightforward. Karna was a renunciant, part of the ascetic tradition of the Dasanami Nagas. Vik was a rational choice, a dazzling emperor of the world of commerce that Karna so despised. Karna was her lucky charm, a miraculous coincidence, he had made Vik's appearance possible. She would go with Vik to India, where she would go to his ashram and meet Karna again. Life had taken a positive turn and she would ride the crest of the wave.

Superstitions, signs and ephemeral connections had conspired to signal a new chapter of experience, a change of gear. The Drama of Depression would diagnose that she was overdoing the similarity between Karna and the painting. But his appearance here, now, added up to a phase of action in which to act positively was the signal her father was sending her. Vik had called her love-in-a-mist and asked her to marry him. Mithu's desperation would be unbearable if Mia refused, on the grounds of the missing ingredient known as love. Mithu came from a long tradition of arranged marriages which had proved far more durable and companionable than the bewildered silences and near-total collapse of understanding that had marked her own romance with Anand. Mithu would find all talk of love outrageous. And in the crowded context in which Vik had appeared in her life, love, or the lack of it, was of negligible importance when compared to the transcendent rightness of the moment.

Her return to India, the rediscovery of her parents' birthplace, this was the natural progression she must make, now that Anand had quit the world and was asking her to take up the baton and run the race that he had abandoned. She could never find solace in London; in London, she would be trapped by the prescriptions of Rosenthal and Silver.

She'd have to seek solace in India, in the now lost footprints of her ancestors. Yes, the road ahead was clear.

※

'Congratulations and jubilations,' Mithu sang. 'Having a home. Having a family. *These* are the things, Goldie. These are the things. Can't just keep running to some office and keep doing computer.'

'Doing computer' was Mithu's term for all professionals, evocative as it was of intercourse with a hard disk.

Vik said he had to go away for a few days. Moksha Herbals was getting ready for a contract with a German chain. He had a couple of business meetings in Berlin. In the meantime, she must start shopping.

Before he left she offered him her grief –

'My father died quite suddenly. They said it was suicide. But he didn't tell me anything or give me any warning even though he knew he was everything to me and I was everything to him. We had this thing going. He thought I was too cynical, I thought he was often just being silly. He said it was important to be silly. That he'd made a mistake by educating me so much. Now I can't let him die away. I've got to preserve his silly world. His way of seeing things is very precious to me, even though I always argued against it.'

Street lamps shone in Vik's eyes when he pulled her towards him. 'My father's dead too, baby,' his voice was soft, like someone speaking through an injured lip. 'He was a soldier. He died before I was born. We have dead fathers in common. We'll be fine together, love-in-a-mist. Just dandy.'

'Shall we,' she said after a pause, 'call and speak to your mother?'

'She doesn't have a phone where she is.' His voice was energetic again. 'We'll go and visit her as soon as we can.'

'But don't you want to call her?'

'I'd love to, baby. Just that she doesn't have a phone where she is.'

She didn't understand the silence that followed. It was a silence that poured out suddenly, as if she had accidentally pushed open the lid of a manhole and the underground had opened beneath her feet and sent up a fountain of silence. She shrugged it off.

❀

'I'm getting married,' she informed Karna the next afternoon.

'Married?' he exclaimed incredulously. 'My god, that was quick. When did this happen? Why are you getting married? It is a big mistake! That giant wheel which sits in the middle of the world's oceans, spinning helpless boys and girls around in different combinations. That's the wheel of death. Why are you dying?'

'But I thought you would approve,' she cried. 'Isn't marriage Pure Love?'

'Human emotions shouldn't be tied to the waistband where they can get dirty, Maya. They should soar with the clouds. Why should one human being expose his dirt to another? Don't you ever feel how meaningless marriage is? Scientists say that billions of years ago life existed on the volcanoes of Venus. Billions of years later someone will visit earth and find a wasteland. Even though lots of people in this wasteland got married, thinking they would be eternally happy if they did. The way to Pure Love is not by getting married.'

'I think I'm doing the right thing. I have a good feeling.'

'Love does not come with things like marriage.'

'I think Vik and I will be fine. This is a good time in my life. I just have a good feeling.'

'Vik?'

'Yah, that's his name.'

'Ah,' smiled Karna. 'Mia and Vik. A nice couple with two short nice names. Transit lounge names that even the airport immigration officer can pronounce, no? Easy names for a globalized world. Except your name is not Mia. Your name is Maya. No, Maya,' he peered at her through his glasses, 'you don't look happy to me. You look like a zombie. A mongoloid idiot.'

'Thanks,' she grinned back, feeling thoroughly appreciated. 'Me with my transit lounge name. How come you're so perfect?'

'I'm sure I am at least better than this Vik. What does he do?'

'He owns a cosmetic company, Moksha Herbals. They supply organic make-up to film studios as well as to cosmetic retailers.'

'Oh no!' Karna hit his forehead with his fist. 'A frivolous tycoon! One who uses philosophy for his commercial needs. Moksha Herbals! How dare he make fun of an eternal principle. Perhaps he paints his face every morning with all his make-up. Perhaps he drinks orange juice every morning and worries about the acidity in his stomach and kisses you with his mouth closed.'

'Hey,' Mia protested. 'Give it a break, okay? He's a great guy. Really great.'

'It's your choice,' he shrugged. 'Your choice of an inferior life. There's no happiness after things like marriage.'

'Then where is there happiness?'

'There is only happiness,' he smiled, 'at the Kumbh Mela.'

He said it before she could. He said it although she had planned to say it. She had known from the moment that she had seen Karna. She had known that the heart-thudding familiarity between them was not simply her imagination playing tricks. That something existed between them which had always existed and would throb to life even if they had been animals incapable of thought. He would never let her get close, this spiritual healer who was himself in need of being healed, he would sit far away from her, keep her at arm's length but he wouldn't be able to deny, however hard he tried, the spark of an ancient recognition. The coincidence was stretching her imagination to breaking point; she wanted to burst into a babble of explanations that perhaps Anand had just seen a picture in a magazine of Karna at the Kumbh Mela or that his was just a typical sadhu face, but at the same time she wanted to stay quiet and let the silence take over. In the stone age, before the coming of human language, memories must have expressed themselves in mental pictures, there was perhaps no felt need for a rational sequence of events.

'Yes,' she said after a pause. 'I know it.'

'You should go,' he said pulling at his shirt. 'You should go there and see.'

'See what?'

'See the sun rise over the Ganga. See how people surrender to the river. How people surrender to life. See how people learn to love each other. You should go there. See the naked sadhu.'

'Yes, my father told me.'

'Those,' his eyes narrowed behind his glasses, 'who have nothing to lose, don't mind shedding their clothes.'

The Grand Pitcher Festival, the Mahakumbh would begin early next year, he said. The largest spiritual fair in the world. Sages, holy men and women, firewalkers, mystics, mediums, ghost-trackers and soothsayers would come. Pilgrims would pray and chant. Naked mystics would show off massive erections. The penis, deadened to all desire, would become an object of pornographic caricature for television cameras, but for those present it would be a kind of liberation. Even Coca Cola and Pepsi salesmen would strip and run naked into the water, hoping for the accidental chance of revelation.

Would Vik ever think of going to the Kumbh Mela? No, he wouldn't. She couldn't imagine it. Vik was a busy executive, he kept the world sane with his normal laughter, dashing from city to city with faxes, emails and mobile phones as the ever-changing unchangeables. Karna was laughable, a freak who had once painted himself blue, stuck a feather in his hair and called himself Krishna. The army of normals versus the army of freaks, the real versus the unreal, the sane versus the insane. She knew where she stood but it was time to peek across enemy lines.

❧

She walked away from him in a daze. On the ride home, she stared blindly out of her window and that evening she sat up late and wrote her resignation letter. Her time at SkyVision had been very fulfilling. But she wished to marry and move. It had been so wonderful to be a part of a great team. She had learnt so much, acquired so many friends. But now she had met somebody wonderful, a soulmate.

She felt as if she could easily step naked off the morning train, like the Dasanami Nagas of the Kumbh Mela. Amidst grey suits and white shirts, would run the journalist as stripper. The shrieks of bystanders would be nothing but harmless birdsong. She would shrug them off, because none of them were as liberated as she was, by the simple power of a painting coming to life.

'Very good news, darling,' – her producer looked at her searchingly – 'lovely news. Congratulations.'

'Thanks,' she smiled.

'All good things in the future, Mia. Only good things.'

'Only good.'

After the initial shocked murmuring, her colleagues planned her farewell party and chatted about what they would wear to her Indian wedding. In the ensuing debate over short black dress versus cream frock, she made an excuse, grabbed her bag and ran out.

अ

'Today, is the day,' Karna said as they sat on their bench, 'that I have to go, Maya. As I told you, I have to go away on my mission.'

'Today? Right now?' She heard herself sound desolate. She saw herself staring at him in an open-mouthed way. He turned towards the rallyists.

'You'll see me again, Maya.'

'Vik's gone too,' she said as if by way of explanation.

'What is this, Maya?' Karna placed his chin in his hands. 'You will miss us both? Me and your tycoon? But don't worry, we'll meet again. Promise you'll come to the ashram.'

'Promise.'

A sudden roar of sun pounded down and converted him into a faceless silhouette. Light blazed in his spectacles masking his eyes. 'You know, Maya, I have very much enjoyed being with you. I have seen how innocent you are. It is very rare, this innocence. You are that rare thing and you have convinced me that innocence exists.'

'And you have convinced me that one doesn't have to find words for certain things. That there's meaning beyond... sensible language. I don't know if that makes any sense.'

'Have I?' he frowned. 'Then I will come and see you even if you don't find your way to the ashram. Leave your address with the Brothers.'

She looked up into his face and found he was studying her through his spectacles. 'I have never met anyone like you, Maya. There is an openness in your face, an honesty I didn't think existed anymore.'

'So I *will* see you again,' she said.

'I will see you again, even if you don't want to see me, Maya. You will be mine one day, part of my life, remember that. One day you will leave your Vik and come with me. But for the moment, I must say goodbye.'

'Bye, Karna.'

She watched him disappear into the crowd. Handsome, happy, this-worldly Vik, had entered her life only so that she could be free to begin her journey with Karna. A stop at the station only to wait for another train. Vik had called her a wildflower, a love-in-a-mist, but Karna was going to take her to the Kumbh Mela. The holy man and the businessman wouldn't understand each other, but she understood them both perfectly.

She understood that she would never be abandoned again, she understood that she had jumped off the lonely wall to find that love was growing at her feet like two trees slanted in two different directions.

For the moment both had gone. One to his Berlin business meeting. The other to his mission. But soon she would go to New Delhi, the city where she would find Karna's ashram. She was alone, but not for long. Karna is my father's painting. I am getting married to Vik and this is some sort of fantasy. My mind has unhinged into a focused acid trip where I'm seeing things I normally wouldn't. A huge amount of history has been crammed into a short space of my otherwise blank existence and is making me crazy. Like a wild night's partying after weeks alone in the desert. Like a screaming day at a non-stop rock concert after a lifetime's solitary confinement. She felt herself spiral upwards towards the sky; as if the satellite overhead was the circling orb of her future.

She would go with Karna to the Kumbh Mela. She would leave the ice rain, the dull-eyed homeless, the heavily-pierced prostitutes in Soho, turn her back forever on this city where she had become a perpetual stranger. Leave Mithu to her life with Tiger.

And find what Anand had seen.

She would understand why her father had chosen death above life.

ALQUERIA, GOA

Justin walked down the zigzag to the police station in Fontainhas to ask if they could provide some police protection for Indi. She was blind, she lived alone, she had insisted on living alone, intruders would see her as a target and she would never know or be able to protect herself. She felt she was being watched, there was someone on the roof, in her house, someone at her elbow, someone stifling a yawn nearby. She had smelt something, a smell of an unidentifiable chemical. There was definitely somebody there.

The incidents at Sharkey's Hotel were worrying and there could be others.

Justin had his own rooms in St. Theresa's Hospital where he was always on call so she was mostly on her own. Once they had caught the person making the blank phone calls and sending the email viruses they could dispense with the guard.

The policeman at the desk, his speech as slow as the Goan afternoon which slides calmly into siesta, agreed to send some help. For the moment, he said, they could make do with Francis Xavier.

Justin frowned. Francis Xavier was useless. Francis Xavier, who every evening stopped off at Nerul fish market to inspect the catch, then for a leisurely beer at Dom's Bar And Rest before ambling back to his duties, slower than a jellyfish undulating its way into the sea. 'Can't you send someone else? Francis Xavier isn't the fastest guy in the world.'

'Don't worry, Mr Justin,' the cops smiled indulgently at the bedraggled American. 'Does anything bad ever happen in Alqueria? Nothing in Alqueria. But don't worry. We'll be on watch.'

What keeps this old foreign man here, the policeman wondered, as Justin walked back down the zigzag. Why does he never go home to where he belongs? Working day and night at the hospital, taking care of the beautiful owner of Sharkey's, totally disregarding his own appearance, he was like a man who had already committed suicide.

❧

Justin went back to Indi's house to tell her what the police had said. Don't worry so much, Justin, said Indi. I'm far better at defending myself than you think. I'm more than a match for the Phantom Listener.

She could no longer see the Alqueria sunset. But she could hear the twilight guitar from the homes, the evensong from Santa Ana, the music from Sharkey's. She could remember the families sitting out in their verandas, under the low tiled roofs and she could smell the coconut toddy. She could remember how cashew trees became luminous in the setting sun and how, very rarely, a pearl floated in with the tide. She could smell the rain on the palms. Palms that were like skinny bent uncles offering chocolates to a child. Avuncular palms.

She could smell the receding tide. She could hear the roar of the sea and the low horn of the barge. Soon the bells of Santa Ana would ring.

As they walked along Capuchine Beach, Justin pushed his spectacles back and put his arms around her shoulders. 'It's the Kumbh Mela again next year,' he said. 'Remember I was there twelve years ago?'

'Don't I just,' laughed Indi. 'Your Oriental trip. Where was I? Ah yes, the Ministry of Social Welfare. Had to have you rescued from the station because you had lost your tickets or something at Allahabad station. You're a gullible gora.'

'Possibly,' said Justin holding her closer. 'I wonder whatever happened to Anand. Remember Anand Bhagat, the painter from London? That oil on canvas of the Kumbh with me as an Indian sadhu? Made me sit still for a whole afternoon on the sand, wouldn't even let me get up for a pee. It came out terrific, I must say.'

'Yes, I remember you telling me about Anand and the painting. Where is he these days?'

Justin shook his head. 'Don't know. He left me his address and contact number but I, I think I lost it. Hilarious, the way he kept following me around. He was teaching in

London if I remember correctly. Anand, super guy, great painter. Wonder if he'll be there again this year.'

'The painting did very well didn't it,' Indi reached for his hand. 'Got some great notices at the time.'

'Yeah, it did,' said Justin. 'Wow...a long time ago. Wonder where it is now. Oh, well...Remember the poem he read out to me?

> *The universe is a horse.*
> *Its eyes are pierced with evil.*
> *Its ears are pierced with evil.*
> *But from its mouth comes... Breath.*
> *And Breath is the Word.*
> *And the Word is... Adi.*
> *Him without Beginning or without End.*
> *Him who is One and Indivisible.'*

Indi laughed again. 'Hey, I remember your Advaita phase. Ramana Maharshi. Advaita, the philosophy of what... non-duality?

'I find it totally unique,' Justin said. 'A single reality, the single being. That two disparate beings can coalesce into a single whole. Individual A, Individual B, actually the same. A man and a woman, the same. Polar opposites, the same. King and subject. The believer and non-believer, the same. God, the brahman, and the human – the atman being the same.'

'"*I am the ever-shining unborn,*" quoted Indi, "*one alone, imperishable, stainless, all-pervading and non-dual – that am I, and I am forever released.*" ...Shankara. Right?'

'Hey, pretty good. You know your Advaita too!'

'Oh, bugger off,' said Indi. 'All very egoistical. The supreme I, me, the one-ness of the Brahman. All very male. The one-ness of the male reality, basically. The single Big Guy.'

'Not male at all,' argued Justin. 'It could be equally applied to the female. She who creates and She who destroys being the same. A bit' – he stroked her thick black and grey hair – 'like someone I know.'

They walked along the water's edge. Glistening sandy flats were streaked with crimson from the setting sun. Drinkers in Sharkey's called out greetings to them, admiring these two unusual individuals who even in old age seemed as urgently excited to be together as secret lovers meeting once a year.

They went back to the house and opened a bottle of Grover's red wine. Indi lay back in her chair and waited for Justin to light her an evening cigarette.

'Vik's getting married,' Justin whispered.

'Really? To whom?'

'Someone called Mia. He met her in London. He phoned me at the hospital.'

She inhaled on the cigarette he had placed between her lips. Then she slid further down on the reclining chair so that his lips brushed her cheek as he bent over her.

'So are you going to attend the marriage?' she asked.

'Are you? Why don't you?'

'I don't want any responsibilities,' she shrugged. 'I'm denying responsibility. I'm not responsible.' She blew a smoke ring in the direction of the sea. 'I want you to take me back to the bedroom and make love to me gently, and then cook me my dinner and make love to me again because I'm so blind I can't read and write and am therefore illiterate. What a sorry end this has been for an upstanding servant of the government who gave her best years to the cause of the people of this country.'

He laughed. 'Excellent idea, Madam Additional Secretary.' None but the brave, he had once written to her from America, deserve the fair. Justin's eyes were still piercingly blue. As blue as the sea on which his forefathers sailed their Viking ships to America. He had always been remarkable looking. But now, after a lifetime of devotion to Indi, he was thin and stooped, his pale skin was mottled, his grey hair hung about his shoulders and his once blond beard and moustache were snowy. His clothes were so bedraggled that he looked like the backwash of a tide.

He walked up and down the zigzag, a fully surrendered man. So surrendered to Indi that he could have been a priest who had given up his life for the love of his own god.

The rain stopped and the stars came out. The veranda of the house looked out on to the curve of the bay, where a year later a plane would break up and fall. Starlight stabbed at the sea as if to prepare it for the assault, to meet the challenge of burning metal.

Justin and Indi didn't know what lay ahead. They couldn't see the drowning plane. They just drank their wine and became as selfish about each other and as contemptuous of those outside themselves as they had always been.

He had listened silently to her rages. He had bent over her, as the palms bend over stormy seas, and placed soothing hands over her eyes. She had deprived him of everything. But he had continued by her side, joking that if he went back to his life in America he would be like a mad stallion trapped in a polite parade of ceremonial ponies.

But even though he had given up everything except his skills at repairing bones and easing aches to be her protector, she would be the cause of his death.

Her eyes turned towards the ocean. She drank her glass of wine feeling its redness stain her throat and shivered with a terrible recollection. A recollection that made her world heave under her chair.

There was that other memory that had been returning to her of late. Her mind floated back to a hot afternoon when the sun had beat on the window panes so hard that its reflection had torn up the last of her eyesight. That afternoon, sunlight had intruded for the last time into her eyes, intruded with biting agony, then disappeared forever.

'Remember that hot afternoon?' he whispered, as if reading her thoughts. 'Somehow I keep thinking of it nowadays. I keep seeing it. I think of it as often as the tide comes in to the beach. That hot afternoon in a hospital. You said a dry breeze had come beating against the windows, when the street outside had been covered in dusty heat. That hot afternoon.'

'No,' lied Indi. 'I don't remember. I remember nothing.'

You are a liar and I'm a prisoner at your side, Justin thought, uncaring of how ridiculous I am, even to myself. Perhaps human beings are not meant to be loved as dementedly as I love Indi. If they do, they became enraged and lure their lover to greater heights of sacrifice and pain. Receiving love never really makes people content, they are only motivated to put their lover through an even tougher obstacle race.

He stroked her hair. There was a new sound in the hush of the waves that scared him. He turned his head. Indi was right. A stranger had come to Alqueria. Someone was standing outside the cottage. There was someone there. He could feel it, he was sure. There was a smell, a funny unrecognizable smell, yes, he could smell it too. Nail-polish remover? Hair dye? Someone whispering through the net door, walking in the beach, yawning outside, as if weary of a long vigil. He squinted towards the waves.

A shiver ran down his shoulder blades at what he thought he saw.

5

LONDON

Mia trailed down Regent Street with Mithu, imagining Karna suddenly darting out from behind Liberty; wondering agitatedly why Vik's hugs were so chaste.

After he came back from Berlin shouting, 'Hey Mia' with the airbus engine behind his voice, she had led him up to her room and assured him that they didn't have to wait. As he began, dutifully, to undress, she saw that strapped to the belt of her athletic emperor was a small monitor which looked like a TV remote, about the size of a deck of cards. A thin plastic tube connected it to a circular disc that sat just above his pelvis.

He studied her expression and explained: 'My Medtronic MiniMed implantable insulin pump. The closest thing to an artificial pancreas. I set the monitor and the pump delivers insulin into my body through a needle or cannula implanted under the skin. Need to change it every three or four days but it only takes ten minutes,' he shrugged. 'The latest technology against diabetes mellitus.'

'You have diabetes?'

'Yup and I'm a pumper. Freedom from insulin shots.'

'Shouldn't you be more careful then, with all this travel?'

'Nah,' he shook his head. 'It's all under control. Was diagnosed when I was ten.'

'Shit!'

'Not shit, piss!' he laughed. 'Went to the loo a lot.'

'Must be tough to live with.'

'Not really. I can disconnect the tubing,' he pointed to the disc, 'when I'm showering or swimming, and a computer controls the insulin level. Sounds complicated but it's not. It doesn't hurt,' he laughed again, 'if that's what you're concerned about. There are many little kids who are pumpers too. People live with these things: Iron in their knees. Pipes in their hearts. Steel in their backbones. The human body is not alien to metal.'

In bed she brought him the full force of her loneliness and heard him gasp in surprise at her dreamily powerful desires. Her body, he said, was the most precious thing he had ever touched. Not only because it was beautiful but because she seemed so far away, as if she was drifting through his arms towards some other planet of limitless eccentricity. He said her narrow hips and soft waist were bewitching. She really was a love-in-a-mist.

She couldn't think of anything to say. His insulin pump clouded her vision. It telescoped the world into a giant capsule which barrelled incongruously through her night-time mind. She imagined the needle positioned in a perpetual pierce of his skin, a spaceship inching through blackness towards the infinite nothing.

His embrace was soft. His palms were light and clammy. His interest lasted for what seemed to her was two seconds before crumbling between his legs like an acrobat with a broken back, sending her thoughts careering back to Karna's muscular silhouette.

As he hurriedly pulled his trousers back on, she felt as if she was part of a triangle with two half men, each one fading at the opposite end into a background of fuzziness which confused her. Her fiancé desired her but was too embarrassed to take his clothes off. Her lover was a renunciant monk. She felt dissatifaction gnaw at her abundance, as if she was shut out of a room filled with riches. The sky, which looked as if it was bursting with stars, was as lifeless as a studio set.

The moon shone down on the cherry tree. Vik lay exhausted while she stood at her window, wondering if she should tell Karna that she was disappointed with her prince. She imagined him skulking under the cherry tree, a troubadour singing for her to open her window and let him in, so he could show her what it really meant to be lovers.

'Sorry, a little out of practice,' Vik coughed. 'Long hours. Travel.'

'Not to worry,' she said. 'I love you. I do.' This is not the time for doubt. This is the time for laughter, for my mother's wedding, for me, for my mother's jewels, for packing, for goodbyes and for new beginnings. The rest will come with time.

After our world's been built, his broken acrobat will be infinitesimal compared to what lies ahead.

🦂

The time, Tiger announced, was at last auspicious. The galaxy had arranged itself into a moment of marriage. The vibrations between continents had become sweet. From Hong Kong to New Jersey to London to Leeds, the beautiful and the successful were being led into excellent unions. Long-dead ancestors would awaken from the smell of frankincense and hot-foot it down from the other dimension to bless this party.

A stream of goodwill wound its way towards her. Emails arrived announcing the flight timings of aunts. The oil-paint-and-turpentine flat filled with wedding gifts.

The Newark aunt and uncle arrived, as did the Californian side of the family, declaring that they supposed this meant a lifetime's free supply of Moksha Herbals even though the stuff was probably manufactured by child labour. Every meal became a feast, a metaphor of cultural fusion. Chicken in onion curry, trout in coconut milk, barbecued vegetables, pumpkin tart. And kheer, with gulabjamun on the side. The table was a gastronomic United Nations. Civilizations didn't clash here, they simply flowed discreetly into the common waters of the tastebuds so that when a wedge of lasagne quivered up between mountains of lemon rice, it was as if the mountains that divided people were just so much cheese.

There was an ashirwaad ceremony followed by a turmeric bath. Some of the rituals were forgotten, but thank god his family wasn't there to notice. Where were they?

He had told her in great detail about his home in Delhi – the pistachio-marble flooring he had recently put in, the leather sofas, the emerald grass of the lawn, the two huge trees in the garden, the jamun or java plum and the semal or silk cotton, and underneath the trees, the flowerbeds lined with triangular brick patterns that his grandfather had made. He said he would take Mia to meet his mother in Alqueria as soon as they arrived in India.

Mithu was in far too much of a hurry to ask questions – too grateful for the opportunity to say goodbye, too caught up in the horoscopic precision of the time to admit to any deficiencies in the proceedings. It was impossible to tell Mithu that it was Karna and not Vik who had begun to dominate her thoughts. That her fiancé's desires were flaccid;

that sometime in the future she was convinced Karna would love her far more passionately than her husband ever could. But then Mithu came running to her in a flurry of fabric, in a tremulously blissful state, and it would have been unforgivable to rebuff her with grim tales of disappointment.

The front door of the flat was hung with garlands and the floor decorated with rangoli. Mithu's sari was the dressiest as she was not only Mother-of-the-Bride but also, herself, Bride-and-New-Yorker-to-be. She rocked back and forth to the drumbeat of 'I am the most fortunate of mothers, the most fortunate.' She sang: 'First my daughter, then me.'

Aunts daubed each others' foreheads with sandalwood paste. They lit lamps and agarbattis and prayed with the combined power of their L'Oreal and Gucci. Then they switched to Ketchup and swung around in their heavy silks. The SkyVision gang came with champagne and eagerly joined in the dancing. Tiger had managed permission for a shamiana. The fire altar was created in the garden at the back. Vik and Mia walked around the fire seven times while the priest's voice rose, shrilly invoking the gods, the elements, all plant life and many minerals and ores to bear witness.

They spent their wedding night in his room at St James Court Hotel where Vik fell asleep almost immediately, apologizing: 'The wedding was such a laugh, baby. I've got to make one last trip to Berlin before we go home. After that, life will be one long party.'

He apologized again the next morning. He simply must make another quick trip to his German clients in Berlin. There was a possibility of a new order from a film studio specializing in cross-cultural cinema.

Once Moksha Herbals was truly on course, once the supply chains were well established, once supervisors in

India and buyers in Europe could interface independently, his travelling would slow down.

爱

She went in search of the Purification Journey as soon as she had seen him off at Gatwick. The Brothers had disappeared, there were no banners to be seen. But the red-haired man who had been making speeches was standing on the pavement talking to what looked like a group of new recruits.

'Hello,' she called.

The red-haired man waved back. 'The Almighty Presence bless you, Sister. How are you?'

'Karna's gone, right?'

'Who?'

'Karna,' she said. 'I interviewed him. I'm a TV journalist, remember? I've been coming to talk to him. Don't you remember? We used to sit on the park bench. He said he had to go on a mission. He spoke about a mission. That's why he's gone.'

'Sorry. I don't know any Karna. Probably just someone in the crowd.'

'You don't know him?'

The red-haired man looked straight at Mia. He had a pink and orange face in which the colours merged and shone. Behind him, tall buildings rose like horns in a Viking's helmet. Mia blinked.

'There is no one here by that name who is part of our group, Sister,' he said again in a loud clear voice. 'You must be mistaken.'

'But I met him here!' Mia cried. 'I've been meeting him here. You've seen me. You said you had seen me. The bearded guy with glasses. He was dressed like you, except he had a toy on his back. He said it was the dress of a novitiate, someone who hasn't yet become a Brother.'

'Yes, I've seen you but I'm very sorry, I have never heard that name.'

'But he was here. Standing right by you. He was right here.'

'Sorry, Sister. I can't help you. I don't know any Karna.'

She looked down at the folded bit of paper in her hand. 'I came here to leave my address. In Delhi. I'm going there.'

'Excuse me, Sister,' his voice was fervent. 'But I really don't know who Karna is.'

'Just keep this,' Mia thrust the paper at him. 'In case he comes for it, okay? I'm sure,' she paused, 'he will.'

The red-haired man nodded. 'By the way,' he held out his hand, 'my name is Sanatkumara. I'm the leader of the Purification Journey here.'

'You sound German,' she said curiously.

'We're a very international group,' he smiled. 'We have pianists from Argentina. Architects from New York. Tour operators from England. So many of us have felt the emptiness of this industry-dominated world. So many of us are seeking other ways to find peace. Many of us want to return to an old world and establish a universal brotherhood. I wish I knew about your friend, but I don't. I'm sorry.'

'I'm sorry too. The name was very clear. He said Karna. I have it on tape.'

'There's no Karna in the Purification Journey, Sister, but I'll ask some of the Brothers. They may know.' Sanatkumara handed her a card. 'When you're in Delhi come to our ashram for a 15-day retreat. We will teach you about ourselves. We have daily prayers and meditation. A simple life. How to serve others. How to achieve true love. This is the war of our times, Sister. The war between our worst and our best selves...here,' he pointed, 'it has our address. Come and purify your love. Don't turn your back on us, Sister. It will be the experience of your life, I promise you.'

Mia nodded, putting the card in her pocket. She went back to the flat to pack her suitcases, feeling remarkably calm. Karna would find her, she was certain of that. She had no idea what Sanatkumara was playing at. But she would see Karna again. As surely as a painting could come to life.

※

Mithu was more content than she had been in years. Anand's flat was to be abandoned! Mithu would move with Tiger to New York. The oil-paint-and-turpentine flat would be locked up. Or rented. Or allowed to rot. Oh, I don't care anymore, sang Mithu. These exposed wires, the grimacing faces of damp, that deadly tree. Bye bye, flat. Bye bye, Goldie. Mithu threw her clothes around. She sipped wine while cooking. She barely noticed Mia. Rose and lily garlands still hung from the doorways and a wayward coconut lay forlornly behind the sofa. The refrigerator was still full of half drunk bottles of wine and boxes of food.

'Best wishes,' Mithu sang distantly. 'Best wishes for your future.'

How happy my mother must have been before I was born, thought Mia. Before I arrived and displaced her as Papa's only treasure.

Vik called to ask if she was packed and ready. His meetings had gone well, they were almost over. Yes, she was packed and looking forward. She took down the Kumbh Mela painting from her wall, wrapped it carefully in bubble wrap and cardboard and slid it under her clothes in her suitcase. Wherever in the world she was, as long as this was up on her wall, Karna would come to her, summoned to it like a spirit to a planchette.

The sceptic takes a holy bath. The unbeliever admits the power of coincidence. The atheist struggles against her own better judgement but falls prey to an ordinary miracle. The believer in the intellect recognizes the power of the intuitive. Damn! Too many well-trodden paths there. She wasn't in any danger of being drained away towards the divine. She, the seeker of vision and the purveyor of vision, the daughter with the dead father, was simply widening the arc of her being, so that it included the intangible and the unseen, because she needed to find out why her father had given up on life.

ALQUERIA, GOA

Justin's voice pierced Indi's blindness. She felt his hand tremble as it touched her shoulder.

'Another disaster!' he cried. 'Let's go.'

'Oh heavens,' she whispered, a magenta cloud leaping at her in the blackness. She reached for her cane. 'Now what?'

'The restaurant is flooded,' said Justin. 'Somebody turned on the pipe and pushed it through the door!'

'So turn the pipe off!' she shouted, trying to get to her feet.

'I did!' he shouted back. 'They're working on it. But how to drain the water out? The sand's getting in.'

He held her by the elbow as they hurried along the zigzag. The restaurant of Sharkey's Hotel was swimming with water. The brick floor was ankle-deep in it. Waiters were running in and out of the kitchen. Others were scooping up water in buckets and splashing it over the low wall that separated the restaurant from the beach. Justin led Indi to the banyan tree, away from the mess, and sat her down under it.

'Water!' shouted Francis Xavier. 'So much water everywhere. The floor will stay wet for days.'

'Turn the main taps off,' Justin cried. 'Turn the main taps off.'

'Swabs! Get some swabs and mop it up, and use brooms to push the water into the drains,' instructed Indi.

'Hey you!' cried Francis Xavier to the other waiters. 'Come on, Madam is saying get swabs and brooms!'

'Justin, see if there's someone near the water tank,' Indi called suddenly from her perch under the banyan. 'I think they may be lurking around there still. Sometimes they stay behind to see the action.'

'They? Who's they?' he asked.

'These madmen. The good-for-nothings. The Phantom Listeners, enemies of society, enemies of those who don't share their constant need.'

'Justin, sir,' shouted Francis Xavier plaintively insistent. 'Please see this way now...'

He appeared before Indi. As the waiters ran about and the guests tried to help and Justin cursed, a man came to stand in front of Indi, as if daring her to see him. She turned her head towards him, smelling that same, strange, chemical smell. The ocean storm light in her eyes was so blinding and assaulted him so sharply that he turned his back to its glare. As Indi reached out in front of her, her fingertips grazed his back, feeling something sharp and wooden. He was here. The Phantom Listener was here. 'Who is that? Who are you?'

'No,' he whispered, turning on his heel to go. 'There's nobody here.'

'Wait!' she tried to stumble to her feet. 'Where are you from? What do you want?'

She knew the smell. An unmistakable wet smell, of something that had rotted, that was breaking down to its chemical components ... She yelled for Justin. He bounded over the wall and ran to her, just in time to see a tall figure in white vanishing down the zigzag.

Justin began to run after him. He wasn't a bad runner. Hadn't he been a quarterback in days long gone? The man was way ahead though and as he ran, it seemed as if he was running on air, as if parts of his body were melting into the evening darkness. Justin squinted through the twilight. Was there something on his back? A wooden staff? Could it be a bow?

The man ran down the zigzag, up the red dust hill, towards the ridge between the Portuguese fort and Santa Ana. Justin chased after him all the way up the hill, but once he came to the top of the ridge, he had to sit down because he was no longer as young as he liked to think he was. His heart was beating far too fast and his breath was steaming out of his ears. The man had disappeared. Justin looked around. He saw only a contorted grin in the sky, a distorted cloud-face.

※

He thought he saw Mia everywhere. He had come here as part of his mission, but all he could think of was her. After having met her, having looked into her face, he felt suddenly as if there was hope in the world, that the world was not just full of evil spirits. He was accustomed to seeing the glint of a knife in the darkness; he was used to scanning the horizon for threats. But Mia's innocence had calmed him.

As had Alqueria. Nothing mattered in Alqueria but the gentle thud of coconuts falling to the ground. Or a monkey swinging from tree to sun-dappled tree. Or bursts of shining sea between the palms. The houses with their china mosaic floors were welcoming. The gardens crowded with abolim, hibiscus, palm and jackfruit trees were comfortingly untidy.

He had made it his mission to destroy Indi, to force Sharkey's Hotel to close down, because such hotels were evil and it was people like Justin and Indi, old and wicked, who corrupted this land. They were not even married, yet the way they carried on. The way they sat out on the veranda and hugged and kissed in full public view. The way they felt each other up as they walked on the beach. They clearly fornicated in that house of hers and didn't care whether anyone knew of it or not. They needed to be taught a lesson. The old woman should be taught about the Pure Love of the Mother Woman. She should be taught how to behave. She seemed to be someone who had pursued her own ego all her life, set bad examples. He had burgled the old woman's house, made blank calls, sent an email virus, thrown dead rats into the hotel office and flooded the hotel dining room. But sometimes he wished he could forget it all and escape. Escape from himself. Because who was it who drove him on in his mission, if not himself?

Mia had charmed him. His voice roared out threats against female immorality but as soon as her face appeared before him, his yells petered into doubt. She seemed hurt. Hurt by her father's death and by the behaviour of her mother. He, who pretended to be the expert on love, would he ever even recognize it? He was a popular figure in the Purification Journey. The Brothers all liked him and took care of him. Sanatkumara was proud of him. Now she was weakening him with her readiness to give and receive love. Her yearning for something new, her fascination for the Kumbh Mela, had captivated him. She had made him doubt his mission.

She should run away with him. She should leave that ridiculous husband of hers and come here to Alqueria. Once they had driven away the sex-crazed fools dancing on the beach, they would find a new way to love.

To love, that was all he had ever wanted to do. To love with compassion. To love without expectation. That's all he had ever wanted. This is what he was to tell Mia.

But by the time he finally told her, it was too late.

⁂

Vik came back from his second trip to Berlin looking tired. She was packed and ready. After one last night in the flat and a final hurried meal with Mithu and Tiger, they set off towards Heathrow.

6

NEW DELHI

Bahadur Shah Zafar was the last badshah of Delhi. He was eighty-two years old and drunk on romantic poetry when Captain Hodson and his British soldiers marched in and captured the city, almost two hundred years ago. The freedom rebels of 1857 had raised old Zafar up as their leader, but he had been no match for Hodson. When he surrendered to Hodson, Zafar was swollen-eyed and helpless with love for his wife. The poets whom he had gathered around him were all either dead or fled. Zafar didn't care any more. He didn't care that in his army the soldiers were so poor that they would have betrayed him for a meal and cared nothing about the complexion of the rulers who sat in Red Fort. His soldiers had starved while the king wrote love songs. .

Hodson killed Zafar's sons, bundled doddering Zafar off to Burma, and took over the city. The Mughals died. The old and mannered ways of Delhi were trampled underfoot first by the British, then by the Socialists who replaced them after Independence – who were so fixated on Five-Year Plans for the economy that they had no time to reawaken Zafar's courtesies and poems.

Few in this city would even recognize Zafar if he reappeared in this new city where the sun sank into putrefying ditches of purple water which supported jigsaws of mosquito eggs and mucus. A sweetly pungent smell of fart hung over the electric wires which dipped towards a neglected mosque. In the mosque, migrant construction workers cooked vegetable paste over a wood fire and cared two hoots for Zafar. The city's wide boulevards and colonial architecture looked helplessly down on screaming new Mercedes and Volvos. Packed buses lurched across the river carrying the workforce back to their apartments. Loudspeakers sent bitter hymns across the neglected bend of river.

Zafar, the romantic, would be lost in this lawless city, a city-village contained in a single tree-lined entity. The countryside burst from skyscrapers, pushing hutments and oxen to take refuge under new flyovers. A skyscraper was reflected in a lily pond in which buffaloes floated. Small patches of mustard fields swayed next to New Instant Fax and Email Centres. A herd of cattle and a leotard-clad jogger were inhabitants of the same fountain park. Open ravines yawned next to glass-and-chrome office blocks. Gypsy women in bright skirts and veils danced past billboards announcing United Colors of Benetton. At traffic lights, illiterate village elders and bejewelled nomads from interior Rajasthan hawked *Cosmopolitan*, *Vanity Fair* and feather dusters, while their skinny livestock waited on road dividers. The cripple in the Stetson hat who ambled about on his arms near the Golf Course was spider-like – useless skeletal limbs supporting a huge head and cowboy hat. But in a sooty apartment block, hung with clotheslines and aerials, Mia spotted a little girl dressed as a fairy queen. Someone bent over her, fixing little white wings as she twirled in a flickering dark neon. An angel in the gloom. She blinked again and rubbed her eyes. She had slipped, as usual, into the familiar can't-shock-me alertness of India.

Death lurked under iron and steel. Giant boulders which had been moved to make way for the new Metro sometimes rolled down and crushed a family. A rattling bus would careen into a waiting bus stop and kill the first half of the queue. Many slipped accidentally into the invisible realm that churned next to every footstep.

At a traffic junction a smiling beggar with huge eyes, closely cropped hair and a single arm offered blessings in return for money. Mia gave her some but the beggar made a face and tossed it away. Mia had mistakenly handed out a Euro.

Men came crowding at her. Men with eyes that bulged out of their heads. Men huddling at roadside tea-stalls. Men with eyes that didn't seem to move from her body. Men strolling in couples with their little fingers linked. Skinny men running along highways with not a care in the world. Fat men standing on pavements sending spirals of snot into the air. A bare-bottomed man astride a fence shooting cylinders of turd into the hedgerows. Men with eyes that stayed fixed on her face or raced up and down her body with expressionless urgency.

There were eyes everywhere. Eyes in Mughal tombs. Eyes on the road that swept towards the colonial palaces where the government sat. Eyes in parks. Eyes behind showers of bougainvillea. Dead eyes, bright eyes, bulbous eyes, eyes that belonged to hands working furiously in loose crotches, eyes in bus windows, eyes that flew at her from from passing cars.

'Vik,' she asked as they craned their necks up the Qutub Minar. 'Who are all these guys?'

'Unemployed buggers, baby,' he grunted, trying to position his camera. 'Nothing to do. And why shouldn't they look at you? You're hot. You know, I'm glad I'm an employer,' he continued. 'I'm glad I'm the job-giver. I've seen the horror of my artisans and workers. You think these guys are ugly, right? But they're ugly because of the horrors they've endured, the horrors they're constantly aware of. The fear of tiny hands reaching for non-existent pots of rice, aching fear that can make a man of dignity turn to a bottle of arrack or journey to the city and become part of the footpath people. Selling plastic cars and glossy magazines at traffic lights, poked and shoved by the police, watching their bewildered wives open their legs to strangers. Setting out every morning with the staffs of beggars and the begging bowls of easily recognizable scum. Industry saves, it doesn't oppress, whatever the fashionable firebrands may say. I'm glad I'm part of the rescue team.'

She was surprised at his unexpected passion. Vik's hidden depths were well hidden, indeed. Karna had judged him too easily.

It's easy, Anand had told Mia, to be deceived by India. To not see that meagre yet intelligent poetry is being murmured in slum colonies. That among migrant gangs of brickworkers there sits a grandmaster of a dying tradition of martial arts. That in the crowd of vendors walks a mathematician. On a footpath, even a beggar carefully peeling a rotten apple as the traffic roars by him, has created an island of a remembered civilization, because the human has tunnelled deep into India's earth. Most westerners have been blinded by India's sun. Only few were different. There was Alexander Cunningham, for example, father of Indian archaeology, who toiled alone in the fields of north India unearthing stupas and attracting the anger of the colonial government because he knew the official records were only partial truths.

※

He obviously took great care of his home. Victoria Villa looked freshly painted, white on the outside, cream walls inside. The living room was furnished in leather and hung with a central chandelier. There were freshly cut flowers in the vases. In the garden were the two trees as he had described. She remembered their names. A silk cotton, the semal and a java plum, the jamun. And they too seemed to have dressed themselves up for her. Sunlight shone through their branches in filigree patterns. Under each tree was a flowerbed ringed with a triangular brick edging.

Yet Victoria Villa was no beautiful Jehangir's palace. It was as emptily immaculate as a company guesthouse. It smelt of lost pride and a nagging grievance that everyone – starting with the British sahibs who'd built it – had deserted it. Inside the house, there was a waiting in the air: something had been brewing here for decades and was about to rise up and crush the house under its weight. The staff – a flashily-dressed male cook with blowdried hair and his wife with plucked eyebrows – Mr and Mrs Krishnaswamy, looked sullen, as if waiting to start an insurgency.

The branches of the semal were like skinny outstretched arms. The bark near its base was pock-marked with hollows. The tree was in bloom. Blossoms the colour of dark blood grew in clusters. She thought she heard a cry from its upper branches, a cry that was frantic and shrill. A sinister tree, branches darting this way and that like rude statements. She turned towards the jamun which seemed far friendlier, its leaves hanging shyly to the ground.

She felt disoriented. Remnants of jet-lag ached like a dormant boil and her skin smelt of Duty Free. She wandered down the front veranda, deciding finally to put up Anand's painting opposite the four-poster bed in the massive master bedroom where she and Vik would sleep off their daily doses of beer and whisky. In a drawer of the dressing table, she placed *The Drama of Depression.*

᚜

She met his friends. There was a skinny runner-up in a Miss Universe pageant with skin lifted from ear to ear, like tarpaulin stretched across crumbling rocks; a gun-trader equipped with a wordless yet stunning wife; a smart politician who carried two mobile phones at the same time and had a face that drooped as liquidly as Salvador Dali's melting clock. There was a construction magnate with a bouncy ponytail who told Mia that it was a relief that Indians no longer felt ashamed of being naked and horny and a massive newspaper baron whose weight was all alcohol induced and who lived in a Moorish-style villa normally seen in the suburbs of Morocco.

Vik's evenings centred around 5-star hotel nightclubs which shone as brightly as his credit cards. At night, he would take her, with his friends, to atmospheric lounges fashioned like caves or tents where security guards kept out those not rich enough to be sexy.

Landlords from the hinterland, newly rich and stuffed into sequinned couture sometimes became filthy drunk here and bludgeoned their chauffeurs to death, though subsequently the cases were fixed, the judges were bought off and everything was forgotten in a couple of days. Despondent beauties climbed to the roof, crawling along the airconditioning ducts clutching bottles of whisky. Then they plunged head-first down sixteen floors, leaving suicide notes on their mobile phones, while only a few miles away in the depths of the countryside, neighbours hacked each other to death because there was a drought and no water to drink, let alone whisky.

※

He took her to the offices of Moksha Herbals. The New Delhi store, after the one in Mumbai, was the biggest in the chain. Two floors of cosmetics, bath oils, perfumes, dyes arranged in glass shelves, their colours enhanced by overhead lights and wooden floors. There were bottles, vials, syringes, gelatinous globs of flesh-like material, lipsticks, even wigs and face masks. There were huge slabs of natural soap, jars of shower-gel made from jasmine and neem, perfumes made from mint and frangipani, moisturizers made from sandalwood and rose. The names of the cosmetics were from Hindu scriptures: Vedic eyeliner, Nirvana face masks, Ganesha balms and Karma shower-gel. Behind every counter stood white-coated make-up artists and shop assistants who smiled and bent in namaste towards her.

'Wow, Vik, this is huge.'

'This is only the retail. Wait until you see the film unit in Mumbai. The office and administration are upstairs, including a salon. But retail is not half as profitable as film. Production houses are bulk consumers and many are ready to try Moksha because it's cheaper than the bigger brands. We do a great deal of film and stage make-up. We have false skin of every colour and texture. Contact lenses, dentures, prosthetic noses, limbs, all made from indigenous herbal products...'

'False skin?' Mia asked.

'Sure,' he laughed. 'False skin. Would give a person a completely different face shape; make a clear complexion look mottled and blotchy. Remember Douglas Fairbanks dyed black in *Thief of Baghdad*? That was Max Factor. Dustin Hoffman in *Tootsie*? Even Kamalhaasan in *Chachi 420.*'

She looked around. The walls of Moksha Herbals were startling. They were covered in murals. On one wall, on a mist-wreathed mountain, Shiva sat meditating. On the opposite, a goddess on a flying tiger with demons at her heels

'Aren't they great?' Vik waved at the gods. 'Murals. My idea. Moksha Herbals in a mythological setting.'

'Fantastic...' she whispered, staring around.

'I like the stories,' he shrugged. 'Good over Evil. Gods killing demons. Easy stuff. Stuff I can understand.'

'The philosophy's quite cool too.'

'Oh,' he waved his hand. 'I don't know about all that. I like the straight stories about the good guys cutting off the heads of the bad guys,' he laughed. 'And some of the gory stuff. Like slicing somebody's head off with a disc. There was this beast called Narasimha, half-man, half lion, who ripped a king's chest open and ate up his heart. Neat, huh? Wouldn't you like to do that to your boss?'

He looked smart. His nails were filed and his shoes were polished. His socks matched his shirt and he smelt recognizably of Azarro. His skin was unusually pale. His cheeks and chin were tinged pink. His hair, brown in the dark, became light-coloured in the sun. He seemed to have grown taller. In London, he had seemed diminished by the traffic, but here his cellphone dangled perpetually from his ear like a lopsided silver earring, making him look callously overdressed in the shabbiness of Delhi.

'It's great,' she said brightly. 'What a great store.'

'Come on.' She felt his hand on her back. 'The staff is waiting to welcome you. Tea for everybody upstairs.'

The semal seemed to scream particularly loudly in the evenings. A tree full of tears, Mia thought, evening tears which only the moon had seen. The tree was watching her. There were shadows it wanted to tell her about. As if some curious fate awaited her that she would never believe if she knew. The waiting that sat in the air of Victoria Villa was drawing her inexorably towards it. Anand had sent her here. What if Anand's spirit had turned against her for some reason and brought her towards some sort of disaster? The murals on the walls at Moksha Herbals were frightening; made her feel like a little English-educated girl who had rushed in where she should have never ventured. Reality and dreams had merged. Had she willed herself into an insane, unreal area of murals and screaming trees because of some whacko attempt at retracing the footsteps of her dead father?

She had a vivid dream that night. A man in faded clothes, working tirelessly among children, cleaning their soiled beds, placing cold compresses on their heads. There had been an outbreak of something... cerebral malaria, perhaps... even though the government claimed it had been eradicated. Local party functionaries arrive, hoping to persuade the man to stand for election... Such a respected social worker, a source of inspiration to so many, a true leader... The children look at him with their dying eyes... She is one of them. He flits in the edge of her vision as he crouches by her bed, feeding her. Then she sees him. A bearded man with round spectacles wearing jeans and carrying a mobile...

She awoke with a start. Karna. Karna who made Vik seem pathetically slight and frivolous.

The next morning her face stared back from the mirror. A normal ordinary face, confident about the reasonableness of the day ahead.

'Here's another one of my favourites coming up,' sang the DJ. 'Today is Cheerful Day!' Her face, still the same, was a spur for normalcy.

That evening, while Vik dressed for another visit to a nightclub, she found herself standing on the lawn and staring at the semal again. She stood under its branches straining to hear its cry. But instead of the voice of the tree, she heard Vik's, calling out from the veranda.

'Hey, love-in-a-mist,' he shouted, half talking on his phone, 'I have to talk to you about something.'

'Yes?' she turned towards him.

'Come here.' Leading off from the front veranda was the semi-circular study with window seats all along the curve. The jamun leant in at the windows, swaying against the glass.

Vik sat down behind the wooden table and waved her to the chair facing his. 'This is where my grandfather used to spend all his time,' he smiled.

'It's a nice room,' Mia acknowledged. 'I love the circle of windows.'

'Mia,' Vik's voice was grave. 'I have to go away for a bit –'

'Go away?'

'– and have a fight with someone.'

'What? Fight with someone?'

'Scary, eh? Look,' he bent under the table. 'Look at these. Then I'll tell you everything. Look. I have paintings too, just like you.'

In the drawers of the antique study table were a dozen canvases. They were oil-paintings of different sizes, unframed and smudged with dust, but clearly new.

'A bit dusty,' he said, drawing out the canvases carefully and wiping them gently with his palms. He drew out the paintings one by one. 'I had them done from family photos when the house was being painted,' he said. 'Here,' he pushed them across the table towards Mia. 'My grandfather' – he pointed to a man in a three-piece suit – 'Ashish Kumar'. A woman in a sari standing on the deck of a ship: 'My grandmother, Shiela Devi. Towards the end of her life she bathed in the Ganga so often that her clothes were always damp and she died of pneumonia.' A couple, with their two children by their side, a vase of rich roses in the corner. The older child, with an arresting face and astonishing eyes, was dressed in shorts and shirt.

'I didn't know you had an uncle,' she said, listening to her voice reach up towards the high ceiling.

'Not uncle, silly!' he laughed. 'That's my mother. They used to dress her as a boy when she was a child because they were so disappointed that she was a girl. Yes, that's my mother, Indira.'

No wonder the air in Victoria Villa was so bereft. Why Vik's brown eyes flickered away when she tried to hold his gaze for too long. Why the garden was sunk in weary anticipation, sunlit but sepulchral. The sounds of the streets were remote and far away. The voices on the streets sounded distant. Where was his family? Where was Indira? He talked about his mother so vaguely. She ran a hotel, was too ill to travel to England, but they would visit her soon. Now that they were here, where was she?

'Aren't we going to meet your mother, Vik? Shouldn't I speak to her at least?'

'Of course, baby,' his voice was cheerful. 'Of course.'

'Where is she?'

'I told you. She's busy running Sharkey's Hotel in Goa. She's having some trouble there. That is, in fact, what I wanted to tell you about. That's the fight I have to have.'

'You have to have a fight? With whom?'

'Some ruffian's been harassing her. A hooligan of some kind. A terrorist.'

'A terrorist?' she gasped.

'Relax,' he laughed. 'Some local ass-hole. Probably wants to drive them off the land.'

'Them?'

'My mother and her staff. She telephoned. She's scared. This man who's stalking her, or hiding, or following her around, apparently he showed up recently. I'll have to go and help her deal with this creep, whoever he is. Here' – he dusted off another painting – 'This is my mother.'

An oil of Indi.

My god, thought Mia, she's a cracker. Tall like Vik. Dressed in a white, high-necked blouse with her hair scraped tightly back in a plait. Mother and son standing back to back. As if in a duel.

'She studied much harder than me, but I got better grades,' Vik tapped his temple. He picked up another painting. Indi wearing thick glasses lying on the lawn under the semal tree with a chubby boy smiling above her.

'Wow,' Mia said. 'She's a knock-out. Even with those glasses you can see she has the most amazing eyes. I've never seen that colour before.'

'They're better in person,' he smiled. 'She's so restless, never sits still long enough to be photographed. Maybe a distant ancestor screwed a Viking adrift in the Indian Ocean, and the result was... my mother.'

'She's absolutely stunning.'

'And I?'

'You, too,' Mia said, a little surprised. 'You said at the wedding that she couldn't travel. Why?'

'I should have told you before,' he shrugged. 'You see, travel is difficult for her. She's completely blind.'

'Jesus!' Mia whispered. 'I wouldn't have guessed, looking at those eyes. Who looks after her? How does she manage to run Sharkey's?'

'She has good help. Lots of friends.' He laughed loudly. 'We're a sorry pair, aren't we, a blind mother and a diabetic son? I bet you're already wanting to escape this fucking hell hole!'

'No,' she turned her face towards his. 'Hey, come on, you musn't keep saying things like that. Don't. I love you very much. We'll make ourselves a wonderful world. It'll be our world. We'll build it. I have nothing else.'

'Baby,' he drew her against him and held her hard against his chest. 'Do I deserve you?'

'You deserve far better,' she said. The disillusioned painter's daughter with a crush on a mad swami. Oh, yes, you deserve far better than me.

'But we'll have everything, you'll see,' he laughed softly. 'Everything and more. Every fucking thing. Just as soon as I've dealt with this hooligan or stalker or terrorist or whatever he is, we'll have every fucking thing.'

'You should try getting her to London, Vik.' Mia's eyes drifted back to the paintings. 'There are so many new treatments available.'

He shook his head, 'Too late. Nothing to be done. Sad,' – he waved his hands – 'a great lady she is. You'll meet her. You'll meet her when we visit her in Alqueria. We'll be there soon, I promise. I promise.'

He picked out another painting. A group of people stood in a laughing tableau in front of a low red-roofed building

on the beach. Sharkey's Hotel, Indi, and next to her –
Karna. An older, whiter, Karna.

'Who is this?' Mia's voice cracked.

'That's my mother's buddy,' said Vik. 'Justin. He's a
doc.'

But the same length of hair. The same beard. The same
height. Everything exactly the same, except for the single
difference that Justin was white and Karna was dark. A
photo and its negative, the same person painted in different
colours.

'That's your mother's friend?'

'Yes, why?'

Dust swirled outside forming hobgoblins of intense
evening heat. Cars honked past, pushing currents of smog
over the lawn. Evening vendors on their way home yelled
their wares: Nose, ear piercing man! The drilling, nailing
sounds of new construction crescendoed to a violent finale.

'He looks like someone I know.'

'Does he really? Hey, he won't be happy to hear that.
Justin thinks of himself as seriously unique.'

'He looks like someone from the Purification Journey,'
she blurted out.

Vik frowned, then smiled. 'Ah...no... I don't think so.'

'Someone....'

'Someone who?'

'Who I ... interviewed once...'

'Nope,' Vik shook his head briskly. 'Justin definitely
ain't someone from any journey.'

✻

She didn't tell Vik how hard she waited for Karna, sitting
under the high ceiling of the bedroom, staring at the painting
and wondering if Sanatkumara had passed on her address.

She didn't tell him that she dreamt of Karna on most nights and that her days in Victoria Villa were becoming a vigil, a countdown to seeing him again.

'My dad would have loved these paintings. Aren't there,' she paused, 'any photographs of your dad?'

'Photos?' he wrinkled his nose. 'I told you, I never keep photos. Only paintings. I chucked all the photos. I had all the photos copied into paintings as soon as I could afford to. Then,' he smiled brightly, 'I tore up the photographs.'

'So aren't there any paintings of your father?'

He came around the table, drew her towards him, led her to the window and put his arm around her waist. They stared out towards the jamun which came sweetly towards them at the window. 'I told you,' he said, 'that my father died before I was born. He was a soldier. When we go to Goa, you'll see pictures of him. My mother has them.'

'What was your father's name?'

'Same as mine,' he said. 'Same name as me. Vik. Vikram.'

She leant up and kissed him. His lips against hers smelt bittersweet. His creaseless clothes and carefully combed hair were flimsy bulwarks of order against the insulin syringe that kept him alive.

'My love-in-a-mist,' his voice resurged with its normal loud energy. 'My wildflower. You'll hear all about my family from my mother, drink wine and go swimming in the sea. And I,' he smiled, 'will go off in search of the ruffian, the troublemaker or whoever he is. God, I wish I didn't have to think about that fucking shit.'

'Do they have any idea who he is?'

'No,' Vik shook his head. 'Justin chased after him to the top of a hill but he apparently just disappeared. They're very worried. I'm worried. Worried about what he might do next. Perhaps,' he turned towards her, 'I should get myself a gun. Would you like that? If I got myself a gun to kill this guy?'

'Would I like it?'

'Would it turn you on? If, for example, I got myself a gun and crawled after that ass-hole, stopping only to replenish my insulin like a soldier on a sugar high? I'd be a real macho man if I did that, wouldn't I?'

'That's a weird thought,' she said after a pause.

He laughed, pulled her hair loose from its clip and arranged it around her face. 'I'll have to do something. Seriously. I mean, I'll have to. I owe it to my mother, to her hotel. Today he's threatening her, tomorrow, he may turn up here and start hassling us, god knows.'

'Hassling us?'

'Hoo! Hoo!' Vik made ghost sounds and twirled his hands. 'Who's that knocking on the door? Open up, it's me, the terrorist who's come to get you!'

'No worries!' she smiled. 'I always know what to do in a crisis. I'm a tough cookie.'

'No, you're not,' he said softly. 'You're a love-in-a-mist. Anyway, forget it. Nothing will happen here. I'm not worried, we have the guards outside, but still,' he frowned, 'you never know. There's some weird stuff happening in the world.'

I'm a ruffian too, she thought. Kicking my tincan of fantasies along two continents. I'm an amoral hoodlum hiding in your house for my own selfish motives. Sadhus may think of the eternal paradise they are about to attain after their death. I'm a pilgrim who thinks only of the eternal paradise I'm about to attain on earth.

'You're lovely, baby. Come, let's go. Fuck all this shit.'

He organized parties in the garden to entertain her. Minarets of cardboard and cloth reached past the trees. Canopies bloomed under the semal, a pink fountain bursting from the centre. There were fancy-dress parties. Rummy parties. Parties controlled by dictatorial DJs. Parties where a line of saluting elephants welcomed the guests. Parties where an illuminated horse sat in the centre of the decorated tent. Parties where kebabs hung from the ceiling on giant skewers, like a morgue full of cadavers. Parties where the gun-trader's wife and her lover were caught making out in a BMW. Parties where lurid masks loomed out through dimly lit rooms.

In a lamp-dark study the chairs were stained with sticky hands and smells of embraces rose out of the cushions. The heavy breath of heartbreak…where? In the money plants clambering up the walls or underneath the wooden dragon table which Vik had brought back from Bali? Silhouettes fell on the bushes. Silhouettes that were permanently attached. Silhouettes with mannequin breasts holding drinks in their hands, with cigarettes burning in their lips.

'Tell me,' Mia asked the skinny Miss Universe runner-up. 'Does Vik have lots of these parties?'

'Good for you, isn't it?' The runner-up's eyes were wide, 'Good for you to come here from London and just slip into this world like a princess. Some Indians love NRIs, although I must say I can't stand them. I just hate NRIs. The demands for mineral water, those cheesy accents. Ugh. You've done well. Look at you. Didn't get a man in England, and now you're living here like a maharani! All the best Indian men go abroad and come back married to the charlady's daughter, happy that they've found someone with an English accent.'

'Hey,' Mia said aggressively. 'Give it a break, okay? My mother's from Kolkata and my dad's from Delhi and was a history teacher in London. And a painter. I'm …'

'Oh, come on,' snapped the runner-up. 'We all know about the kind of life you people live over there in your little ghettoes. All you Asians with your Bollywood obsession. You're all religious fanatics, you immigrants. We're not immigrants here. This is our land. We do what we want.'

'Good for you.'

'You NRIs always get fooled in India. We can easily fool you. You think you understand, but you don't. You can't see anything. You're blind.'

Mia thought of Mithu's phone calls from New York which were blissful, delighted at the loss of her daughter. Tiger was doing well. There was so much to see in New York. The bagels and cream cheese were delicious. They might even buy an apartment and settle down permanently. The oil-paint-and-turpentine flat was an orphan now. It was dark, its eyes were closed and it was alone except for the cherry tree. She wasn't sure what to say.

'You're pretty rude, d'you know that?' inquired Mia.

'Yes, but I'm also pretty,' beamed the runner-up. 'And so would you be if you made just a little effort.'

'Nobody here is exactly a great beauty,' Mia smiled back, relieved that friendship had been forged by fire. 'Not like Vik's mother.'

'Ah, Vik's mother,' breathed the runner-up, staring at the semal tree. 'Indira. Indira, the great Indira. Must be hard to have a mother like Indira. By the way,' she paused, 'Vik's really angry. Totally pissed off...'

'Why?'

'Why? God, where are you living, yaar? Come on, he's been working really hard, Moksha's finally, like, up and running, he gets married and now suddenly his mother lands up with this problem which he has to sort out. She's blind, she needs protection, all that. Did he tell you? Some guy who's been making life miserable for his mother and her hotel in Goa. He's been doing all kinds of things. I told him,' the runner-up lit a cigarette, 'to just have him finished off. Once and for all.'

'Which man?'

'The guy threatening his mother, of course. Jesus, where the fuck are you from, man? Set a ... you know,' the runner-up shrugged, 'supari on him. A supari, understand? Guys who kill for money? One of those velahs who hang about near the railway station and can be paid to get rid of people? Organize a fake police encounter. You know, just send some cop to shoot him out. I mean, how dare he threaten Sharkey's Hotel? Shit, does he know who he's dealing with? When Vik gets angry,' the runner-up shuddered, 'it's time to watch out.'

'You can't just have somebody killed. I don't think Vik would do that.' Mia's eyes had become huge. 'That would be a mistake, an over-reaction, I would say. I mean, maybe he can just talk to him.'

The runner-up laughed. 'Oh, come on, yaar. This is not your little immigrant neighbourhood. This is a different strata of society, okay, this is the big league. Big money, big shit. You never know who this guy could be, there could be some kidnapping thing happening, some ransom demand. The last thing Vik needs is to have this on his head now. He's got tons on his plate already with Moksha.' The runner-up threw her cigarette into the grass, stamped on it and marched off towards the bar.

The party sighed to an end. The guests swayed to their feet and disappeared past the bowing trees. The runner-up had rapidly become drunk and weaved off into the house. After a while Mia spotted her crawling out from behind a leather sofa with a garland of lilies around her neck. Vik helped her to her feet and half carried her to the bathroom where she threw up and passed out in the guest bedroom, her legs splayed out. He stood over her and grinned at Mia. 'I'm the protector of all women,' he said. 'They feel safe in my house.'

On the four-poster bed, he stroked her tenderly, his insulin pump glancing against her skin. She prowled around him, her mind full of dark fantasies of Karna. When Vik kissed her mouth, she imagined drawing Karna's face into her stomach. When Vik encircled her belly with his arms, she pushed his hands roughly against her thighs, imagining he was Karna. Vik's chest was soft and covered with light springy fluff but she imagined it hard and spare. He would be here soon. She had already seen him in this other painting. It wasn't just a coincidence that Justin looked like Karna. Coincidences were patterns of things to come.

'Mia...?' he whispered.

'Yes?'

'I had no idea you were so sexy.'

'Yes,' she confirmed.

'Wonderful,' he murmured.

Wonderful? You call me, wonderful? She muttered silent warnings about herself: I am a latent sorceress biding my time, pretending delight in your tender ministrations that will never satisfy me. One day, I will rear up from the bathtub and drown you in sensual rage. All I wish to do is watch the sun fall in different ways against Karna's white clothes. All I want is to go with Karna to the Kumbh Mela and see for myself that India's contribution to world civilization is the idea that the naked human body is not a pornographic product but an ascetic ideal.

The next morning over a breakfast of fruit and dosas, Mia said that she had been in Delhi for two months and all she had done was go to parties at night and sleep all day while Vik was at work. Perhaps she should try and find a job of some kind? Some freelance work for a channel? Nothing doing, said Vik, nothing until they had been to Alqueria. He still hadn't decided when they would go. There were some schedules to be met and a couple of trips planned. Once he was able to make sure he had enough time, they would go and visit Indi, who, he said, was waiting to welcome Mia. And he would find out who this weirdo was who was harassing his mother and her friend. In the meantime, why didn't she just make herself at home, wander around the city, meet the runner-up and the wordless wife for lunch, walk in the lawn, do whatever she wanted? It was far too hot to go anywhere in the afternoon and in the evenings, of course, he would take her out. Summer's a pretty time, she should see the amaltas and gulmohar ablaze in yellow and orange in the streets.

She drifted through the days. Waking to hear Vik's presence in the bathroom, to smell his Azarro and his damp towels and see his insulin pump neatly disappear into his waistband, turning over the past six months in her head. She flipped through news channels desultorily, following debates on the Kargil war and Sonia Gandhi's leadership of the Congress. She ate lonely lunches served by the coiffeured chef, read, walked in the garden and stared at the semal tree. She was waiting. A waiting in the air and a waiting inside her. The semal tree seemed to burst with words. There was so much she didn't know, so much about Victoria Villa that was hidden from her. She positioned herself on the lawn, twisting her head so that the house looked like the great white jaw of a shark breaking out of a blue-green sea of grass.

The Delhi summer was a carnival of different types of heat: damp in the mornings, crackling dry in the afternoons, fever-hot in the evenings as if constantly running a temperature of a 102. The road outside Victoria Villa became a molten river of tarmac. She watched the floors of the house being swept, then swabbed, watched the pistachio marble flooring spin away transparently, marvelling at how instantaneously the water dried. She bathed with Karma shower gel, washed her hair with Tantra shampoo, then lay under the ceiling fan on the four-poster bed, letting the towel-like air carry away the moisture from her body in minutes.

Where could Karna have gone? What mission was so urgent that he could deny the eerie recognition between them and just leave? And how could Sanatkumara not have even known his name? Had he given her a false name and just stormed off in his crazy way?

Vik had had a comfortable life. His home, his successful business and his psychedelic friends. Karna had nothing. He probably smoked ganja by the banks of the river, lived among the poorest and dressed like a blue-painted Krishna. But Vik's India made her anxious with its many lost, solipsistic souls perched on glasses brimful with champagne. Would Vik ever call her Maya? Probably not. He would always want to see her as the mini-skirted Mia. Hollywood heroine Mia.

She yearned instead for Anand's India, for Karna's India. Running off into wheat fields in search of a Mughal descendant. Jumping off an old steam train to sit with banjaras, scribbling notes on the back of cigarette packs. Going to the Kumbh Mela. Perhaps when Anand drowned in the river he imagined he was walking into the Ganga for a dip before being impolitely swallowed up by the freezing Thames. Perhaps like the Dasanami Nagas, he had calculated that this was the right astrological moment of the Kumbh bath. When they had found his body, his expression had been serene.

One afternoon, sandwiched between the runner-up and
the construction magnate at one of Vik's favourite lunchtime
restaurants, Mia looked out of the windows to see a fantastic
sight. The sky had begun to darken. Brown swathes of
burning dust were rising. Stilt-walkers of hot earth were
teetering past, pursued by a gleeful wind. People shouted
for cover as the stilt-walkers went wafting past like
participants in a summer parade. After the parade, came
the grand finale, a flourish of rain. Muddy drops at first,
then slicing slivers of freshness, slanted against the breeze.
Lightning illuminated treetops in flashing chiaroscuro.

'Wow!' said Mia. 'Look at that.'

'Aandhi,' smiled the construction magnate. 'Now it'll
get cool in the evening.'

As the tall dust-walkers strode past, she was dazzled at
how rich with elements the city had become in the midst of
the summer stupor; a vibrant poem from the earth after a
dull drone of heat.

She set off in pursuit of those tall stilt-walkers of dust.
Shaking off the smells of Duty Free, she rediscovered her
father's city. Flaming yellow amaltas and burnt orange
gulmohar trees marked her way as she drove and pelted
along in scooties. She saw grand farmhouses with spiky
metal gates to keep out the poor and the potentially
villainous. She visited the villages surrounding Delhi, Tata
Safaris nuzzling bullock-carts. She met Munshi Gopalchand
who had retired from bailiff service to a big Haryana landlord,
come back to a double-storeyed house in Khirkee village
and bought his son a cyber café. She saw call centres with
their windows blackened, export houses sending fabric to
California and Brussels. She juggled contradictory images of
brutality and normalcy. There was an older rational life, a
long continuum of human existence under the daily clamour.

In every touch and gesture and shout she fancied she saw empires and royal courts and kite-flying rooftops. She tried to trace the gestures back to where they must have come from but she was soon lost.

Summer flared into the monsoon. Sheets of hot rain came spraying into the Victoria Villa veranda. The jamun was covered in fruit and Vik called in the children from the surrounding shanties to shake the tree free of its riches and fill up their tins. Mia's first taste of jamun was so tangy and satisfying that she couldn't get enough of its purple pleasures and looked with camraderie at the friendly tree.

Vik kept up with his travels, Kerala, Kolkata, Berlin and Paris – promising every day that Goa awaited at the end of the year, his mother waited, a long break waited. She visited her grandmother's home, St Stephen's College where Anand had been a student and rebel, met his old friends who lamented his death, and because they were all important government personages now, laughed away their forgotten revolution. She spent some afternoons at Moksha Herbals gazing at the fresh stock arriving nearly every day. The make-up studio was specially impressive. One afternoon, she volunteered to have herself transformed into Naomi Campbell and was stunned at the near-perfect likeness.

The monsoon made the air as thick as a hot wet towel and the power cuts in Victoria Villa made for some desperate conversations with Mithu. Wait for October and November, Vik told her. Wait for Delhi's prettiest months.

Sure enough, October then November, came with their air rich with festival. Chrysanthemums smiled to life. The city became crowded with religious renewal and consumer excitement. Deities pranced through marketplaces: Durga, Ganesh, effigies of Ravana. Mothers trailed through traffic dragging weepily reluctant Rams and Sitas to school Ram

Lilas. Mia went to card parties at the runner-up's plant-strewn flat, another card party at the home of the newspaper baron and another Diwali party where a fireworks display sent flashes of fire shaving closely past her ears. The smell of candles, dry fruit and silk reminded her so strongly of Karna that she realized she hadn't stopped thinking of him in the past six months. Where was he?

She pulled out Sanatkumara's card from the bottom of her suitcase and stared at the address. Pavitra Ashram, Bijwasan, Delhi.

The wait for Karna and the Kumbh Mela was a long one, but she wouldn't have to wait much longer.

It was her duty to visit the Kumbh.

I must hollow out a crater and fill it with my revelations, cover it with sand and leave it for others to discover after I'm gone.

Sitting at the computer in the semi-circular study, she had already accumulated print-outs from the Net on the Mahakumbh Mela. The Grand Pitcher Festival, the first Mahakumbh of the new millennium was to start on January 9. Less than two months away. But where was her guide?

ALQUERIA, GOA

Francis Xavier had lots of stories about Goa. He would sit on the beach and tell long histories of his homeland to anyone who cared to listen: Goa was Portugal's golden land, informed Francis Xavier. Up the Mandovi river, which wound its way through mangroves and coconut forests, Velha Goa became the Rome of the East. Golden Goa. Arabs, Jews and Persians came to the cobblestone marketplaces outside the huge cathedrals to sell horses, carpets, diamonds and rose water. A Portuguese carpenter from Lisbon would come to Goa and get so rich that he could become a fidalgo overnight and add Dom to his name.

For a while, the Portuguese had a grand time. They raced about on horseback or jolted about in palanquins in their own little strip of the Orient, building churches, marrying local beauties and converting whomever they could to Catholicism. But they spared little thought for mundane things like sanitation and after the torrential Goan monsoon, when the rain came thundering out of the sea flattening the palms and shacks, the gutters outside the villas and churches began to run with filthy water and dead leaves. Malaria and plague began. The Inquisition arrived and drove away the fun loving traders. Golden Goa began to fade.

Yet, buried deep behind the palms, in the Catholic villas and the Hindu mansions, a new civility was born. Hindus and Christians lived separate lives yet they learnt to coexist in this new civility. Paddy, coconuts and oil were offered to Jesus, richly gilded churches sat along Shiva temples. Feast days were like festival days. Garlands and diyas decorated roadside crucifixes. In Alqueria, civilizations had learnt to live together in peace. In Alqueria, Father Rudy made plans to visit the Kumbh Mela.

'Right, let's go through this again,' Justin said to Indi for the hundredth time, as he had over the past months. 'The guy whispered something? He said something?'

It was late. Outside, Francis Xavier snored against the wall of Indi's house. The intruder hadn't come for several weeks and probably never would return, although for Indi his presence was intangibly constant.

'I've told you a thousand times, Justin,' Indi threw up her hands. 'He said there's no one here. But he whispered it. I told you, I couldn't make out his voice. He smelt of something. Nail-polish remover. Something like that.'

'All I saw,' Justin said, 'was this tall guy rushing off down the road, running up the hill wearing some sort of costume, something, a bow, can't be sure ... and then suddenly ... nothing.' He sighed, 'This world is full of scary creatures. Young, scary creatures. Much younger than me, to be able to run so fast.'

'Well, at least Francis Xavier is here.'

'What the hell did the creep want?' exclaimed Justin. 'Why was he so bothered by little Sharkey's Hotel? We've just got to get through to him somehow, if he comes back. There has to be a reason why he's doing this. There has to be.'

'There doesn't,' Indi's brows were arched. 'Nothing needs a reason. Disasters are as much part of our lives as the sun and moon.'

'Some sort of very angry crank,' he said. 'A costumed clown. Listen, do you want me to come and live with you here? I've been wanting to do so for months!'

'Oh rubbish! Of course not. How many times do we need to discuss this. Nothing' – she waved her cane – 'nothing will happen to me here. You're needed at the hospital. I don't think it's me he's after, anyway. It's the hotel. Besides,' she smiled, 'there's Francis Xavier.'

'That guy was terrifying,' Justin said. 'Could be an extremist. An extremist, you understand? Don't you read the newspapers? Are you,' Justin shouted, 'by any chance, blind?'

'No, I am not blind,' Indi said calmly. 'You're talking to a former Additional Secretary. I know a troublemaker when I smell one. They say it's unemployment, but I think it's a crazed sense of... something else. The LTTE picks them even before they're ten. The Khalistan movement was all mostly young. How old was Bhindranwale? Late thirties, if

I remember right. No matter if their cause is just or unjust, they somehow feel they're constantly up against an enemy; that they need to destroy the enemy before the enemy gets them. The energy of a hormonally charged young male is a great asset or a lethal weapon. If harnessed to the good it leads on to great things. If not,' she ran a hand across her unseeing eyes, 'nothing is more destructive.'

There was a pause before Justin spoke. A pause in which faint choir music from Santa Ana could be heard. 'I don't think this guy's anything like that, for heaven's sake. Probably just a small time criminal. But I'm confused,' Justin said quietly. 'What's he got against us?' He got to his feet, his eyes on her face, 'I think I'll go to the station again. I'll tell them about the other incidents. They need to send out an alert. We'll put it in the newspapers. Just to be on the safe side.'

'We need to talk to him,' she said briskly. 'We need to negotiate, find out what he wants and what we can offer. There has to be some meeting ground, some reasonable compromise solution without loss of life and limb. Perhaps I should ask him to bathe the next time I smell him. A good bath always helps clear the mind and might ease his delusions. Lux and Dettol will provide him with some values, or perhaps a sense of belonging.'

Justin laughed. 'Madam, you are one in a million.'

'I hope so!'

Indi cared about nothing but Justin's continued obsession with her. She, hated by the world and loved only by Justin, fed his obsession with her as a zookeeper feeds a hungry tiger. Her own mind raced off in many different directions, back into the past or forward into the future. But her worst fear of all was the loss of Justin's attention. She was grateful for her blindness at such times because even if he ever forgot her in his preoccupation with his duty towards his patients, he would never be free of the suzerainty of her blind eyes.

❧

Indi's vision, now completely obliterated, had narrowed into a long tube and stabilized as such in the early years of her career as an IAS officer.

She was easily incensed, unable to sit still, impatient with everyone and everything except her private abyss. *I'm going blind,* she thought. The brown paper, the neon light, the semal tree, they will all exist but I will not know it. I'll have to smell my way around like a cur, feel my way around like a leper. The ticking clock rings out my death every second of the day but no one can hear it except me. The darkness will be impenetrable. I'll die airless at the bottom of a black ocean. What means will I have to live? Nothing, but my probing hands and feet, my ears straining to catch the faintest of sounds to stay ahead of my sighted adversaries, my nose twitching for the smells of people, cataloguing them by the smell of their burps and farts, no maroon or azure except in memory.

She felt trapped in an airless vault, gasping for oxygen, then felt relieved that her lungs at least were letting in air even if her eyes were shutting out light.

She developed a rigid formula about dress, yelling out warnings to her maid that there must never be any deviation from the dress code. She scraped her hair back into the tightest possible plait which hung down to her hips like a thick length of blue-black yarn. She scrubbed her face mercilessly with soap and covered herself from head to toe in white, nun-like saris with high-necked blouses. Yet her physical perfection, the audacious sensuality of her face, made Indi's presence unbearable to almost everyone who saw her.

Her furious energy manifested in long hours of work. And in a secret life which was self-destroyingly perverse.

One night the floor gleamed with a lunar pallor.

Vikram, an old admirer, had pushed her breathlessly into bed. She had surrendered wickedly, knowing that Justin was about to arrive. When Justin walked into her Victoria Villa bedroom she had laughed.

Vikram jumped to his feet, hurriedly pulled on his pants, and left as soon as Justin entered. Indi remained on the bed with her nightdress hitched up above her knees and calmly told Justin that he couldn't ask for explanations because she didn't belong to him. He couldn't expect anything from her, least of all fidelity. She was incapable of natural goodness, gratitude and other virtues

'This is how it is, Justin,' she said matter-of-factly. 'This is just how it is. You can get out if you want.'

'You needlessly cheapen yourself,' was the only thing he said before catching a plane back to America.

Her need was to convince herself that she was invincible. She had to prove that she would never be destroyed, however hard people tried. But her invincibility depended on Justin's love and his care – however bored she may have occasionally become of his devotion and however wearisome the burden of being his chosen instrument in righting the world's wrongs.

She knew that she was his 'cause', his crusade, his expiation of guilt. His selfish way of compensating for his country's mistakes, his atonement for the sins against the Third World. She knew he would never be free of her, not just because of herself, but because she was his bludgeon against his own world.

As he turned on his heels and left her bedroom, she knew that she had won again. That her rejection had only made his love stronger. He went back to New York, telling herself that he would never ever see her again, but felt trapped and could no longer concentrate. He fled to Viet Nam as an army doctor where memories of her dominated every minute of his days.

A few lines of latitude down from Viet Nam, Indi plunged into care of her country. After a few months in Delhi, she was posted to a small town in North Bengal, where whispering rivers ran through pine forests. She was Madam District Collector, with her own office, staff and bungalow. Her monsoon eyes gave her a semi-divine quality among the locals. When Madam District Collector swept into courtrooms and sorted out disputes, or strode fearlessly out towards a riotous mob, or quelled a belligerent protestor with an unseeing stare, her booming voice and flashing eyes became an incarnation of goddess Durga. Like the blind saints of the past, Indi passed into the local pantheon as an avatar of Shakti.

She devised secret ways to master her surroundings. Exactly counting the number of steps from her desk to the door. Never being afraid to stop in her tracks if the light in her eyes suddenly went out. Laughing when someone said, 'look out'. For the government, her – at this stage – partial blindness made her doubly formidable. She seemed so outwardly good humored about her failing eyesight, so tall, capable and clever despite it. She started schools, laid new water pipes, sanctioned roads and bridge building projects. She was the showpiece of the service. Her name was recommended for the Ramon Magsaysay Award. Even the prime minister wrote to her saying how proud the country was of so courageous a public servant, who struggled daily against such a terrifying disease. On occasion, her eyes seemed to suddenly improve. The two prison bars became fuzzy at the edges and she woke up some mornings convinced that the doctors had been wrong. But by afternoon, there they were again, black welts against two sides of daylight, forcing her to peer into a railway tunnel ahead.

She dictated a letter to Justin, in the manner that civil servants dictate notes to their secretaries. She didn't apologize for what she had done. She didn't mention her vow of promiscuity. Instead, she wrote that she was getting married. And Justin forgave her as soon as her letter arrived. His heart, full of resolutions for a future without her, returned to her again.

She married Vikram, now a major in the army. He wore a turban for the wedding and his body was flat and bronzed. She sent Justin a hilarious account of the wedding – how the priest kept sniffing at the wafts of brandy in her breath, how she was barely able to see Vikram. Their lovemaking, she wrote, was progressing superbly. But then they went to Haridwar for their honeymoon. In the bus down from Dehra Dun, Vikram complained of pain in the chest and threw up a few times. He arched, stretched and pushed his legs through the window of the moving bus. By the time she got him to a hospital, Indi's soldier husband, her spouse for a week, was dead.

Shiela Devi and Ashish Kumar rushed to the Dehra Dun hospital.

'Do you have any idea what you are doing to your parents?' Ashish Kumar's voice cracked. 'Don't you care? God curse the day you were born!'

'But this is not my fault!' Indi yelled back. 'Is it my fault that he died? Is it my fault that I'm blind? Am I also the God of Death on top of everything else?'

'It *is* your fault,' wailed Shiela Devi. 'Who will marry poor Pom when they know she has an older sister like you who is blind and a widow after only one week of marriage? Ill-fated girl! Source of my unhappiness!'

'Demoness!' shouted Ashish Kumar. 'You've eaten up your husband and your mouth is running with his blood. You never looked after him. You killed him! You're the worst person I've ever set eyes on! The *worst*. A bad character. The way you carry on! Everyone knows what you are.'

'Oh, stop talking like idiots,' shouted Indi. 'He had a heart attack, that's all. Now get lost and let me make the funeral arrangements in peace. Carrying on like a pair of uneducated rustics! Mouth running with blood, if you please. Demoness. Such words! Very picturesque... but is this the language of educated people? Aren't you ashamed of the way you talk? What is this, some sort of gothic drama, folk theatre? No thought for me as usual. Concerned only with yourselves. I'll eat you up next if you're not careful.'

'Oh, god,' wept Shiela Devi. 'Now she's even talking like the Four-Armed-One. The way she ate up a decent man for no reason at all.'

As punishment, when Pom's marriage was arranged, Ashish Kumar and Shiela Devi didn't invite their older daughter to their younger daughter's wedding.

'Why?' Indi demanded on the telephone. 'Why don't you want me to come for my younger sister's marriage? Because my husband happened to die? Because I'm a widow? Because I'm polluted? Come off it, you can't be serious.'

'Your mother does not want you to come,' Ashish Kumar's voice was triumphant. 'She feels you might cast the evil eye. Or whatever eye you have.'

She swallowed hard and shouted to camouflage the tremor in her throat: 'I can't believe you. The double standards. The public posture of sanity and your private sickness. The way you go on about being a progressive. I believe in the Constitution, I believe in the Constitution. Yet you're nothing but a village bumpkin. You exemplify the gap between public stance and personal belief. You talk of progress but you're in the Stone Age.'

'Lecture me all you want,' Ashish Kumar minced. 'I will not allow you to come.'

'But Pom's my sister!' Indi shouted again. 'We're supposed to be a family.'

'Don't let her come!' screamed Pom in floods of tears from behind the curtains. 'Don't let the shameless one come to my wedding!'

'Keep away!' 'Shiela Devi quivered. 'Keep away, Four-Armed-One.'

'You,' said Ashish Kumar to Indi, 'cannot come. I'm sorry.'

'Is this your final word?'

She had her career, didn't she? Her successful, wonderful career. Her looks, her whore-like looks. Wasn't that enough for her? She had heard she had been recommended for the Magsaysay Award, one of the youngest names ever to be considered. He had heard of the prime minister's partiality towards her. He had heard that the road she had been supervising was one of the best highways in the country. 'Your mother and sister do not want you to come,' side-stepped Ashish Kumar.

All right, thought Indi, leave me out. Leave me out with my blind eyes and my widow's weeds. Leave me alone with my highway construction with nobody to keep me company but construction engineers and road-repair men and my secretaries. And the Constitution. But I will have my revenge on you. She dictated another letter to Justin, her words transcribed by stenographers who worshipped Madam District Collector too much to ask questions.

It's lovely here in this little mountain town where I live. I'm working with the local government supervising the construction of a new bridge. D'you feel like a trip? Love. XX

He was still in Saigon. As soon as he received her letter he telephoned his parents in New York to say he was going to be with her because at last she had asked to see him.

'But she is so awful to you,' complained his mother. 'She betrayed you. Now her husband's dead, she wants you again?'

'Yes.'

'And you're still running to comfort her?'

'Yes.'

'So, if you and your girl love each other so much why don't you settle down?' asked his mother. 'We could get her some treatment here.'

'I can never marry this woman,' Justin said resolutely to his mother. 'Never.'

His parents couldn't help but admire this toweringly hostile love.

He flew to her side. With his unshaven face, tattered rubber sandals and army rucksack, Indi's betrayed lover came to stand by her looking like a ragged street performer. He forgave her instantly for that night in Victoria Villa. He craved to see her made repugnant, so he might love her for her inner ugliness instead of her outer radiance which others inevitably worshipped.

He remarked at the change in her. The clinging saris tied inches below the navel and skimpy blouses were gone.

Instead she wore high-necked shirts and starched white saris with her hair tied by her maids in a waist-length plait down her back. To Justin she looked like a clothed Venus De Milo.

One early morning, they went down to the banks of the icy transparent river He let his hands slide under her blouse and along her back so he could pull her against his thighs. He brought her face against his and kissed her untidily. That made her laugh, but he kissed her again, more skilfully this time. She giggled against his mouth letting the smell of his blond beard and moustache flood into her face. He clutched her breasts, she winced, shifted and eased herself against his palms so that his touch became softer.

'My god, Indira,' Justin whispered. 'You're so fucking beautiful.'

'So I am told,' she whispered back.

A huge snowy profile of mountain floated in the clouds. Shiva's profile, asleep, with his icy nose against the sky. The sun dazzled down on them as they made love at midday. Justin was the sun, bending towards her in the brilliant light, his fair hair ablaze. He was Surya and she was Kunti, and they were the parents of the unknown.

There was a new vision in her eyes when they said goodbye. He went back to Saigon. And she stayed on with her construction team in the little mountain town.

When she doubled up with nausea a few weeks later she knew that her moment of revenge had come.

※

The Catastrophe came to Victoria Villa.

Indi's revenge on her parents for not being brave enough to love her, was so swift and so final that Ashish Kumar and Shiela Devi died within a year of each other.

Now that Pom was securely married and Indi working far away at her job, Ashish Kumar and Shiela Devi had thrown themselves happily into a daughter-less idyll. Ashish Kumar had started on the *Complete Works of Tolstoy*. And Shiela Devi had begun to flavour his yoghurt with little pieces of fruit.

Then Indi came to Victoria Villa and announced that she was pregnant.

Victoria Villa was shaken to its foundations. The semal tree trembled and the jamun's branches sank closer to the ground. Shiela Devi flew into a panic and croaked that unless she bathed in the Ganga this very second, kaliyug would descend on the family. Ashish Kumar contracted mild diphtheria and lay in his study wishing the Four-Armed-One would come for him without further delay.

A nerve-edged silence sat in the living room. The bedrooms were darkened by a softly playing transistor-radio gloom. This was a shock of monumental proportions.

'It can all be set right,' said Ashish Kumar defeatedly lying on the sofa in his study. 'You know it can be set right. Nobody need ever know. Why don't you go and get it taken out?'

'Taken out? Set right?' Indi cried. 'But there's nothing wrong for anything to be set right. I'll take care of everything. If anyone asks any questions, I'll say I conceived on my honeymoon.'

'Conceived on your honeymoon? Are you mad or what? That was almost two years ago,' whined Ashish Kumar, frantically rotating his eyes. 'Everybody can calculate. Not everybody is blind.'

She stood next to her father's bed like a tall sentinel. 'I'm not a helpless woman. I'm an IAS officer. I'll take care of everything. The government has too much sympathy for me. They won't touch me. Nobody will calculate dates.'

'Monstrous girl!' burbled Ashish Kumar. 'Destroyer of my existence!'

'Who? Who? Who?' Shiela Devi wailed after she came back from her baths in the Ganga. 'Who is the child's father?'

'I can't remember.'

'You can't *remember*?'

'I'm single. I sleep with a number of men. It could have been any of them.'

'Any of them?'

'Because I can't see! Understand? I can't see anything at all sometimes. I could hardly see who it was. I don't know who. Maybe a construction engineer. Maybe the postman.'

This was too much for Shiela Devi. She gave up trying to make yoghurt for Ashish Kumar. She gave up trying to get Indi to keep her voice down, and trying to keep her blindness at bay. She travelled to Benares every week to bathe in the Ganga, sometimes forgetting to dry her clothes. Eventually, she contracted pneumonia and died, telling herself with her dying breath that you had to be truly cursed to be consumed by your own child.

Ashish Kumar took to his bed with high blood pressure and breathing difficulties. Murmurings about Indi circulated busily in Delhi's salons.

Then Indi found an unexpected protector. None other than India's prime minister and Indi's namesake reached down from her highest office to come to Indi's rescue. Indira Ray is the jewel of the service, the prime minister snapped. Is everyone not impressed with her? Her hard work, her dedication, the dignity with which she battles blindness every day. The prime minister put an angry end to the rumours, saying Indira was an extraordinary woman who lived by her own rules. When Indi went to thank her, she found a hard palm cupping her chin with a whispered chuckle, 'We Indiras understand things, my dear. We're not very nice people but there's no getting away from us, is there?'

In Victoria Villa, oxygen cylinders were brought in for Ashish Kumar. Shelves of syringes and tablets teetered over the bed. Pom came to stay with her dying father while Indi chose that moment to announce she was going on holiday.

Justin took Indi to his home in New York. New York exhilarated her: a booming, plentiful city of love, peace and protests against Viet Nam. He took her to see the new skyscrapers that had transformed the city's skyline. The Sixties were drawing to a close but hippies played music on street corners. Lovers held hands under posters of the nuclear bomb. Flowers came flying out against the Pentagon and the sky was alight with youth. Her eyes flickered in the sunlight. The black bars had thickened slightly, but she could still see if she looked straight ahead. She coveted the mini skirts and bell bottoms that she couldn't wear in her swollen condition. The peace marchers outside the United Nations building were enviably slim. The first migrants from Asia had begun to arrive and directed openly curious looks at her. She was pregnant yet she was obviously alone and walked with a stick. Where was her husband?

'Marry me,' Justin said.

'No. I'll have to leave the IAS if I do. And I can't do that. I can't do that for my country's sake. I can't do it. India is my destiny.'

'The child?'

'Who cares?' She squared her shoulders and held herself upright. 'It'll grow up in its own way. The way I did. On my own. Why does it need any help? Did I have any? Did I

have any help? Any doting parents? Did I have eyesight?
How did I pass my exams? Did anybody help me?'

'My child too,' he reasoned.

'No.'

'No?'

'No. I'll do what I want with it. It's mine. I'll give it to
an orphanage if need be.'

'Why?'

'Children don't need much. Food from time to time.
And shelter. That's all a child needs. Like an animal. The
rest is an elaborate myth, created by self-indulgent people
who want to escape into their children. Because they can't
make a go of their own lives.'

'But I want to be a part of your life.'

'I and the child will be fine. You can do what you want.
You can get out if you want.'

'Never.'

'My palms were burnt by my own father, Justin. I still
got on in the world, didn't I? I have no eyes. Yet I made
what I could of myself. Man was created to forge civilization
from the jungle. He didn't have anyone washing his nappies
and slavering over his baby bum. All I have is myself. You
get out of my life. Go on, get out!'

'I'll never get out, baby. Not even when I die.'

'I don't need you in this. I'll do it my way.'

'Then I'll go with you. I can't be separated from you or
my child. I shall come back with you.'

She shrugged. 'As you like.'

'Let me be my child's father.'

'No.'

He fell to his feet: 'Please.'

'I won't ever see you again if you tell the child you are
its father. Remember that, Justin. My child is the only thing

I have. It's mine. Only mine. I will be everything to it. It doesn't belong to anyone else. It's either the child or me, Justin. You choose. Choose me or your child. If you take it away from me and keep it here in America and tell it that you are its father, I'll never see you again.'

'Why? Why, Indi?'

'Because I'll be everything for my baby. I'll be its father and mother. I'll see it to it that it learns how to grow up, without this cloying stuff they call love and family life and all that rubbish. Families are nothing but traps; they weaken you. Weaken you into a morass of emotional need. Freedom from attachment was the message of the sages. And I reject all attachment and all the needless weeping and wailing. There are greater battles to be fought, for god's sake. I'd like my son to be strong enough.'

She would resist him with her dying breath and the potential of her womb. She knew they would never be equal. She knew they would never be the same in the eyes of the world. But she would never surrender. She would go on fighting her guerilla war. Because she feared that if she stopped he would stop loving her.

'Choose. Me or your child.'

My love for her is so desperate and so egoistical that even our child is an irrelevant pawn, he told himself. It is only by loving her that I am able to redeem myself. She is my redemption, my only hope against the cruelty of my culture. She's the cross I want to bear, the burden I'm determined to carry.

He chose Indi over himself because loving her was the only way he could save himself from self-loathing. Nothing about her would ever repel him. He dared her to become more repellent, drove her to declare a red-eyed war on goodness, so that he could love her with self-indulgent selflessness. He had yearned to lose himself in love and his passions would have vapourised if she had ever made the mistake of being ordinary.

Perhaps she was right. Perhaps attachment was weakening.

It had certainly weakened him.

⚜

The child was born in a New York hospital with his father's blond hair and pale skin. Indi snatched him away from Justin and went back to Victoria Villa with her baby, after a phone call from Pom that Ashish Kumar was sinking fast. Her eyes sparkled as her taxi drew up at the Victoria Villa gate. She walked down the veranda to the semi-circular study, with her baby boy in her arms.

She sat beside Ashish Kumar and stroked his head. But her father edged away from her to the extent that his airless limbs would permit. 'Go away,' he croaked, gazing at her in open disgust. 'Get out with your bastard.'

'But it's a boy, baba,' she said. 'A golden-haired baby boy. Not a girl.'

'Get out!' His voice cracked. 'I don't want to see any golden child. Any dirty golden child. Get out of here, get out of my room and let me die.'

Ashish Kumar looked at the foot of his bed to see if the Four-Armed ancestress was still there. He had seen her a few moments ago standing with her head bowed. But with the entry of Indi, the Four-Armed-One had gone, scared off by Ashish Kumar's elder daughter. Not even a deadly, many-limbed great-granny dared come near Ashish Kumar when Indira sat by his side.

'You,' Ashish Kumar pointed a shaking finger. 'You killed me.'

She gathered the baby into her arms and stepped back from the bed. The Four-Armed-One slunk back into the room and Ashish Kumar was gone. Death had saved him from surrender to Indi.

She went running out of the room with the baby in her arms. She flung the baby towards one of the maids and marched away to her office. 'Do what you want with the boy,' she tossed over her shoulder before stepping out to work. 'Feed him if he cries. No, he doesn't have a name. Why don't you think of something?'

All over the land, first-born sons were named with fanfare. Naming ceremonies involved priests and families clucking in robust approval at the infant's penis. Heaven has blessed us with a boy! Sandalwood pens were used to inscribe the boy's name on betel leaves. His father or grandfather held him aloft, while his mother bathed his head and the gathered priests recited prayers. Planets clashed vigorously in the solar system to announce that the boy was destined to be a doctor. If he was to be a professor (hopefully at MIT), then all the trees bowed in obeisance.

But Indi's boy was different.

Indi's boy was named by giggling servants.

They held him against the semal tree and whispered a name. Let's call him Vikram, they decided. After the dead Vikram who had been married to Indi for a week.

In New York, Justin squashed a lit cigarette into his palm to feel the same pain that Indi had many years ago. He hardly slept, worked himself to the bone, and went for long walks at night. He wrote to his hospital submitting his resignation. After considering many possibilities, he decided on St. Theresa's Hospital in Goa, near the scenic town of Alqueria, far away from the city. Perhaps Indi would visit him and or he could visit the child in Delhi. The government had brought her back from her district posting in view of her eyesight and her enormous capacity for work; by prime ministerial decree, Indira Ray was stationed permanently in Delhi.

When Justin left America, he vowed to his mother that this was the only thing in the world that would make him happy. You have abandoned and lost all rights over your child because you're so addicted to the wicked Indi, his mother said. Yes, he agreed, but he needed her like a life-giving drug. No child could ever compete with his adoration for his child's mother, adoration which was fleshed out by a revulsion of himself. Obsession that degraded them both and let him wallow in degradation, helpless to get out of the trench into which he had dug himself.

The child crawled between the semal and the jamun. Nobody heard its hopelessness but the trees. Nobody saw its gums bleed, or its knees buckle, or its first stumbling steps.

Their child mourned. But Indi and Justin felt ecstatic in each others' presence. A burning desire freed their spirits and sent them bounding over the clouds. Their perpetually intoxicated love made everything else, even their own flesh and blood, negligible.

The way her bra strap sometimes hung out of her blouse, her wet body in a swimsuit when he took her swimming, her hopeless culinary skills, her mannish roughness and extraordinary mind – these were his universe and heaven. They looked on at their child with detached bemusement, from afar, without emotion, because they had no love left to give anyone but each other.

※

Winter was in the air. A few months later, the Kumbh Mela would begin in Allahabad. 'I'm thinking of going,' said Justin as they sat in Indi's veranda in Alqueria. 'Maybe I'll meet Anand Bhagat again.'

'You should.'

'You come with me.'

'Why d'you want to go anyway?' she asked.

'Because of the dope of course!' he laughed. 'What else does an ageing hippie like me need? No, seriously. Just thought it would be good, you know. Wash away my sins.'

They cooked themselves pomfret curry and ate it on her veranda while Francis Xavier patrolled the beach. Then they went to her bedroom and made love in the life-giving way that they had always done, even though they knew that their tomorrows were diminishing. Her eyes sent tremors down his back. Their unseeing depths made him want to cry out in joy.

The bow and arrow man was their nemesis. He had come to punish them for their love. Punish Justin. Punish Indi.

If either one of us were to die, thought Justin, the pain would be physical. Grief would manifest itself in physical ways. A knife permanently wedged in the skin.

'You haven't sinned Justin.'

'Yes, I have, Indi. We both have.'

'No, I haven't,' she said. 'I believed in everything that I did. If I have to pay a price for it, I'm willing to. But I'm not going to apologize. I'm prepared to defend myself for my values and for everything I believe I stood for. I will never apologize or beg for forgiveness. Forgiveness from whom? Apologize to whom? It is I who should be the recipient of remorse and forgiveness. I refuse to also be a provider of sympathy.'

He stroked her hair, convinced there wasn't much time. Those four decades of grand obsession were churning away into a gutter where weakness and compromise flowed.

7

NEW DELHI

Winter came to Victoria Villa garden. The semal had started to shed its leaves. The jamun's fruits were gone. Almost seven months had passed since she had arrived in New Delhi and with every passing week, the waiting in the air had become stronger.

One night there was an unexpected shower bringing with it a blanket of cold. Vik was away at a wedding. Mia sat alone on the four-poster bed watching the rain spray off the jamun leaves making them shine in the moonlight. Suddenly, there was a screeching sound of brakes and then another long sound. A human scream? Or was it the familiar imagined scream from the semal? She ran out into the living room and peered through the doors down the veranda. Another shout wavered through the rain, a human voice punctuated by the sound of falling water. Vik? Perhaps the wedding had been rained out.

She called out for the guards. There was no answer. She pulled on her dressing gown and crept into the windswept driveway. Clouds powered out of the horizon. She ran down the lawn and out of the gate. The guards were asleep behind the bolted door of their wooden cabin near the gate. A truck stood on the road, its headlights glaring onto the verge.

There he was at last. The painting of Justin had been a sign. The rain had been a herald. He was sprawled on the grass next to the road. His eyes were closed and the moonlight ran off his face. His beard had grown almost to his chest and his hair was down to his shoulders. His glasses sat crookedly on his nose and she noticed he wasn't wearing the wooden bow and arrow. It might have simply been an exotic toy to lure the Londoner.

A long streak of blood was beginning to emerge on his thigh, through his white pyjamas. In the darkness, she knelt down next to him and held her hand over his forehead. He opened his eyes, raised himself on his elbow and gazed at her.

'Maya?'

'I went back to give my address to the Purification Journey Brothers,' she blurted out. 'Sanatkumara said he'd never heard of you.'

'The Brothers are protecting me.' The whites of his eyes shone in the darkness. 'Protecting' – he winced and raised himself on his elbow – 'me because of my mission.'

The wind boiled up again. The storm penetrated the ditch next to the road and howled in its depths. The truck stood under the sky like a metallic Tyrannosaurus Rex, searchlights on for the next prey. The rain slowed and became less sharp as they shook hands awkwardly.

'I've been waiting for you for almost an entire year.'

'Maya, as honest as ever. You haven't changed. You're thinner but just as pretty.'

Crusader for purity, Karna.

Innocent Maya, who married even though she knew marriage is meaningless.

She led him past the semal – grinning, she thought, as it stood upright in the storm – through the veranda, into the leathery living room. She brought him water, Savlon, cotton and bandages, and he turned his back to her so she wouldn't see his upper thigh. He dressed his injury with expert soldierly gestures and then he turned towards her and smiled. He was so unkempt, so covered in beard and hair, that she could barely make out the expression on his face. He kept far away from her, as if she was a precious object that would be damaged if he went near.

'So,' he sat gingerly down on the sofa and looked around. 'What a big house. Your new home. Your new home with…Vik?…Vik, you said his name was? That would be an abbreviation for Vikram. Vik, who sells make-up to film studios, worries about the acidity in his stomach and kisses you with his mouth closed. How is your life with him in this huge place? Is he a fat pig?'

'He's not!' she protested indignantly, surprised at how readily she sprang to Vik's defence. 'And this is a beautiful house, I'm lucky to be here. I think he genuinely believes in what he's doing. Creating employment. Giving people jobs. And he loves paintings too, like me. He's shown me some lovely ones, oils on canvas, of his mother. And there's a painting of someone called Justin who looks just like you.'

'Well, then, an artistic pig,' Karna smiled again, hitting the centre of his forehead with his fist. The gesture was heart-stoppingly familiar. Someone else had made a similar gesture but Mia couldn't remember who it was. 'The owner of Moksha Herbals. Yes, I remember the name. That name which makes a mockery of faith.'

'It's a very successful company,' she said resolutely.

'A frivolous tycoon, Maya,' moaned Karna. 'A CEO of money. Come with me. Leave him. It's easy. It's very easy to leave and begin again. You'll be surprised how easy it is. You left your life in London. You can leave this life. Now. Immediately.'

'Karna, no! That wouldn't be right. I like, I love Vik. He's been good to me. I have no complaints. We need to make plans, though. The Kumbh Mela. Remember?'

'Ah,' his eyes widened. 'The Festival of the Pitcher, as you call it in English. Of course, you must come with me, Maya. Embark on a new and much more fulfilling life as my assistant in faith. I,' he smiled, 'being the CEO of faith, while your husband is the CEO of Moksha. My gods are beggars who wear imitation jewellery and sleep in railway stations. His gods are the snowy deities in his deep freeze next to his … what is it… tubs of Haagen Daz ice cream.'

Outside the garden was velvety with rain. The semal tree seemed to come marching out through the moonshine like an African mask, elongated and dark.

She laughed. 'Poor Vik. You're very unjust to him. Right, come on, let's fix the dates. I've looked it all up on the Net. Jan 9 is Paush Purnima.'

She didn't tell him about Anand's painting because she was afraid of a prosaic explanation. Afraid of an explanation that would make her miraculous coincidence into an ordinary one. She would much rather remain with the fantasy than hear an explanatory account of Karna's chance meeting with a London-based historian and painter who had perhaps seen him at the previous Maha Kumbh in '89 and decided to paint him. Instead, she told him about Vik's paintings. The painting in which there was a white-haired man named Justin, an American doctor, who looked exactly like him.

'Nothing but an artist's impression,' he brushed away her enthusiasm. 'Of little consequence.' He turned away from her and stared out of the window. 'Let's not talk of these other things, Maya.' His voice was soft: 'Of course I remember about the Kumbh Mela. In fact, that's why I came to see you, because we don't have much time. We must make our preparations. First I'll show you Pavitra Ashram, then you come with me to the Kumbh. There are three main days of the bath. Paush Purnima, Mauni Amavasya and Basant Panchami. Cleansing baths, the bath that purifies, washes, cleanses. We'll fix a date. Then...' he turned, 'you'll join me.'

'Join you?' she asked. 'Where?'

'Join me on my road,' his voice dropped and became hoarser than normal. 'I'm walking a long road, Maya. It could even be a deadly road. But there is joy at the end of it. Immense joy. I have given myself this mission. And you know why? Because you can go mad thinking what kind of world we'll leave for our children. You can go mad thinking we can be snuffed out at any time and there will be absolutely nothing left. Nullity and void. Nothing. We have to act, we have to act because it's all in our hands. We have to act now. Will you walk the last deadliest mile with me, Maya?'

How do I want to spend the days allotted on this earth? Either by cynicism and reducing every true word of life lived to a joke about weight-loss or bad sex. Or by edging away from the prison of jokes and information, leaving the oil-paint-and-turpentine flat in London and Victoria Villa behind, knowing that the world, this colony of humans like any colony of ants, is really a very small place where those who tell us what to do are not wise, but simply expert at playing the necessary games. The wiser way is to seek out the other crazier moments because everything is lopsided and tilted off balance.

Involuntarily, she stepped closer to him but he pushed her away, almost violently. He would not let her get close; never stood less than a couple of feet away from her.

'The vow of a brahmachari, or renunciant, can be broken one day, Maya,' he smiled sheepishly. 'After my mission is over you will see the true depth of my love.'

She had never had missions. She didn't know what people in political movements or nation-building projects felt, what sort of purposeful energy filled up their days; whether they hurtled from one intense experience to another without ever having time to stop and lapse into superstitious schemes. She had interviewed such people – the oracles, the activists for world peace, the zealous leaders of people – she knew their lives were centred on a higher purpose, that many risked death so that others could vote, many starved in solitary confinement so that their countries got their own rulers. Others stood in neck-deep water so villagers were given land or took a bullet in the neck simply to convince others that the present system of government was squashing their rights. But she had never explored these individuals beyond the eighty-word limit of a TV script. The only semblance of mission in her life was the one charted by Anand, which was to look at the world with an artist's eye. To find a vision that came not just from the light of a television camera but from the darkness of the spirit. A vision like Homer's who wrote epics in blindness. Vision in which a naked human being next to a billion-year-old river was seen for what he was. A neglected memory, not a joke.

'So what's this mission about?' she asked.

'Before I tell you, I need to know,' he said. 'I need to know if you will come with me, Maya. Will you come with me down the last deadliest mile?'

Yes. She wasn't scared of the deadliest mile, whatever it was. She listened to him tell her about his plans to rid the world of pornography, the ill-effects of the female ego, the need to purify society, while her mind spun out a double-life of a homestead with him on a mountainside.

The darkness became darker. The moon struggled up through the settling dust and positioned itself above the semal. Smoke rose from the wood fires in the slums surrounding Victoria Villa. The night grew cold.

'The rain's stopped,' he said. 'Come, let's go out. I'll bring you back before your chief executive officer comes home, I promise.'

'Go out now? But if Vik comes back, he'll be frantic.'

'He won't, Maya. I promise you he won't.'

He took her to the Hanuman Temple. In the assault of colour and crowds she forgot to ask him how he could be so sure that Vik wouldn't return. Even at night, the wet courtyard of the temple was bright and bursting with soaked people trying to catch a glimpse of the garlanded deity through the crowd. Women held up glass bangles gleaming with rain, for sale. Piles of damp marigolds lay abandoned near the temple steps.

They sat down in a corner of the courtyard under a tamarind tree hung with paper flags. He was distinctive, encased in a flame, a man set apart from the crowd because he was touched by some some extraordinary current of air.

Vik? Vik was a corporate guerilla. Party hard, play hard, work through daily rituals of money, sex and booze. Karna was different. Karna had called her Maya. How had he known that Anand's name for her was Maya? Because Anand and Karna were made of the same stuff and it was no accident that after her father died, the young priest from his painting had walked into her life. She would abandon all of it one day – London, Vik's parties, SkyVision – and spend her days playing footpath whore to his footpath prophet. The world would rush by with its meaningless preoccupations but Karna would travel with her into monsoon nights 'fragrant with flowers and bursting with honey' – as she had read in the Oxford translation of Tamil Sangam poetry.

Karna was a gateway to literature; Vik was a clubby sex symbol with attention deficiency syndrome whose highs and lows depended on his balance sheets, his effect on a glamorous crowd, and whether or not his beer was foamy enough.

Back in the taxi, as they neared Victoria Villa, Karna said, 'If your CEO comes home and sees me here, he will call me a loser and a thug and call the police.'

'He might.'

'Strange, isn't it? Someone who is trapped is perceived as a success, while he who is most free is perceived as a failure. A success at what, a failure at what?'

'An eternal paradox,' she agreed. 'Thanks, Karna. Thanks for the ride.'

'We will not see each other for a few days, Maya,' he said, saluting her in a soldierly way. 'But I'll be back to show you the ashram and I'll make arrangements for the Kumbh. We will leave on New Year's day. You'll stay for a few days at the ashram and then I'll meet you in Allahabad. In the meantime, think of what lies ahead. Think of whether you can keep your promise to me to travel the last mile.'

She waved at him from the gate as he drove away in the taxi. Tendrils of cloud slipped across the moon.

She lay down in bed again. Vik was a threatening rich kid. Concerned only with how to organize his evenings. And his need to decorate things. He led a boxed-in life in a neurotic world, a needy yet dismissive world. A few hours later, at the tail-end of her first dream, she smelt the faint smell of make-up and sensed him slide into bed. With a

dreamer's fuzzy conviction, she decided it was the latest
Moksha range.

※

'I've been thinking,' she said to Vik the next morning,
watching him put on his tie after he had finished an exciting
account of a politician who had spat into the construction
magnate's plate of food in the course of an argument, 'about'
– she gestured towards the painting – 'the Kumbh Mela. I'd
like to go. Maybe after we've been to Alqueria, once you
get back to work, I can make a trip.'

'Trip?' he cried, hitting his forehead with his fist, 'To
the Kumbh Mela? Hell, not your father's painting again!
No, never, we're going to Goa!' He always looked freshly
bathed, his eyes and teeth shining, his hair neatly combed.
He looked so confident as he strode off to work every
morning; in the evenings he was wet-haired and flushed,
after his workouts

'After Goa, Vik. It's happening in January. Just another
two months away. It's the Mahakumbh this time, after twelve
years, in Allahabad. I've been pretty obsessed with it, you
know that.'

'I know you've been obsessed,' he stared at her in
horrified astonishment. 'But you actually want to go there?
It's no place for you. You'll fall ill. Nude sadhus with big
dicks strutting around pulling trucks with ropes attached to
their dicks. Bending them around swords. It's fucking awful,
man. There's no way you can go there, Mia. Never.'

'But why not?'

'I told you, baby, it's crazy! Thousands and thousands
of people. Stinking toilets. Shit and piss everywhere. There
are always stampedes. People die. It's ghastly. It's filthy.
No, no,' he splashed on furious amounts of Azarro. 'There's

no way I'll let you go there. You'd get hurt. It's not safe.'

'But my father went.'

'Your father was a Sixties type, Mia. An expat in search of his "true" Indian self, or some such shit. And it was different in those days. It's awful now. Believe me, it's not for you. You're not some foreigner searching for the mystic East and all that crap. You,' he ruffled her hair, 'are my wildflower. My wild party flower. My love-in-a-mist. Come on, put on some of the new stuff I got for you. Did you see what those women were wearing that evening? Hot, eh? No question of going to the Kumbh Mela. Don't even think of it, okay? Besides,' he stroked her cheek, 'we have a big night tonight, right?'

He was always so full of energy.

She would watch him every night showering, changing and splashing Azarro on his closely shaven cheeks. She would watch him strap the insulin pump to his belt and key in the dosage. She would watch him button his shirt and smooth down his trousers and wet and comb back his hair. He was very neat. He folded away the bed-covers carefully, plumped his pillows, smoothed down the sheets and tucked every little wedge into the mattress.

🦚

That night, a pre-dawn light grew behind the semal tree. Vik stood in the light, his shadow reaching up towards the sobbing heights of the tree. He stood very still. The party lights were running low. The cooks were asleep behind their skewers.

'Hey,' he cried out, suddenly bursting into the living room. 'Let's have a game. Let's act the bloodied sheet!'

The runner-up, the gun-trader and the wordless beauty clapped sleepily.

'Blood?' giggled the construction magnate. 'Oooh! I mean eeyew!'

'What's the bloodied sheet?' whispered the runner-up to the wordless beauty.

'The bloodied sheet!' Vik held Mia's shoulders. 'Come on, you guys, don't you know? Celebration of the new wife, the blood on the sheet thing. The Rajput stuff.'

Long ago, marriages of Rajput princes were confirmed by bloodstains on the wedding bedsheet. The prince would emerge after the wedding night and display a bloodstained bedsheet to family and friends to prove that the marriage had been consummated and that his wife had been a virgin.

'Blood on the sheet?' Mia asked in confusion

'Not for real, baby! We'll just act it. Come on, it'll be fun!'

'Everything Vik does is fun,' said the newspaper baron hopefully.

'So where do we get blood?' inquired the runner-up.

The friends sat glassily upright as Vik screamed for Mrs Krishnaswamy to bring him a clean white sheet. He shepherded Mia back to their bedroom and pushed her down on the four-poster bed. As she lay on the bed, he unbuttoned his trousers. Running along the side of his thigh, half way to his knees, was a long strip of bandage.

'Vik?' she cried. 'Vik, shit, what are you doing? What happened to your leg?'

'Relax,' he said excitedly. 'Nothing to worry about. Just want to spill some of my blood, you know. Some of my own sweet, sugary blood. I got this a few days ago moving some equipment. My cuts take ages to heal.' He ripped off the bandage to reveal a neat gash, still oozing with blood, purplish along the sides with bruises.

'Vik! What the hell happened?' Mia shouted, jumping out of bed. But he pushed her back against the pillows.

'Relax. Relax, love-in-a-mist.'

He pumped the sides of his thigh like a nurse searching for a vein. A little blood oozed out of the wound. He grabbed the sheet and wiped off the blood with it, dashing the sheet energetically this way and that so tiny smudges of blood dotted its whiteness. Then he tore off a strip of the sheet and tied it across the cut.

The bloodstained sheet was a torn teenage hymen.

Daubs of sticky red crumpled across virgin white tissue.

Mia sat on the four-poster bed, watching Vik bind his leg again firmly.

'How did you get this cut, Vik?' she whispered.

'I told you,' he grunted, smoothening down the sheet. 'Moving some crates in the office. Don't worry, it's almost healed.'

An injury on the leg, a cut, running about three inches down the thigh. Vik's skin was pale, almost white and the hairs on his legs were golden.

'There,' Vik smiled, pulling his trousers back on and gazing at the sheet in satisfaction. 'See, the bloodstained sheet? Now I'll pretend you're my recently deflowered virgin bride. Cool, eh? Come on, baby, stop looking so spooked.'

She stared at him. He looked excited and calm at the same time. Like a chef who had just completed the finishing touches on a complicated entrée. A party manager, signing off the decorations with a trademark bunch of flowers. The expression in his eyes was distant. His mouth smiled but his skin was very pale, like someone who had been drinking so hard that his face had drained of colour. She felt her palms turn cold. She shivered with fear at the sight of his pale face. She shivered as she had at the casual way he used the word 'terrorist' for the man in Goa. Again, she sensed the waiting in the air of Victoria Villa. Some secret feelings had squeezed themselves into every crack of these walls. Victoria Villa was a foul spirit tempting its inhabitants into unspeakable crimes. The semal had been a witness, that's why it shrieked.

He held the sheet above her for a few seconds then rushed back to his friends in the living room where they sat edgily on the leather sofas.

'Look she's a virgin, she's a virgin!'

She ran after him, exhaling in relief. She was too brave and too experienced a journalist to lapse into a ghost world. *The Drama of Depression* would say she was hallucinating again. Vik had just been making a joke. A harmless party prank. One of those tricks he had told her about. He had nicked his leg somewhere, that's all, it didn't matter. It was like someone holding his hand above a candle. These things happened at parties. People did these things at parties. Parties were a kind of circus where each guest performed a set of tricks to keep the others amused. Parties were a play where actors performed according to the needs of the audience. She clapped as Vik flapped the sheet over his head and bellowed in a mock-Rajput voice: 'Hey, I'm a Rajput warrior and my wife's a virgin. The woman's a virgin!' The friends clapped and giggled.

In bed, afterwards, she kept her eyes tightly shut. He kissed her with familiar tiredness and touched her neck with his mouth in a word she could only describe as nipping. He's nipping at me like someone picking raisins off a pudding. Like a rabbit. His hands were soft. He patted her about like a baker patting dough into shape. She felt bready. Doughy. She hated him.

Should I run through the garden yelling that I think I've made a mistake in my marriage? Should I run back to London? What reasons will I give to Mithu? That my husband has lots of parties, buys me presents all the time

and has a naughty sense of humour? That he cuts his leg,
then drizzles his blood on a sheet to amuse his friends?
Mithu wouldn't believe me. She would think I telling nasty
stories about Indian men.

The weight of the party hung over her like heavy
pollution. He was an extravaganza of afflictions, with his
insulin pump and his bandaged leg. Her hands and feet
were ice cold. The clatter of the hot air blower rang out a
coded message. Far away from London, in a dark room
with a man with a bleeding leg, she felt as threatened as she
had once been on assignment in Sri Lanka, when on the
train back from Vavuniya to Colombo, she had been
interrogated by a soldier whose voice had been hysterical
but whose eyes had been bored.

She had been over-confident about India. She had
married Vik armed with the preconception that a dashing
young man from her parents' land was bound to suit her
just fine; that he was a cheery businessman who fell in love
easily. That he was Jehangir, the handsome emperor. That
his good looks and hearty handshake were as predictable as
airport check-in counters, no surprises there. She had even
felt a little superior to Vik, had sat on judgement on his
parallels between cities and movies-stars and mentally given
them grades. In the hierarchy of experience, she had placed
him many notches below Karna, as the flighty opposite
number of a sage.

Now she felt annoyed at his metamorphosis into a figure
of fear. Why was Vik, of all people, trying to scare her?

'I have to go to London again, love-in-a-mist,' he said in
a sleepy voice. 'The very last trip before we head for our
holiday in Goa. I'm sorry.'

'London? Again?' she focused her eyes on his face.

'Moksha. Again. Back to London.'

'London.' Her rain-grey city with Anand's absence jumping at her from every corner. 'Do check on the flat.' The oil-paint-and-turpentine smelling flat with the wet grimaces in the wallpaper. 'And could you please get me some...'

'Sure, anything. What would you like?'

'Liquorice.'

He laughed. 'Absolutely.'

Thoughts of London drove out her fear. She was being silly. There was nothing to be scared of. He just hadn't grown up. He lived for momentary excitements, the empty pleasure of a party trick, quick sex, quick sleep, up again, another party trick. A roller-coaster existence, with no part imbued with anything as dark and dreadful as she imagined.

'Lovely,' she reached across and hugged him. 'Thanks!'

'Sure,' he kissed her forehead. 'Will look in on the flat too. Bet Mithu left it in a mess. Not to worry. Hey,' he reached for her, 'I would never leave my love-in-a-mist for even a second. But the guards are here round the clock. If this new deal comes through for Moksha, we'll be rocking. Really rocking. They can close Sharkey's. My mother will have enough money. She'll never have to worry about the... that man.'

'Did he show up again?'

'No,' Vik sighed. 'But he might. After I come back we'll go to Goa. You'll have the best holiday and I'll sort out the mess. I'll take care of him once and for all.'

Mia turned her face towards the window and the silhouette of the semal. She felt as if the air inside the bedroom had become thick and that Victoria Villa's memories were bubbling out of the wall, in the manner in which water spirals out of the hull of a sinking ship.

The Kumbh Mela, the Kumbh Mela. The answers were all there. After she came back, she would have to get back to the drawing-board of her life and chart the blueprint of a new future. The inglorious reasons for her marriage to Vik had begun to assert themselves like weeds sprouting from a camouflage of artificial flowers. She would have to either find another garden or replant this one.

But first she had to make the journey inside her father's painting, the painting that had been the parent of her adventure.

꽃

Tunnel vision negates the dimensions. Light appears sometimes as a glare, a 'white out'. Sometimes light is concentrated in a doughnut-shaped ring in the centre of the eye. At this time Indi wore eyeglasses with dark filters to block the sudden white-out glares when she went into the sunlight. She sometimes saw two separate worlds. The world in front, and another just above it, leaving her to claw her way to the correct image. Justin read out passages from books on how to deal with the madness of retina loss. *'The Madness of Usher's Syndrome: Dealing with the Threat of Loss'*. But the books were of no help.

She turned on her boy. The flat-chested boy, with six by six vision blazing from his eyes as he pranced around her, flexing his muscles and turning cartwheels under the trees.

She had always secretly wished to be a thin, hairy, ordinary man. A rangy man with laser power in her eyes. Someone who could simply throw off his shirt and bask bare chested on a park bench, not skulk around in bathrooms, covering herself up for fear of the rage of strangers. In comparison to her son, she felt perpetually ill, handicapped, dragging her stupendous body along dim corridors, while he hopped and skipped in a pool of sunlight, his coiled energy promising to take him far ahead of her, to places she could never venture. Rangy men with vision in their eyes were born to win the war against Indi.

She vaguely registered his school teachers as dumpy women who smelt of hair oil. 'He's trying too hard,' his teacher once said, glancing at the composed boy who stood with his back to his mother. 'He puts himself under enormous pressure to succeed.'

'He should,' she replied. 'I had far better marks than him even though I had failing eyesight.'

'But he doesn't have to, he's good enough at his work already.'

'He should be as good as he can possibly be. Sometimes he opens and closes his mouth like a dumb goldfish.'

'He's not a dumb goldfish!' His shocked teacher put out a hand to grasp the boy's shoulder.

'He's not as cerebral as he should be.'

'He's a fine boy,' the teacher said hotly as the boy turned his face away. 'You misunderstand him.'

'He appears to associate with all manner of scum.'

'No, he doesn't,' his teacher was confused. 'He has very nice friends and is working far too hard.'

'Hey, dumb-as-a-goldfish!' the children shouted in the school playground, delighting in his mother's description of him. 'Hey, goldfish!'

His mother's friend Justin always had lots of nice things and showered him with gifts. He gave him a mountain bike. He bought him clothes from America. He had books and toys and games and a transistor radio. He had books on Viet Nam and he had army boots.

She sensed no love from him. All she got from him were demands, demands of who his father was, demands to attend his school, to interact with his foolish teachers, to attend to his needs. He wasn't as impressed by her as he should have been, her formidable reputation didn't seem to arouse the sort of admiration in him that it should have. The government had given her a special assistant, on the prime minister's orders, a special secretariat had been created so that all her important documents were converted to Braille for Madam Indi and she could labour over files without pause. She had won the Ramon Magsaysay Award for community leadership. Standing on stage in Manila, rays of gold light from the portrait of the Philippine president flashing through the black prison bars in her eyes, she had enthralled the audience with her movie-star looks and social commitment – India's partially-sighted woman civil servant who had toiled so remarkably at building roads in north Bengal. Dressed in her severe uniform of white sari and blouse, with her hair piled into a thick crown on her head and aided by tinted lenses on her eyes, Indi had looked so tall and aristocratic that the crowd had gasped in disbelief. She had shown Vik the photographs but he had tossed them away disinterestedly. Why did the boy not admire her, she whispered agitatedly to herself? Why did he not admire how hard she worked?

Sometimes she saw red flames flickering in the dark, which the doctors said were possibly the beginnings of a cataract. Sometimes she saw grey concrete slabs even in the round circle of vision directly ahead. Sometimes she couldn't hear and voices became jumbled in her head. Justin had told her that the disease could affect her hearing so she should expect it and report it immediately. There was nothing to be done, she bellowed to herself, standing in front of a mirror she couldn't see, there was nothing to be done.

There was nothing to be done but wreak revenge.

Revenge on those who could see the sky change colour or concentrate on a crow about to take flight, those who saw everything and achieved everything while she curved out from every imaginable place and blundered across streets, a breasty cow. She cringed at herself.

She hated her body. Perversely, she tried to make her son equally voluptuous by feeding him sweets and cakes, so he wouldn't taunt her with his thinness. She forced sweets, lozenges, toffees and lollies at him. She gave him cakes when she wanted to keep him quiet for the night. She gave him pastries so he wouldn't cry when she was working. She watched while he ate, screaming out, unconvincingly, how much she cared for him. Juvenile diabetes was diagnosed when Vik was ten and gave her cause for some devilish triumph; just as her blindness must have been some consolation for Ashish Kumar.

She began to take LSD. She had taken some as a student and remembered how it had helped her not only make sense of her world but also to hallucinate about an imaginary eyesight that lasted forever. She went searching for it again, in secret, telling her secretaries she was going to meet an old retainer, tap-tapping with her cane down the dingy alleys of Paharganj where the dealers lived.

Every evening after work she began to pop a tablet so that at home she was almost perpetually high, barely registering the boy's presence and absently shoving chocolates in his direction every time she noticed him. She came alive at night when, in drug-induced energy, she would either laugh through the nights with her hallucinations or speed through her files as if the words were pouring themselves into her brain without need of sight. She wandered, cigarette dangling from her lips, groping her way along the walls and the windows, or peering at dates on calendars or the brushstrokes on a painting. The drug made the prison bars blurry, so she could fool herself that they were just eyelashes caught in the white of her eyes which would go away if she blinked hard enough.

She scared Vik.

One night, when he was just about thirteen and was asleep in his room he heard a strange sound, a sound like someone laughing. He turned over in his sleep reaching involuntarily for his lollypop. He listened again for the sound. Yes, it was a woman's laugh broken by bouts of coughing. He got out of bed and padded across the veranda towards the living room. He saw an orange light coming from under the door. His heart almost stopped at what he saw. He stood there, in his nightshirt and pyjamas, staring at his mother as she sat on a sofa, in flames.

She sat laughing in her nightie while the sofa burned all around her. She laughed then coughed and he could see all the way down into her throat, white with dehydration.

'Wake up!' he shouted. 'Hey, wake up!'

Indi opened her eyes at the sound of his voice. She blinked at him unseeingly and went on laughing.

He ran into the veranda and out into the garden. He pulled out the hosepipe that lay coiled up near the garage door. He dragged it in with all his strength, grunting and sweating as he came hurtling into the study.

The fire flamed all around her. She went on laughing, her hair spread over her shoulders. Any minute she too would begin to burn but she didn't seem to be able to see the fire. He ran back to the garden and turned on the water. Then he sprayed and sprayed with all his might. Sprayed until the water crushed the sofa. Sprayed until she slid, unconscious, onto the floor, sprayed the curtains which were untouched by fire. Sprayed the walls, sprayed the paintings, sprayed the lamps. Sprayed everything, cleaned everything.

She blinked awake, lying spreadeagled on the carpet, waving an airy palm at him to go away. He tried to drag her out but couldn't as his heart had begun to thud far too fast. In the end, he ran breathlessly to her bedroom, got her sheet and covered her up. He sat by her side all night, watching her toss and turn and cry out for water. In the drenched living room, the burnt sofa looked like a beheaded animal. He sat crouched by her, sucking his lollypop, while the servants whispered horrified in the kitchen and her secretaries telephoned her doctor...

※

Justin had burst in the next day, off the morning train from Goa and gathered Vik up in his arms as he sat stockstill in his room. 'Stop this drug-taking,' Justin pleaded to Indi. 'Please stop.'

'It helps me,' she cried. 'Don't you understand, it helps me? Does nobody understand?'

But she did stop, flushing the tablets down the pot... Blind, blind, I'm going blind and nobody in the whole world can stop it. Fatally beautiful; fatally cursed.

Justin sat with Indi in their silent universe, as he had always done, his arm around her shaking shoulders while she shuddered and knelt before him, her mouth slavering for her tablets, and kissed her until she fell asleep, sprawled against his chest.

'When will he ever get lost?' she murmured, listening to the boy tearing open more chocolate wrappers in his room. 'When will he go away and leave me alone?'

The unwanted boy, once the unwanted baby grieving under the semal tree, had begun to acquire a glow in his eyes.

His eyes darted. They flamed. When Justin was around he kept his eyes downcast so Justin wouldn't see the smouldering coals. But when Indi walked by, he turned his eyes on her and it was just as well that she wasn't able to see them.

If you write to your father and leave the letters in the hollow of the semal tree, Justin had whispered to him, be sure he'll write back.

So he wrote a love letter to his imaginary father:

Dear Daddy. How are you in heaven? I miss you. When it rains, you and I could huddle under a blanket. When it rains, you and I could go splashing in a puddle. Lots of love.

He left it in the tree and found a reply a few days later.

God looks after me well, little son. And you are an angel who has come along to remind me of the magnificence of this world! Lots of love, Daddy.

He found the letter in the hollow of the semal.

Indi would wake up in the morning and rush away to work. She was in charge of army widows. She marched with them from door to door, from minister to minister, from official committee to official committee. Women came to her in great numbers for help. Some with bawling babies in their arms. Some with their bones rotting from lack of calcium. She marched through the day and often late into the night, tapping with her cane into committees and parliamentary inquiries. She was tireless, sleepless, and she never gave up until every widow had received her due. Indi was awarded the Sarojini Naidu Award for Professional Excellence, the Commonwealth Prize for Leadership and the Jawaharlal Nehru Award for Social Achievement. The citations and awards crowded Ashish Kumar's study but she never gave up her work.

She led other women to prosperity. Women who needed small loans to set up businesses. Women who needed money so that they could leave their violent husbands. She moved ministries. She dispatched teams of administrators into the countryside to stop child marriage and dowry killings. She collected money for a hospice for homeless women and supervised its construction. She started a neighbourhood watch scheme where citizens were asked to keep an eye out and report the ill treatment of little girls. She wrote letters. So many letters.

But she never saw the other letters that were written under a blue light in Victoria Villa. The child's letters which were always titled 'You and I.' Under the semal tree, the letters came thick and fast:

Dear Dad, what's your favourite country? Lots of love.

Little son, my favourite country is Antarctica. Imagine living in an igloo? Love, Dad.

Over the years, she patchily tried to make amends. Once after he had come back from school with medals in maths and football, she bought him a computer and promised to take him out. She had been strictly forbidden to drive but in an urge to impress him, had tried to reverse the old Ambassador out of its musty garage, the same Ambassador in which she had first driven past Justin in Connaught Place. She didn't see that Vik had run out from behind the car. When he screamed, she braked hard but it was too late. He had already fallen down with his leg twisted under the rear tyre. In hospital, she ran her hands along his leg strapped in a plaster cast and scorned him for his mere temporary injury. It would heal. It was a mere fracture. But nothing would heal her. She would never be cured. She left him to the nurses, refusing to stay with him in hospital.

He heard the nurses say, 'Hé bhagwan, what sort of mother is this who breaks her child's leg and doesn't even come to see him?'

Anger when it comes, is not just a noisy tantrum. Anger focuses the mind, quietens the soul, sharpens the intelligence. Anger bides its time, anger is polite, anger is well-behaved because anger grows into a conviction, a belief and then it starts to find ways to express itself in the most efficient manner. Vik looked up at the high ceiling and saw the face of his dead grandfather smiling at him from the cobwebs. Ashish Kumar had become a spider and come to crawl around Victoria Villa, his antennae up for the same anger that Indi aroused in generations of men.

By the time he was eighteen, his anger was not irrational. On the contrary, his anger was now becoming cool and deliberate as he worked out various plans in his head. His anger worked at great speed. Anger was a plan of action that had been incubated for a lifetime.

He was a good-looking boy and made friends easily. The friends came to Victoria Villa, played football under the semal tree, drank beer and smoked cigarettes because there was no one ever around in his house except the servants. Sometimes they saw a tall, bespectacled woman drive up in a government car, get out escorted by helpers and assistants and tap her away to the semi-circular study where she remained while a silent line of assistants took in tea, lemon juice and an evening whisky. He ruled the rest of the house; his music, his books, his happy loud laugh. He had an imitation pistol. A wooden bow and arrow. And albums of family photos of his grandparents, his aunt and the woman in the study who he said was his mother. His birthday parties were most fun for his friends because they were always efficiently organized by a group of staff, who he said, worked for his mother. But his parents were never present, nor were there ever any relatives, and the boys could do whatever they liked, including smoke.

Prime ministers came and went, all expressing their admiration for Indi in personal letters of appreciation. She outdid her father in her dedication, her incorruptibility, the long hours she was willing to spend at work and the frantic energy she developed as a compensation for her eyes. She conquered her drug addiction and began a course in homeopathy that slowed her disease and sharpened the circle of light. Her special assistants brought her as many Braille documents as the administration could manage. Her once scandalous reputation was forgotten in admiration for her work. The tap-tap of her cane around the office buildings acquired a moral ring. Madam Indira was a model officer, a blind woman of steel.

⁂

In Victoria Villa, a blue light fell around a boy writing a letter. The light shone through a flowery glass shade. The shade was curly and painted with a sprig of lemon grass. The boy couldn't sleep. He was an insomniac who ate chocolates through the night.

He kept the night light on because sometimes he woke at night retching and trying to squeeze sticky vomit from his throat. If the vomit was sweet enough he would swallow it and write to his father. He never gave up writing to his father, as he had done when he was little. As he grew up, he sent him messages about The Who, Deep Purple, Sunil Gavaskar and Mohammad Ali. He watched the film *2001– A Space Odyssey* half-a-dozen times and sent a detailed treatise. When he grew older, he said he'd like to go to America. His father replied that he certainly should.

Dad, I wrote a poem, he wrote in a letter. *Here it is:*

I dreamed there was a convent in the ocean. And the nuns robes were floating like underwater weeds.

That's a strange poem, kid. But keep it up, son.
Love Dad.

He grew convinced that it was her, the woman, who was the obstacle between him and his father. If his father was dead, then how come he was writing the letters? They were typed letters. Did dead people use typewriters? Then why did she say he was dead? She was obviously lying. She was a liar on top of everything else. He did have a father and his father wrote him letters. The letters were a secret between him and the semal tree and they drove him, unintentionally, into mania. A mania that he lived with alone, a secret which was so fantastic that it must be real.

'There must have been someone,' he nagged Indi.

'I told you,' she snapped, 'there wasn't.'

'But it's not possible. According to the laws of biology.'

'He died.'

'But what was his name?'

'I don't remember.'

'Why?'

'Why?' she shouted feeling for her torch so she could shine them on the files balanced on her knees. 'What d'you mean, why? Don't you think there's enough I have to remember? What my father did to me? What my mother did to me? I knew their names but believe me, it would have been better if I hadn't. I have a great deal on my mind. There's a need to change mindsets. Not be imprisoned in an old way of thinking. To be independent, there's a need to strike out towards the new, towards newer ways of seeing things. That's how reform is created, that's how change comes, that's how new societies are built. This house is yours, everything I earn, all yours. Why do you keep asking about the past? Erase the hankering, look forward.'

'What was his name?'

'Look, it doesn't matter!' she roared. 'It really doesn't. What should it matter what his name was? Just do what you have to do and get on with it. Make a life for yourself. Go forward and make a life for yourself instead of fretting about names. There's so much to be done. You must grow up and become a good citizen. Do your bit for the country that nurtures you. Progress may be tortuous but it must come. Progress won't make you popular, but you must sacrifice yourself at its altar for the next generation. Try and think of others. Try and concentrate on the work you must leave behind. Not only yourself. Think of me. Don't you have any idea what I'm living with?'

'He sends me letters. I get letters from someone who says he's my father.'

'Oh rubbish!' she peered at him through her glasses. 'Must be one of my secretaries playing a trick on you. They all know what a dumb fellow you are.'

He frowned at her. She told him to think about others but all she ever did was think about herself. She told him not to think of his father, but all she did was think of her own father. He hated the way she filled the house, her blind presence looming into every room like an ogre. She was a

giantess, a demoness, a chudail, one of those women with
her feet turned back to front. In a huge house, she left him
no space to move with her harangues about creating a new
country and a new way of thinking.

'Tell me,' he whispered to her, showing only the whites
of his eyes and standing under the semal tree, possessed
with a menacing spirit which only the tree could see. 'What's
your name?'

Revenge need not be impetuous. Revenge can become
fanciful and imaginative, reflecting the twists and turns of
the growing up years. Revenge is not just a silly bout of
crying; revenge plots silently and becomes a reason for
survival.

He leapt across the line of normalcy. If she had reached
out for his help, he might have been moved to sympathy, he
might have read up on retinitis pigmentosa, might have
assisted Justin in his care of her. But she assaulted him,
pushed him against a precipice and held her cane to his
chest as if she would quite happily ease him over the cliff
with her hatred of him clearly visible in her eyes. She hated
him for his existence. Hated him for his eyes. Hated him
almost as much as much as she had hated Ashish Kumar.
Her father and son fused, in her blindness, into a malevolent
single entity whom she must subdue.

He read a book entitled *Inside the Mind of a Terrorist*
based on the author's experiences of travels with young
Sikhs who joined the Khalistan movement for an independent
homeland. He read: *Most of the militants are young men,
battling a powerful sense of victimhood. The feeling is that
life on earth is nothing compared to the paradise available
for all eternity if one sacrifices one's life for a greater cause...
Death is a reassertion of glorious manhood, of heroic glory.*

He realized the definition described him.

8

ALQUERIA, GOA

The man swam between sky and sea in a place where one could be the other. He had been swimming for about half an hour and his calves and shoulders ached. On the shore he could see smoke curling up from Sharkey's Hotel. What a time it was here in the sea. A peaceful stretch of twilight after an afternoon nap. The water against his chest was cool.

Sharkey's Hotel was filling up with the usual finance consultants and fashion models. Lights glimmered on and off and music began to pump out over the sand. If he was god – a giant reclining god in the ocean – he would simply lift his heel and an avalanche of water would rush from his toes and flood out all those filthy little pleasure spots. The cretins gyrating obscenely to their music would be washed away. Seekers of sex. Sex to the power of infinity. Menstruating, constantly pregnant. Using the pure ocean for their mucky activities.

If he could, he would wring their dirty necks one by one.

He had been angry all his life.

He swam towards the beach, dried himself, and lay on his back on a rock.

Mia was different. She loved her dead father in the old-fashioned way. She had been abandoned by her mother and read psychology books to cure her depression because there was no one to help her. He would keep her safe. The minute he'd seen her in London he had known that he had to preserve her. Preserve her vulnerability and her ability to believe in things. Her intelligence was eccentric, idealistic, innocent. She was just like himself. Seeing her again reminded him of how much he loved her. One minute he had been lying on the road gazing at the underbelly of the truck, the next her face was hovering above his. She had agreed to walk with him down the deadliest mile. He would vault over her marriage as a jumper pole-vaults the highest heights. He would crush the jellyfish she had married; in whose rich villa she was a prisoner. One day he would confront her husband face to face, and snatch Mia away. What would their confrontation be like? What would the jellyfish bring against him? A machine gun against his bow and arrow?

He lifted his head to the trees and screamed a shrill scream. Where are you, Mia? He threw himself back on the rock. He ran his hands over his chest and neck. He ached for her. He screamed her name again, feeling the rock's sharp grain pierce his skin. When he rose to go, his back was dotted with blood.

He crept along the zigzag and up the red dust hill to the small abandoned outhouse in the courtyard of Santa Ana. He used the outhouse as his hidden home whenever he came to this village, which was pretty often these days. He had been making his plans for a long time. His mission to destroy Sharkey's Hotel was meticulously planned. The outhouse had been a good place to hide. He gathered his things... a can of paint, a brush, some palm leaves, a fruit cake, rope, screwdriver, torch, some make-up, a bunch of hibiscus flowers and a Canon instamatic.

And his other favourite toy. His revolver – a Smith & Wesson Model 640-1.

Tonight, he had tryst with the repulsive old woman who lived by the sea and ran the sleazy hotel. The one with the barely covered breasts. The one who was the opposite of the Pure Love of the Mother Woman. The one who looked as if her hands had travelled to unimaginable places; as if there was a treacherous cavity between her legs that would lead to the ruination of all men. If there was any example in the world of a woman with a big ego, it was her. She ordered people around in an imperious way. She was an enemy of society, an instrument of squalor. She was the reason why the world was becoming dirty. She was a putrid rotting piece of meat who thought far too much of herself.

He waited until the moon sailed out and then began its descent into the sea. It was raining. Slinging a canvas bag on his shoulder, he slipped out of the outhouse and ran down the red dust hill, across the zigzag, to the sea front. He ran past the lagoon to Indi's house. Francis Xavier, dozing outside and reeking of rum and tobacco, was easy to kill. All he had to do was aim his revolver, watch Francis Xavier surface from sleep as slowly as the seaside afternoon lengthens into twilight, and then fire a single shot into his head.

The sound of the sea and rain camouflaged the sound and Francis Xavier fell forward.

He ran up the wooden steps leading to her veranda. Inside, the rooms were pitch dark and she was asleep. He pushed lightly at the front door. It was locked. He pushed it again. Noise didn't matter, she'd never be able to see him. Using his screwdriver and torch, he unscrewed the hinges

which were large and easy to take apart. The door came
loose. He propped it up on one side and stepped in with the
rain and wind streaming in behind him. He switched on a
lamp. She was asleep, lying stretched out on her bed. He
dumped his bag near the door went through the bedroom
into the hall, through it to the kitchen. He opened the fridge
and found three bottles of wine. He unscrewed them and
dunked the wine in the sink. Then he carried them back
and arranged them in a neat line at the foot of the bed. In
front of the wine bottles he placed pieces of fruitcake. He
had brought armfuls of palm leaves. He arranged them in
the corners of her room, propping them up against the wall.

❦

Indi woke up.

He heard her fumble in bed, then saw her sit up with
her hair down her back.

'Justin?' she whispered.

'Yes,' he whispered back. 'It's Justin.'

There was a long pause. She snatched up her cane which
rested against her pillow and held it in front of her like a
spear. He laughed to himself. The Purification Journey
Brothers couldn't have given him a softer target. An old
blind woman as his chosen enemy. What a joke! He walked
towards her and pushed her against the head rail of the bed.

'Who are you?' she screamed. 'What do you want? Why
have you been following me for so long?'

'Relax,' he whispered. 'It's Justin. It's the man you want.'

Again, the same smell. A wan, woebegone smell,
something chemical, something doomed. Hair dye, or
foundation or was it some sort of hair lacquer? If only she
could get to touch his face, she would know for sure who
the Phantom Listener was.

'No, nooo!' She started to get up. He pushed her down again. He held her pinned against the headrail, twisted her hands behind her and tied them against the bedpost.

'Help!' she screamed. 'Francis Xavier!'

'Francis Xavier is dead,' he whispered. 'Why do you want Justin so badly? Won't I do instead?'

'Who are you?' she shouted back, struggling hard. 'What are you doing? Do you want money? Is it money? Bring the key, haan? I'll give you money. I have money. I'll give it to you. What do you want in Sharkey's Hotel? You can come and see, you can see what we do, you can see that it doesn't offend anyone. You' – she tried to negotiate as she had with the violent trade-unionists of a sick company – 'need to tell us what you're after. What cause you believe you're fighting for. What you hope to achieve. Your objectives, as far as I can make out, are too short term. An attack on me won't get you anywhere, won't help you to gain your freedom or help you escape from your sense of being the target of injustice. Tell me, tell me what you are looking for.'

He let her ramble on as he tied her legs together. Then he started to work on her. It was difficult because she kept struggling. He drew out a lipstick from his pocket, bent her head back and painted her lips bright red. He painted two red circles on her pale cheeks. 'Hold still!' he hissed. 'You're looking wonderful. Let's see your eyes. They're the most amazing eyes anyone has ever seen. The sea in a storm. A downpour in a deserted ocean. I've never seen such eyes in an Indian woman before. Hold still!'

He painted her eyes black. He braided her hair and stuck hibiscus flowers in them and placed some in her nightdress.

'Beautiful, Madam,' he whispered. 'You look beautiful. Even more beautiful than you already are.'

She shouted so loudly in her hoarse voice that he had to shut his ears.

'Help!' she screamed, 'Help me! Get out, you scoundrel!' She shook her head violently so the hibiscus flowers fell out.

'Oh lord,' he mouthed. 'Now look what she's gone and done.'

He stuck the hibiscus on again; she shook her head and sent them flying. He hit her hard across the face, so her head whipped around and blood spurted from her gums. She started to cry in low guttural sounds.

'I have nothing against you personally,' his gaze on her face was calm. 'It's not me. It's the Brothers, basically. The Brothers of the Purification Journey say they've been watching you at your work and your home. They say you are one of those women who are a threat to our world, understand? You are ruining, no, *murdering*, human civilization. Your ego is too big. You neglect your children. You compete with your children because you can't control your own ego. We are working to create the Pure Love of the Mother Woman. We'll have to decide your fate soon. We haven't decided yet. When we decide, we'll tell you, okay? Don't worry. We'll make sure we tell you.'

On the wall opposite her bed, along with some photos and prints, was a gilt-framed citation of her Magsaysay Award. He brought them all crashing down. Then he took out his brush and his can of paint and painted a giant bow and arrow. A black curving bow with a string. In the centre a long arrow aimed at the ceiling.

The sea growled outside and the rain came thumping down on the roof. He turned to look at her. She was tossing and yelping, straining at the ropes around her wrists and ankles. But she looked nice, he thought. Her cheeks with their bright red blotches, her blackened eyes and her violently red lips. Another touch was needed, a cleavage to make sure she looked as if she was attending a dinner party. He tore open the front of her nightdress. There, now she looked as if she was having a wonderful time, as if she had had a party with the wine bottles arranged in a row at the foot of her bed and the flowers in her hair.

He took out his Canon and clicked some photos. Several of her from the front and sides. Close-ups. Long shots. The flash went off against her face as tears ran down her eyes, the black liner streaking the red circles on her cheeks.

'Who are you?' she sobbed. 'What's your purpose? Don't you realize how foolish all this is, what a short term measure it is?'

He said nothing. He spotted her cigarettes next to her bed. He lit one and put it in her mouth. She coughed and spat it out. He pushed it in again, but it fell out. He held it in her mouth so she blanched and inhaled as much as she could. Then he snatched it away and threw it out of the window.

He stared at her for a few moments. Then he dusted himself off, switched off the light and went out the way he had come, with Francis Xavier's body outside leaking blood into the wet sand.

Indi sat upright in bed, bound, coloured and dressed with flowers. The wine bottles were knocked over by the wind blowing in through the open door. Outside the rain stormed into the sea.

When Justin found her the next morning she couldn't stop shaking. They locked up the house and she moved into his hospital room. They decided to close Sharkey's, send a written apology to the guests and refund advances.

A case of murder was registered and two police jeeps came tooting down the zigzag. A small police picket took up station at Sharkey's, waiting for him to come back.

The villagers gathered together. There was a special mass for Francis Xavier at Santa Ana and for poor Indi who had lived through such an unimaginable assault.

Lord, negotiated Father Rudy, let this be the end.

🦋

Justin crept under the semal leaving gifts in its hollows. Justin watched him wobble past on his tricycle.

'Hello,' said Justin, under the semal.

'Hello,' said the boy running up towards the semal. Little boy in his father's hair. Little boy in his father's eyes.

'Hey big guy! Hey cowboy!'

'Hey!'

'Are you being fine? Are you being good?'

'Can, can I ask one question?'

'Course you can, little person!'

'Am I a normal human being?'

'Now what made you think otherwise?'

'Then why doesn't my dad want to see me? Doesn't he even *want* to see me?'

Avenging angel Justin shouted fiercely: 'Of course he does. Your dad sees you. Believe me, he does. Do you believe me?'

'And who's that woman who sits in the house? She keeps walking around. She's blind. Who is she?'

'She?' Justin's brows were puzzled. 'Don't you know who she is?'

'No. Who is she, Justin? I know you. But who is she?'

Sometimes Justin's anger at Indi grew into a dark mountain. At other times he told himself that he understood her better than she understood herself.

The boy had always been a good student so when the warden rang that evening from his college saying she should come as quickly as she could, she was impatient at being disturbed at work. Perhaps he had won another prize.

The warden took her to his room and when she peered through her glasses she fell back in shock. He was sitting up in bed, white-faced. Down his shirt front a thick ochre-coloured liquid looked like the worst bout of vomiting she had ever seen. She blinked in the half-light, the beige stripes criss-crossing his chin. His body was rigid and his jaw set fiercely. Next to him, a steel bucket stood full to the brim with vomit.

'My god,' she shuddered. 'How ugly he is.'

The boys outside the dorm sniggered. 'Hospital and then drug addiction treatment, Madam,' the warden said. 'God knows from where they get it. He needs to go to hospital immediately.'

'Then take him, for god's sake!' Indi shouted. 'Somebody clean him up. I'll make a mess of it if I try.'

The ambulance drove through the night, past the ridge, past the Inter-State Bus Terminus towards the 24-hour Emergency at the Medical Institute. They had wheeled him in, pumped his stomach and let her see him after twenty-four hours.

'What have you to say for yourself, you?' she drew herself up into a figure of authority. 'After that disgusting episode?'

'What do I have to say?'

'Yes?'

His answer made her head spin. 'Tell me, who are you?'

'Who am I?'

'Yes, who are you? Why do you dominate the house? Why is everything centred around you?'

'I'm trying to get on with my life in the best way I can!' her voice broke. 'I feed you. I pay your fees. Have you no gratitude for what I've done? Don't you see how much work I'm doing? What do you mean, you don't know me? What's your problem? Twittering around like a ballerina... I'm going blind, Vikram. I'm struggling to keep my eyes and my sanity and my independence. It's a struggle, believe me, because most of the time, yes, I admit, I am deranged about the fate that awaits me. I cannot deal with it. I cannot read books and calm myself. I want to be independent because I don't want anybody to feel sorry for me. I work hard so there'll be enough money for you. I'll leave you everything. The house, all yours. What do you know what it is to suffer. You're spoilt. Pampered!'

'You don't care for anyone but yourself,' he said calmly.

'Listen!' she shrieked back, red flashes darting in front of her vision. 'You listen to *me*. Why can't you just endure? Endure like me. Do you know that my own father squashed a cigarette into my palm because he couldn't stand me? And you know why he couldn't stand me? He couldn't stand me simply because I was a girl and because I was going blind and because I refused to become a pitiable creature on whom he could pour his sympathy and his condescension ... I'm disabled but I don't act like I am, you know what I mean? I don't act as if I am handicapped and this makes a lot of people very very angry. People want to be sympathetic to me but they can't. I refuse to be a figure of pity. Partly because of the way I look. If I was ugly, I would be better off. But I'm not. I'm not ugly and I choose to live my life. That's what gets people angry. That I choose. That I *can* choose, when in fact I should be taken care of, or hospitalized or institutionalized. I don't play the right games. I proved my father wrong. I endured. I rose above it. I had no eyes, I lived alone, away from family weddings. And I endured and I brought myself up. You're a boy. You're supposedly the apple of everybody's eye, are you not? You're the right sex, the right gender, so why do you need all this attention from me? Why do you come crawling to me, looking for me to make your life better? You're not going to get it from me, because yes, let me tell you, let me honestly admit that I resent you for your advantages. I resent you for your natural advantages of gender and eyesight, both of which I have to fight for almost every day. Did anybody make *my* life better? Listen, I didn't want to be your mother. This *mother* thing is a terrible trap. Mother is a category without change, without dynamism, without democracy. Everything else can change. The world can change. But mother cannot change. Just *Mother.* Mother Mary. Mother Earth. Mary is every man's secret fantasy, is she not? The woman who gave birth without sex? Without any dirty sex. But immaculate conception is not enough for some people, understand? It's not enough for me.'

'How vulgar you are,' he remarked. 'You're vulgar. I don't know who you are and I can't spend any more time talking to a vulgar woman whom I've never seen before in my life.'

As she turned on her heel, he was suddenly at her side, his face long and strange. He pushed her down on the hospital floor and brought his hands to her throat. Her tongue ran dry as his grip began to close around her neck. His sweat dripped down on her glasses. She felt a savagery in his arms, in the spittle collecting in the corners of his mouth, in the rough strange slaps he gave her on both cheeks. 'My god, what is this, what are you doing? Stop it, Vikram! At once do you hear me?'

'Why does it always have to be you?' he kept inquiring. 'Why are you always the centre of everything? Why are you the one so famous, oh-so-beautiful, oh-so-brilliant, so whatever? You, you, *you*. *You* the blind amazing goddess. *You*, the centre of attention. *You* the only human being, while everyone else is just nothing, less than animals. *You*, the goddess. *You*, the superstar. You want to live; you want to live but your life is my death, do you understand? Your life is my death!'

'Stop this!' she coughed back. 'Stop it, you low life, you mongrel.'

'It's always you.' Tears collected in his eyes and dripped down on to her face. 'Everyone wants you. Everyone talks about you. My father wants you and not me, you're the only star. Why? What's so great about you, anyway?'

Poor sad Victoria Villa. With its mournful shadows and its sobbing tree. Victoria Villa where love died in strange ways. He looked like his own father. But to Indi, he sounded identical to Ashish Kumar. So identical that she had fought him as hard as she fought her father.

Prince Jehangir was an aesthete and a poet, but numbed all his life by the immense presence of his father, Akbar. Akbar, who built an empire with such force, such masculine energy, that poor artistically-inclined Jehangir had to fall back on opium and liquor to give him the personal style that could match Akbar's valour and wisdom. The sheer strength of Akbar's character led Jehangir in later life to acts of vicious cruelty towards others, in an attempt to bring some proof, some succour, to his own achievements. Jehangir found his father intolerable. And over 400 years later Vik found Indi similarly unendurable.

Her courage, the smashing beauty and the mind that leapt forward into contructive acts of public welfare, the grandeur of Indi, made him desperate. He felt as if she was a giant sun that was hurtling towards him, uncaring that she would burn him to death, as long as her own flames remained fiery. He brought his face closer to hers; his open mouth like a dead star. Her hands were pinned to the floor but she began to howl like a kicked dog.

It was a hot afternoon. A hot afternoon in a hospital with the sun beating against the white curtains. She howled like a cur in an alleyway, in broken barks. Her eyes became bloodshot with the pressure of her screams. The sound of the nurses' running feet sent him jack-knifing back to the bed, cheekbones protruding out of his skin.

'You bastard!' she screamed, groping for her cane and raising it as the nurses helped her up. 'You tried to strangle me! I could bring the police against you for attempted assault! I could have you put away for ever! Physical assault is a crime, don't you know that?'

'You go to hell!' he stared at her calmly.

Mother and son readied themselves for mutual annihilation.

※

After that hot afternoon, Indi left Victoria Villa forever. She had her assistants pack her suitcases and stumbled out through the gates, her eyesight now completely gone. She dictated her resignation letter from the Civil Service in a barely audible voice and fled to Justin who was working at St Theresa's Hospital in Fontainhas, near Alqueria. The government was co-operative. They begged her not to resign but when they realized she was adamant she was given every help with her papers; her pension was expedited and the chief secretary of Goa himself helped her buy a patch of land in Alqueria next to the cottage Justin already owned. Indi and Justin started Sharkey's Hotel together.

She never went back to Victoria Villa. He never came
to Alqueria. He stayed on alone with the servants and the
two haunted trees, with Justin for regular company. After
he passed his exams, Justin arranged for him to go to The
Wharton School where he not only got his MBA but also
read a great deal of Hegel and Nietzsche. He read
translations of the works of Ernst Junger who wrote of the
flabby, comfort-seeking ways of the middle class, as
contrasted with the higher principle of pleasure which came
from adventures that are close to death. Death was an ideal,
while comfort was mediocre and centred around money.

When he came back, he was raring to go. His diabetes
was fully controlled with his new insulin pump and monitor.
Moksha Herbals already existed as a promising business
owned by a Kerala landowner and contracts with a number
of film studios in the south had already been signed. He
bought the business with the money Justin's parents loaned
him. Since the supply chains and workshops were already
established, he was able to upgrade the scale of operations
by securing a clutch of international clients whom the
Reylanders set him up with through their friends in California
and New York.

By the time he met and married Mia, Moksha Herbals
had become a rollicking concern, poised for even greater
success.

He kept up his reading of Junger.

☙

Under the semal, when evening slanted across the lawn, the
eight-year-old boy asked his father,

'Justin?'

'Yes, big guy?'

'Do you have a son of your own?'

'Do I have a son?'

'Yes.'

'Yes I believe I do.'

'Who is he? Why don't you care for him?'

'My son is Cupid. He shot me with an arrow and I fell in love with his mother. My son has fluffy pink cheeks and has a bow and arrow strapped to his back.'

'What's a bow and arrow?'

'You want one, big guy?'

'Yes, I do.'

'Okay, kid. I'll get you a bow and arrow. A toy one. But be careful with it, all right? Very careful.'

'Is a bow and arrow dangerous?'

'It can be, kid. It can be.'

⁂

Since Indi couldn't describe him except that he had a whispering voice, smelt of chemicals and talked of some Brothers belonging to the Purification Journey who had some plans for her and were on a mission to create the Pure Love of the Mother Woman, the police had no idea where to look for him. They searched up and down all the way from Loutolim to Colva, but what could they do without a description, with nothing to go on other than Justin's sight of someone tall, long-haired and dressed in white? The police detachment posted at Sharkey's dragged some chairs out to the waterfront and dozed off by the purple sunset.

Justin called Vik, speaking to him for the first time after Vik had telephoned him from London to tell him about his marriage, and listened to his shocked silence. Yes, yes, he said after a while, he would try and come straightaway. He would come as soon as he could.

How dutiful he was, Indi told Justin.

Her mind returned once again to that hot afternoon. That hot afternoon; the final act in her blindness. That hot afternoon when the sun, or was it her son, had burst into her eyes for the last time.

Justin was not taking any chances with the police. At Panjim market, he designed and bought Indi a special cane. The cane was as long as the previous one but when you pressed a clasp, the outer covering came rolling down to reveal a sharp inner spear.

'You may never need to use it,' Justin said, loyal only to her; unrepentant of the choice he had made in his life. 'But just keep it.'

9

NEW DELHI

Mia sat on the four-poster bed, replying to sms messages from the runner-up. Yes, Vik had called from London. Yes, she was fine, nothing to worry about, she was well looked after by Mr and Mrs Krishnaswamy. Yes, she was missing him.

The lamp next to her bed cast a pyramidal glow on the Kumbh Mela painting. Karna hadn't come again after that rainy night, although he had been calling every day to say he was in the process of completing his mission and would take her to Pavitra Ashram as soon as he returned.

She had waited for him for three days, counting the precious time they were losing while Vik had been away. She had gone shopping to Ansal Plaza with the runner-up, been to lunch at Basel and Thyme with the wordless beauty, wandered through Victoria Villa and sipped tea in the garden. She had studied Justin's portrait, leafed through *The Drama of Depression* and surfed the Net for more information on the Kumbh. Mithu called to enquire whether Mia was pregnant and to announce that America, not England, was the First World: Brooklyn Heights was *so* stylish, the people *so* friendly. She had been to see the World Trade Center and the Statue of Liberty. She had already been to Victoria's Secret and Banana Republic. In Jackson Heights everything was available, from paan to papad. And at the Lincoln Center there was even a festival of Satyajit Ray films.

Not long now, she thought as her mother rang off. Not long before her date with her father's painting. Once she had returned, she would re-assess her headlong rush to India, she would write to SkyVision asking if she could return, she would cut her losses and write off her incursion into Vik's life as a temporary period of instability after her father's death.

After an eternity of a four-day wait, Karna appeared. He seemed pleased with himself and said the 'mission' was proceeding well. His hair, beard, and moustache camouflaged the shape of his mouth, the contours of his cheeks – everything except his sharp eyes behind his glasses and his indigo-dark skin. A dark-skinned John Lennon in the guru phase. A Hindu Che Guevara. Jesus with glasses experimenting for a while with another religion.

※

Pavitra Ashram was located in a small village on the outskirts of the city where tarmac tapered into wheat fields and yellow-painted buildings gave way to cottages with buffaloes tied in the courtyards. Down a dirt track, leading into an area of woodland, a painted board announced, 'Pavitra Ashram'.

'Walk in,' said Karna.

'And you?'

'I'm in retreat. I won't come with you. You go in. Don't worry.'

'You won't come with me?'

'No.'

'But why?'

'Don't worry. Just go in. Don't mention my name. Don't say I brought you here. Just say you've come because you want to learn.'

'But why hide from the Brothers?'

'Because I don't want them to think I brought you. I'd like them to believe that you're here for your own reasons, that there is no intermediary between you and the Purification Journey. Besides, I don't want them to know that I've come back. I've come back' – his eyes smiled – 'only to see you. Go on. Go in.'

She walked down the dirt track to an arc of mud-daubed huts standing around a calm lake. In the centre of the lake was a building which looked like a seaside church in Greece – white-painted with a blue dome. The whiteness of the building stood out starkly against the inky blue lake. Lilies and ducks floated on the water. Water hyacinths bloomed in clumps. The water in the lake was so still that the temple island looked as if it was suspended from the clouds by invisible threads.

Water and land met in featherlight calm.

Mia walked towards the smoky stillness of the ashram and found herself in an open courtyard in front of a cluster of huts. Groups of men, some in white kurtas and pyjamas, others in jeans and T-shirts, some clean-shaven others with beards, sat on the ground chatting and laughing. The red-haired man whom Mia had seen at the Purification Rally in London twirled a rounded bamboo stick in the air. He recognized Mia at once and stood up and folded his hands, as if he had been expecting her.

'The Almighty Presence bless you, Sister,' said Sanatkumara. 'Thank you for coming.' All the Brothers rose to their feet, folded their hands and bowed. As they stood up, she saw that many of them, like Sanatkumara, carried rounded bamboo sticks.

'Please don't be afraid,' said Sanatkumara. 'These are not weapons. It's a part of our dress. We feel it takes us closer to our forefathers.'

'Interesting,' Mia smiled. No less absurd than a suit and tie. No less foolish than strings and thongs.

'Please come, you are welcome,' said Sanatkumara again. 'I remember you very well, Sister. You asked about someone I could not tell you about. You mentioned a name I could not place.'

Sanatakumara, he explained when she expressed curiosity about his name, was a famous yogi who, many centuries before Jesus, renounced the world to live like a beggar. This Sanatkumara said, he was born on the banks of the Danube but had been so inspired by the Purification Journey that he had come to the ashram to spend the rest of his life.

The ashram was surrounded by mustard and wheat fields. A line of men marched into them in single file, while others bent into the earth, their faces bobbing between the stalks. Everywhere there was a smell of woodsmoke, horse-dung and freshly-cut grass. Horse-drawn carts clip-clopped past the huts. Children sat quietly next to their mothers, reverentially touching the feet of the Brothers as they walked past with Mia. A group of boys stood patiently next to a well. The Brothers took her to a long dining hall where Mia was served a breakfast of milky dalia and rotis. The warm smell of the first chapattis of the day came wafting out of the community kitchen. She looked out of the window and saw a blue-painted child wearing peacock feathers in his hair, playing a flute by the lake. 'That child,' she asked. 'Who is he?'

'Oh,' laughed Sanatakumara. 'That's our little Krishna. We've adopted him. We dress him up like that for fun.' A blue-painted orphan Krishna with a talent for telling stories, abandoned on the footpath and adopted by the Brothers. She had heard the story in London.

The women in the ashram all wore bright saris with their pallus drawn over their heads, some with their veils pulled down to their lips. They sat in the doorways of the huts, cradling their children. There were women with baby boys riding on their shoulders or strapped to their backs. She noticed an adolescent being suckled in a tiny woman's lap, although the child was almost as tall as her. The women were all silent but smiling, their heads covered, their bosoms uniformly large, their hips maternally rounded, their heads bowed.

'We have a regular routine here. We sleep in our huts. Our beloved sisters sleep separately in their own huts. We eat two meals a day and we take turns cleaning each others' toilets,' smiled Sanatkumara. 'Once in six months we abstain from speech for two or three weeks. We have our own cows for fresh milk and cheese and no medicines.'

'No medicines?'

'The human body cures itself, Sister. All we need is the goodness of the plants left behind by our ancestors. And all we need is the Pure Love of our Mother Women.'

'And do the women all cover their heads?' She felt herself clutch instinctively for an absent notepad and pen.

'It's our belief that the Mother Woman should be protected. Protected, because the lust of men is neither beautiful nor poetic, as the advertisers are trying to make out. The lust of men is simply ugly and such lust gives women too much unhealthy power. We are the protectors of the Mother Woman. We protect women from themselves.

In the world of the Mother Woman, women are sheltered
and not savaged. In the world of men they are treated like
servants and whores but don't realize it because their egos
are so big. The ego of a woman must be controlled, Sister.
The female ego is the most destructive force today.'

The Purification Journey offered a unique 15-day
introductory package to interested visitors. Guests could
come for a fortnight, attend yoga classes, eat simple meals
and learn about the Purification Journey. It was a unique
experiment. It helped return lost individuals to their values
and to fight their way back to their own better selves.

Mia sat with the Brothers on their charpoys in the
courtyard, wishing fervently she had her notebook and
camera. SkyVision would have been in raptures over Pavitra
Ashram. Sanatkumara told her about how international their
movement was, how people from many parts of the world
had joined them and how their membership was growing.
Another of India's secrets, she thought. Inside a jungle on
the city outskirts, where there is apparently nothing but
trees, is in fact a spiritual community aiming to wage the
Inner War.

They told her a story about Aditi. Aditi was the mother
of the gods. She had eight sons. The last was Martanda
whom she tested the most. She buried him alive under the
earth with an elephant for company, but he survived and
grew up and became stronger than she could have imagined.

And then, of course, there was the story of Kunti. Did
Mia know the story of Kunti? Kunti was a wayward teenager
who lived in those uncertain times when gods walked among
men. One afternoon, she ran into swaying fields out by the
river and spread her legs to the sun. The sun obliged and
Kunti became pregnant. But as soon as her son was born
she floated him away in a basket and when he grew up and

became a brilliant warrior she tormented him and made him promise that he would never fight against her own legitimate children. Her son grew into a very sad very angry man. Karna was a very sad and angry man because his mother had floated him away in a basket.

'Karna?' she blinked.

'Yes, Sister,' Sanatakumara nodded approvingly at her interest. 'Kunti's son's name was Karna.'

The mythological Karna never had much of a chance, she remembered him telling her in London, but he would.

'You see, Kunti was not a Mother Woman in the right sense of the term,' explained Sanatkumara. 'She was too promiscuous, too busy with her lover, the sun, to love her own son. Kunti had too much of an ego. Karna never got a chance to get his revenge on Kunti.'

Bells sounded at noon. Down the dirt track, Mia saw groups of villagers making their way towards the blue-domed temple. Mia walked along with the Brothers across the pebbly path over the lake, but when they entered the temple she was sharply shepherded away from them. Men and women sat in separate enclosures, children in a common central corral. The villagers settled down comfortably, clearly this was one of their regular visits to the ashram. Women with bright tikas and flowered saris smiled at Mia and made place for her among them. In the centre of the dome was an idol of a female deity in white marble cradling an infant. A sharp light focused on it from the ceiling. The temple floors were white and sparkling and shone with mesmerizing whiteness.

Prayers began with a humming chant. Sanatkumara whirled around like a dervish with his lamp held above his head. Then back again to heaven and down to hell. Bells rose in crescendo. He whirled to the ground and the earth rose up to touch his forehead. The burning incense brought tears to Mia's eyes.

After the prayers, Sanatakumara gave a sermon.

'What is the meaning of the Inner War? What is the implication of the Mahabharat? It is the war within, the war for your better self. If you fight your bad self, you will give birth to a society where we can return to the Pure Love of the Mother Woman. It is a violation of the Almighty Presence's law that girls should show off every inch of their bodies to men. Men and women are not the same and they cannot be. Is this why your forefathers brought you into this world? So that your daughters cease to have dignity, grace and affection and become instead seekers of sex?'

The crowd murmured unhappily.

'Look around you. Your old values are ruined, your morals are at sea, your children's marriages torn asunder by distant journeys in search of employment. Machines are tearing down your shops and constructing new malls where you cannot buy anything. And above all, your daughters have become slaves. They no longer decorate their hair with flowers or carry sweets to the temple. Instead, your daughters laugh and swagger on the streets and spill their breasts and navels for any passing stranger.

'People with rich lives are engaging in sexual fetishes. They can even kill just to get sexual excitement. At their parties, everyone drowns in their own egos. They are converting the beaches of the world into hell-holes of drugs and fornication, where under the glitter there is the pure evil born from extreme affluence and extreme boredom. They scour the world for bodies, for bodies to have intercourse with and then kill, because their lives are so far away from everything that is true or simple. They look alive. In truth, they are dead.

'This shallowness is a form of evil. Those who are unthinking have no idea of what is right and wrong, are incapable of honest friendships or attachments. They have turned their backs on the Inner War. They have ceased to fight. That's why they have forgotten why humans were created.'

Anand would have been in a sweat of curiosity about the Pavitra Ashram, thought Mia. The beauty of the surroundings, the outlandish Brotherhood preaching a schizophrenic battle, would have sent him into a welter of analyses. He would have sat on the banks of the lake watching the water hyacinths and uncovering the layers of life that must have existed here before him, trying to find the human stamp on stones and plants.

What would Vik do if he saw her here? He would cringe in disgust. He would titter at Karna and try to offer him champagne. Vik would never be able to sit still and watch the sun rise over a lily lake. Vik would squirm at the sight of the buffaloes and bury his face in his Azarro-scented shirt. When Vik called on her mobile in the middle of Sanatkumara's sermon to find out where she was and to tell her that he was about to leave his hotel for the Belsize Park flat, she whispered that she was at a movie.

❦

Karna was waiting for her outside the ashram and they both took a taxi back to Victoria Villa. It was early evening. The winter sun was fading and a cold breeze had begun to blow across the grass. They sat together in silence as they had in London on the park bench in Hyde Park.

'Thank you for taking me,' she told him. 'It was captivating.'

'The Kumbh Mela,' said Karna slowly, 'is even more wonderful than the ashram. I won't be going with you. But all the arrangements have been made. You will stay at the ashram for a few days. Before I leave I'll call you there to tell you where to meet me on the festival ground.'

'So,' she said, 'we're off and away, Karna, son of Kunti.'

'Ha,' he laughed. 'The Brothers told you Karna's story. Bad things happened to my mythological namesake.'

'It's a sad story.'

'Sad? No, not sad. These things happen. You can never tell about people.'

'No, you can't,' she agreed.

'Not even about your tycoon husband.'

'Vik's' – she glanced upwards at the semal – 'been talking about some man. He says he wants to fight someone.'

'Fight someone?' Karna frowned. 'Who?'

'Someone threatening his mother.'

'His mother? Why?'

'They don't know. Someone. A man. Vik calls him a thug. He's been harassing her. In Goa.'

'His mother lives in Goa?'

'Yes, she runs a hotel there, Sharkey's Hotel.'

There was a pause. 'What sort of man?' he asked. 'Do they know?'

'He didn't tell me. But Vik says he'll hunt him down if the police can't catch him. One of his friends told me at a party that he was even considering hiring someone to finish him off, a supari.'

'Outrageous!' Karna threw up his hands. 'Just listen to the way the rich and powerful talk! It's shocking! Shameful! You can't just go out and shoot a man down! Just because your husband happens to be rich he thinks he can do what he likes? Is your husband mad?'

'But why should he be trying to scare me?'

'He sounds like a loose talker, this husband of yours. You can walk miles with him into the water and still be in only ankle-deep. You'll never reach the ocean with him, Maya.'

She looked down at her hands. 'After I come back from the Kumbh, I'll write to him and tell him the whole thing was a mistake. I should never have got into it. I can't understand him at all sometimes. We don't really have anything in common. I was deluded. It was my mother's obsession with getting me married and me trying to make her happy. Trying to make up to her. My father's death... I've just not been myself this past year. I've been reading too much into things. That damn book. It's like I'm on a drug or something.' She looked up at him, 'Maybe I should go back to London and try and get my old job back.'

'No, Maya!' he sprang to his feet, his glasses reflecting the branches of the tree. 'You can't go back to London. You promised to come with me. Don't you remember? You promised that you would walk with me down the deadliest mile. You can't forget. You can't walk away now.'

No, to be separated from him now would be an impossible act. He seemed so vulnerable, so unmindful of himself. Yet his eyes were sharp, as if he saw her stripped to the bone. She was far away from her childhood, far away from her home and her mother. She was her father now. She was Anand, her painter-historian father with his artist's satchel and water-bottle, clambering onto an ox-cart to bump his way towards a remote tribe. On an impulse, she tried to walk into Karna's arms again. What would his lovemaking be like? Intense one moment, joyful the next? But he pushed her gently away.

'I can't tell you any more, Maya,' he smiled. 'But you must trust me. Your father would have wanted you to trust me. After I've completed my mission, you'll see how much I love you, Maya. You will see. But you will catch only a glimpse because my love is so large you will not be able to see all of it with the human eye.'

'Vik will be back from London soon,' Mia said after a pause.

'Will he?'

'Yes.'

'Let's teach him a lesson, this fat pig of yours. If he wants to kill a man, let me first kill his house.'

'What d'you mean?'

'Let's see...' He stood up and walked around the semal, like a soothsayer on the verge of a prophecy. 'There's something ugly about this tree, don't you think?' he asked suddenly.

'Ugly? This tree? The semal? No, it's a beautiful tree. It's Vik's favourite tree. Someone used to leave letters in its hollows for him when he was a kid.'

'It's haunted.'

'Haunted?'

'Yes.'

'How do you know?'

'I can feel it.'

'But Vik loves this tree. There are hollows in it. As I told you, somebody used to leave letters in this tree. He thinks it was someone pretending to be his dad.'

They stared up at the tree.

'Semal or silk cotton is called the devil tree in parts of Africa,' said Karna. 'Devil tree. They believe the spirits of the dead live in it.'

They walked around the tree. She pointed to the inscriptions in the smooth bark. RAM for Vikram. And PM, Vik's aunt, Pom.

'What's this?' Karna asked suddenly. 'There's something here.'

In one of the hollows of the tree was a bunch of crumpled papers. The sheets were old and damp with small dead cockroaches in their crevices.

'What is it?' Mia asked.

Between the damp sheets of crumpled paper was a photograph. A photograph that looked new, which had been folded several times but had still survived.

'My god,' Karna whispered. 'My god.'

'What?' Mia asked.

'Look at this photograph.'

Mia recognized Vik's mother's face. It was unmistakably Indi. The cyclonic dead eyes and the mass of grey-streaked black hair. But what had happened to her? She was bound and strapped to a bed. There were bright red circles on her cheeks. There were two hibiscus flowers behind her ears. Long black lines under her eyes. And her nightdress was torn. She looked as if she was in awful pain, her mouth open in a terrified scream.

'Jesus,' gasped Mia.

'Who is this lady?'

'It's Vik's mother.'

'The fat pig's *mother*?'

'Yes.'

'What is this photo doing here?'

'I have no idea. Vik told me that he didn't keep any photos of his mother in the house. There are no photos of anyone. Only paintings. I don't know what this photo...this...oh god...it looks as if she's been attacked...'

'Attacked?'

'This photograph…could it be? Doesn't it look like she's been beaten or something? My god, how could it have come here?'

'What an obscenity!' Karna exclaimed. 'Let's destroy the photograph and the tree. You tear up the photo. I'll destroy this immoral tree.'

'*What?* Destroy the tree?'

'Yes, let's get rid of this tree.'

'Destroy the tree? Are you crazy, Karna? What's the tree got to do with it? No, Karna, wait, I have to think about this a little. How did this photo get here? I just can't think straight any more…'

'No thinking!' he shouted. 'Action! Your husband is a fiend! He lives in this huge house and keeps pictures of his mother inside a tree. I'm surprised you haven't escaped this place. I'm surprised you haven't run away!'

Mia shut her eyes. How had this photograph of Indi appeared here? How could it have? She must call Vik and ask.

'The semal is a lovely tree, Karna,' she said in a haze of conflicting images, babbling like a baby. 'Its branches are arranged in whorls around the trunk. The red flowers will appear soon, it'll bloom in a couple of months. We can't just chop it down. What'll Vik say? What'll he think? No, this is his tree. It's very old. That's why its bark is so smooth. Vik told me. He said when it was young, its bark was covered in thorns, but as it got older it became smooth. He knows the tree so well.'

'It's ugly,' Karna's voice was distant. 'You said he doesn't like ugly things. Stupid, dumb tree. The spindly stupidity of it. It can do nothing but be a receptacle. It can't act. It has no agency. Its muteness is grotesque. All it is, all it can be, is simply outrageously beautiful. But tell me, Maya, what good is beauty, if it can't shield, if it can't nurture? The flowers of the semal are useless, good for nothing. It's unhelpful, oblivious to everything around it. Just a tall beautiful thing which doesn't help anyone.' His voice grew agitated. 'It never does anything. It just stands. It just watches. It can't do anything. It can't help. Can't help those who are in need. Beauty! What good is beauty? Why do poets say that beauty is a force of good? Beauty is a force of evil, constructed by malevolence, beauty aims to destroy goodness. Look at this tree. It's beautiful but it can't act.'

'Act?' her voice was faint, the voice of a heart patient, of a dehydrated child. 'But why should a tree act? A tree should be beautiful. No, no, it's a beautiful tree. Vik loves the semal. He says it is his childhood friend. He says it was where he used to keep letters for his father. He said his mother and he used to have a relay race between the semal and the jamun.'

And now there was a photograph in the semal which had scrunched together a whole lot of memories and became a crumpled technicolour clown-face, mocking her ability to understand anything at all.

She felt herself start to cry. Cry, because the bark of the semal was pitch dark inside, yet it was a tunnel of all kinds of life. There were glow-worms inside the tree. There were illuminated dragon masks with tongues flicking in and out. There were fathers and mothers and sons and daughters inside the tree. There was a goddess in the tree; a goddess impelling those who saw her to run to the horizons of sanity. The goddess was Indi. Indi was an evil goddess who lived in the semal tree. Heavens, she was going around the bend.

Her sobbing trailed off. Through a curtain of tears, Mia saw Karna rush around until he found the garden shed and return with a drill and chainsaw. She saw him push his glasses back and work furiously with the drill, until the semal began to shudder. It's easy to kill a tree. The sap drips like bits of human flesh, the roots are upturned like human muscle.

He tied his robes around his waist. Sweat dripped off his forehead. By sunset, the tree began to creak.

Karna shouted: 'Run!'

They ran towards the house and with a shrill, swishing sound, the semal lay face down on the lawn. The semal spread its branches as if in its death throes and Mia thought she heard it shriek. She tore up Indi's photograph and then ripped through the shreds again. The dead tree gave off one last sigh, which trailed off into a grating laugh. *They killed me, Vik,* she heard it complain. *Your wife and her lover killed me.* In the emptiness of the murdered tree, Mia sat with her lover in a depleted garden.

Karna stood staring down at her as she slumped on the grass. She couldn't see his eyes, only the reflection of Victoria Villa in his spectacles. The rich and sheltered, he said, need to feel the misery of the poor and unloved. Your husband needs to know what else is going on in the world beside his parties and his money, outside his glass cocoon. He, Karna, was here to destroy these abominations. The world is like this tree; this world in which people rush around trying to become bankers and doctors and accountants and fund managers so that the rich can become richer and find new ways of killing each other.

The best way is to uproot the tree and destroy it by its roots, he cried. That's the only way.

❦

Mia sat up all night, staring at Anand's painting, rigid with expectation. She was hurtling, like Alice in Wonderland, down a chute, into fantasia. Something was about to happen. An upheaval awaited her. She made up a story about the tree for Vik. It had been chopped down by the municipality because it was blocking electrical wires for a new building complex. Certain trees in the neighbourhood had been earmarked and it had been one of them. Mr Krishnaswamy stared askance at her the next morning and shook his head in disbelief when she told him the same story.

Vik called that afternoon from London saying he was cutting short his trip. He arrived in Victoria Villa the next day. He came back with his suitcase crammed with gifts. Chocolates, Body Shop soaps, blouses from Warehouse, Lavagulin whisky, liquorice sticks; he had called Mithu in New York to make sure she was fine and had made arrangements for the oil-paint-and-turpentine flat to be cleaned every weekend. The owner of the Eagle and Flag had promised to dispatch his cleaning lady every Saturday and had sent Mia his love. Poor girl, had she recovered yet from her father's death? Mithu and Tiger were fine in New York. And the cherry tree was fine too, bare of leaves, but alive.

As he talked, she noticed he looked preoccupied. He slumped on the bed and said he had had some bad news just as he was going in for a meeting and hadn't been able to concentrate. He had caught the next available flight back. He couldn't stay very long in Victoria Villa either. It was time for them to go to Goa. Christmas was around the corner. Illuminated paper stars would be hung up all through Alqueria and coconut trees would be wound with strands of light. It was time to go, for her to meet Indi and for him, for the final confrontation with the ruffian.

A final confrontation with the ruffian, she frowned. What happened? She heard a story she already knew. An unspeakable and weird attack, an assault whose photograph she had already seen. There were no suspects yet. Francis Xavier had been murdered so this guy would stop at nothing. His mother hadn't been able to see who it was but, obviously, it was the same guy or member of the group who had been harassing them. The police had no leads, nothing to go on except a hoarse voice.

She couldn't tell him about the photograph. It was a secret between Karna and herself. It was a secret that was the key to everything that was going to happen. She was drunk with possibility, feverish with what awaited her. She was trapped in a neurosis in which a set of events was conspiring to push her over the edge. She knew what it was. It was Anand's plan. He was the puppeteer who was controlling her destiny, bringing in this horror here and this threat there and shoving her towards the end. Her father was trying to kill her to bring her wherever he had gone. The photograph no longer existed, its physical presence was finished, it was eliminated. It had been put there to taunt her, to create a hall of mirrors in which everything was twisted out of shape. There were mysterious presences in Victoria Villa, presences waiting to trip her up, to push her into a trap. She didn't know the history here. She knew nothing. The tree knew, and had died for it. Perhaps it was best not to know and not to ask and think only of the journey ahead. She, already a prime patient of *The Drama of Depression*, was being driven mad by India. An epidemic of madness was afoot in this country where the past was a shambles but the future had not yet dawned; light had dimmed but day had not yet broken. A penumbral area of change where schizophrenia had become the national option, a country at war with itself. Vik's parties were, in fact, ceremonies of mourning; wakes held to mark the confusion, vigils to mark an endless night.

The small flutter of soul was elsewhere. It was on the banks of a faraway river among pilgrims of all faiths. It was on a pilgrimage to a spot that was millions of years old. But because it was not profitable, not dazzling enough, it was ignored and prevented from giving succour and purpose. A village fair on the banks of an old river was considered irrelevant and dirty, when, in fact, it was the key to renewal.

'Why didn't you call me, Vik?' she asked in a small voice, 'I would have gone down there. I mean with you so far away, I could have just jumped on a flight to Goa and...'

'No, no,' Vik exhaled. 'You couldn't have done anything. It's all always down to me. It's always me, the dutiful son. I'm the bugger who's going to bail her out of this one. Get the police and track this prick down. Whoever he is.'

She had already abandoned the son of a blind mother. Him, with his insulin monitor and his plans to fight a prowler. She had kissed his soft chest, killed his favourite tree and wandered far away. She was a courtesan and her thoughts were turning to her jungle man. The emperor went on loving her, stroking her face gently, but the courtesan's face was turned towards someone else waiting outside the window.

She felt an ache of love for Vik suddenly. All the gifts, the care he had always taken of her, the kindness of his regard, the constant kindness. He had made arrangements for her life, he had checked her flat, he had called her mother in America and now he was off to do his duty unknowing that she had left him months before, hating him for Moksha Herbals and for his parties. She had listened to him being abused, called a fat pig, a shallow tycoon. She felt a sob of love before she gave everything up and left him with Karna to walk the last and deadliest mile. She hadn't meant to harm him, she needed to find out why Anand had died, she needed to understand why fate was pushing her to the Kumbh.

I've never thanked you for marrying me, Vik. Never thanked you for rescuing me from Mithu and Tiger and from the loneliness of Papa's death. Never thanked you for the scores of presents and for bringing me to Karna.

'Vik,' she asked. 'How are you feeling?'

'How am I feeling?'

'Yes. You travel so much. You must be exhausted. When's your next appointment with the doctor?'

'Hey, you know' – he ducked under the bed to retrieve a shoe – 'nobody ever asks me how I am. Because I,' he grunted, 'am always fine.'

'I know that, Vik, that's why I'm asking.'

She wanted to ask if he was scared. She wanted to hold his arm and pray for his well-being, as a soldier's wife does before her husband goes off to fight. She wanted to confess to him that the apocalypse was coming, that they were tumbling headlong into an unknown axis where the world would turn upside down for a split second, but he had found his shoe and was no longer listening.

'Everybody wants Mia,' he said. 'Everybody wants my English wildflower wife. My love-in-a-mist.'

'Really?' she blinked, unnerved by how he had seemed to deduce her thoughts.

'Are you happy here?'

'Yes. Vik?'

'Yah?'

'Do you ever miss your father? Do you miss him the way I miss mine?

'My father?' He said it like a toddler at school reciting a poem entitled 'My Father'.

'Yes, d'you miss him?'

'You know,' he murmured, 'I'm glad my father died young.'

'Glad?'

There was a pause, and then Vik laughed and shrugged. 'Parents who die young do their children a favour by sparing them the humiliation of their own unravelling,' he replied. 'The glucose drip, the bedpan, better to go with all guns blazing.'

When his voice changed everytime he spoke of his father– changed from loud and hearty to a shy lisp– she had at first thought that this was the Indian way of showing respect to the dead. Or perhaps imitating the way his father had talked to him. But hearing it now, she realized that it was a pantomime act, an actor playing the part of a child, an actor performing a role about which he had no idea and it coming out all wrong on stage. He acted out the part of his father's son, as if to convince himself that he was. He was a manufactured personality. His life was a series of dramatic tableaux. He was the perfect actor. The successful businessman, the party trickster, the loving husband, all of it underwritten by a private battle with diabetes, a war with an injured acrobat.

'Am I disappointing to you?'

'Disappointing? No, why disappointing?'

'You know why,' he chuckled. 'You know very well why. You don't think I'll win, right? You don't think that I'll be able to get the better of him. You think I'll be defeated by this terrorist or this hoodlum, right? You don't think I have the strength.'

'I'm worried for you, Vik. The way you talk sometimes is frightening. You talk of killing him. But why talk of killing him? That's a joke, right?'

'Why, don't you want me to kill him?'

'Of course not! You can't.'

'I can do anything.' He held up his hand. In it was a revolver. 'Look.'

'Vik!'

'Oh, sorry,' he laughed. 'I scared you. This is just my new present to myself. I bought it from my friend before I went to London. If all else fails. If the Goan police are unable to manage it. If Justin can't manage it. If the hired hands can't manage. Then who else will it be but me? Just for self defence. Only if he attacks me. Come on,' he grabbed her arm, 'let's have some fun before we meet the criminal. I must bury this criminal forever, Mia. Otherwise, there's no knowing what he might do next. He must be destroyed. The final' – he sang – 'countdown.' He tucked the revolver away under his clothes and went in for a shower.

Mia changed into the black dress he had bought her, and sat down to wait for his welcome home party to start. She didn't care about him any more. She was on her way to a celebration of bedraggled mystics and Vik was nothing but a laughing boy, constantly hopeful of her happiness. He had been hospitable, generous. But how could he possibly comprehend Karna? He would be bewildered by him, he would wonder how the dirty drop-out could be more alluring to her, to anyone.

For this party, the guests came in masks. The runner-up came in a Catwoman mask, the wordless beauty came with a mermaid's head and the politician wore a dinosaur disguise. Mia stared at Vik in his clown mask. Perhaps he was the Henry Ford or John D Rockefeller of India. The country relied on people like him. The nation relied on him to flesh out its evolving corners.

In the midst of the party, with the curtains twitching with stolen kisses and tears of betrayal falling into the swimming pool, Karna stared out at her from the trees. He had said she was not meant to be imprisoned here. She wasn't.

⁂

That night, as she lay next to him, exhausted, wondering why he didn't have any jet lag and how he had had the energy to leap off the plane and organize another party, Vik asked, 'What will you do, my dear, if I die?'

'Die?' she whispered. 'Why do you say that?'

'What if the thug kills me?'

'Of course not,' she said firmly. 'It won't happen. You'll have the police with you.'

'Will you be sad?'

'Vik, let's not talk like this. What do you mean, sad? Of course I will be sad.'

'That's nice, my dear. I thought maybe you would just be relieved. Relieved to be rid of a frivolous tycoon. A fat pig.'

She sat bolt upright in bed. 'What did you say? *A fat pig?*'

He laughed, 'Just kidding. Just kidding, my love-in-a-mist.'

Layers of quiet stretched around the room. Victoria Villa was spooky at night, sending her mind hurtling off in all sorts of directions. A circle of anxiety formed in her stomach, drawing all her feelings into it. A man's eyes were piercing her from the semal tree. A man hung back, away from the crowd, seducing her with the promise of a Purification Journey, and handing her a pamphlet. One man had a cut on his leg, so did another man, on the same leg. Moksha Herbals, a company selling make-up to film studios.

What sort of disguises did actors require? Did they have false skin, or contact lenses or teeth that could look like someone else's? Another man was taking her to a party, but leaving her alone and going to stand under the same tree as if the tree was known to him, as if the tree was his parent. She turned in bed, to find, with a shock, that Vik was staring straight at her.

'Anything the matter?' she asked quickly.

'Don't be sad, Mia,' he whispered. 'Never be sad, okay? Promise you'll never be sad?'

'Sad, no, I'm not sad, Vik.'

'If I'm ever not here,' he whispered again. 'If I'm ever not here to protect you, you promise me you won't ever be sad?'

'Silly!' she laughed uncertainly. 'Don't be silly.'

'No, I want you to promise me, Mia. Never feel sad if I'm not around, okay? Because I'm going where I want to go. Nobody's forcing me to do anything. I'm happy to do it and I'm happy to die for what I do. I want to get rid of this ruffian forever. I have to prove that I'm stronger than he is. I have to fight him so he never rears his head again.'

'Where are you going?' she cried in a panic. 'Where?'

'Why, down the road to Moksha Herbals.'

They laughed into the darkness. There was something in his voice that she had heard before. The sheet felt cold against her thigh. Its clamminess reminded her of cold rainy days in England. Once, when it was raining hard, Anand had taken her down to the street to perform a rain dance for the slowly edging cars. In her raincoat and boots, she had jigged around, a small Good Samaritan, providing rain entertainment for the unhappy folk crawling through a mighty jam. There's that word which reminds me of the flaming

arc of a falling comet. What's the word? Ah, yes. Trajectory.
That's the word. Trajectory.

My life has taken a trajectory which I could never have
imagined.

⁂

The bleakness of the night fled with the sunlight of the
next day. In train stations all over India, a wintry dawn
brought a cup of tea and the latest chartbuster on the
radio. Vik's Azarro was all over the house; he had already
left. The jamun stood forlorn but upright. She showered,
changed into a bright skirt and blouse and waited for Karna.
He came a little later than he had promised, his eyes
twinkling, his white pyjama kurta looking freshly ironed.
He stared around the garden and grinned. 'So did you tell
him? Did you tell your husband about the photograph and
the tree?'

'No,' said Mia.

'Why? his spectacles flashed. 'Didn't he notice?'

'No,' she lied. 'There was no time, there was another
party here last night.'

Karna threw up his hands. 'I think the garden looks
much better without the tree. Much cleaner.'

'We're going to Goa. In a few weeks.'

'No, you're not, Maya. You're not going. You're coming
with me. You're not going with him.'

She didn't answer. Vik didn't deserve Karna's scorn. He
cut his leg to entertain his friends and held masked parties
but she couldn't punish him with her scorn when he loved
her so terribly.

As she looked at Karna, he seemed to fade from view.
Somebody else stood in his place. Someone who awaited
her at the Kumbh Mela. There was somebody there she

would see, she knew it. Not Karna, not the pilgrims, not her father, but somebody else altogether, distant from her life at the moment. Somebody – this person – was waiting for her. And he had always been waiting for her to come and see him. She would outwit them all. She would conspire against those conspiring against her. She would persecute all those trying to persecute her. She knew their plans. She knew everybody's plans. She was the jabbering madcap in a corner who would rise up and trap them all.

'*A heightened sense of persecution, the feeling of a uniformly hostile environment, a focus on coincidences and schemes, is another dangerous sign that the mind is breaking up into delusion and that the patient might require drugs simply to slow down the rate of thought.*'

Delhi slid into Christmas and New Year spirit. Silver ribbons formed a canopy across Khan Market. The walkway leading to Greater Kailash market was strung with coloured streamers. Roses bloomed in colonial gardens and cake shops laid out cookies, marzipan and Christmas pudding in their windows. Vik took her to see the Christmas decorations at Moksha Herbals – one of the windows decorated with lots of woolly snow and a clay Santa Claus painted with herbal colours. And then they went to sing carols during midnight mass at Sacred Heart Cathedral.

Their last night in Victoria Villa before they were to leave for Goa was New Year's eve. The Kumbh Mela was set to start in three days. Karna called Mia saying all the arrangements had been made, she was not to say a word to Vik, she was get a taxi to Pavitra Ashram on the first day of the New Year, stay there for a couple of days so Vik didn't find her, then the Brothers would give her a ticket to

Allahabad, take her to the airport and give her instructions about where to meet Karna at the festival site. Nothing to worry about, Mia had whispered back. I'll be there. I'll be there after Vik's New Year party.

On the last night of the most tumultuous year in Mia's life, there were bonfires and popcorn machines along the brick-edged flowerbeds of Victoria Villa. The twilight sky was ripe and bursting with colour like a mango split by the force of its own juice. The runner-up stalked past covered in gold glitter. The gun-trader, who declared that it was he who had given Vik the Smith & Wesson Model 640-1 revolver and that he had divorced his wordless wife, was wearing a flowing white toga and a wreath of leaves positioned on his sweating baldness. The newspaper baron wore leather trousers and sipped a whisky. A group of girls, their bodies sheathed in synthetic fire-proof gel, set themselves alight and danced with limbs aflame.

'Remember, you once said we'll have our own beautiful world?' Vik said rushing past her, his hands full of glasses. 'This is it, right? Once you see the sea, you'll see how beautiful our world is.'

'Vik, I want to tell you…'

'What, baby, what?'

'A photograph I saw… it was just like how you described the way the intruder, the prowler, no, whoever he is, a photo…'

'Yes, baby,' he turned to her smiling distractedly. 'What of the photograph? Did you find it?'

'In the tree…'

'The police sent it to me,' he said, still smiling, like synchronized swimmers whose lips are clamped in a perpetual grin as they emerge through the water. 'The police sent it to me, the servants must have crumpled it and put it in the tree. But, tell me Mia,' his smile widened, his voice turned a little shrill. 'Where is the tree?'

'Vik, I...'

Before she could tell him, the runner-up came marching through the door and fell in a straight line on the dance floor. Vik dragged her to a chair and sat her down. Her head fell forward like a doll broken at the waist. 'Can't wait for you to meet everybody, love-in-a-mist,' Vik grunted, trying to position the runner-up at a stable equilibrium. 'You'll love my mother and Justin. You'll love Alqueria.'

'You don't fool me!' the runner-up screamed suddenly from a snarling red mouth. 'I know everything about you!'

The music rose to a crescendo. Bright flowers came charging out of the darkness, touched by champagne froth. The trees were dressed up with lights as usual. All around there was the joyful noise of heartache. People began to dance and so did Mia, feeling the earth judder, watching the runner-up slide in slow motion down the chair and onto the floor like perfectly intact glass. She noticed after a while that Vik wasn't dancing any more. She would tell him. She would tell him that she wouldn't be coming with him to Alqueria. That she had somewhere else to go.

Where was he? She searched among the crowd. He was nowhere to be seen. The runner-up jumped to her feet like an electrocuted corpse and went straight to the toilet to vomit. The wordless beauty swayed from the waist like a performing king cobra.

She couldn't see him anywhere. In the living room, where he had once pranced with the bloodstained sheet, bodies sweltered under a mercilessly hot strobe while the screaming DJ barked instructions. She found him at last in the study. His grandfather's study now lined with paintings of his life.

'Vik?' She crept in.

'Yes, I'm here,' she had heard that hoarse voice somewhere before.

He sat on a chair, upright, bright-eyed and shaking with what looked like euphoria. His pupils were dilated and his hair was uncharacteristically messy. Down his shirt front was a thick ochre-coloured rivulet. Moonlight fell in stripes across his face. She recognized immediately the little pyramids of white powder on the study table and started back.

'Hello, Mia! My love-in-a-mist.'

'Vik, what are you doing here? Why are you sitting like that?'

'I'm sitting here, waiting for you. Waiting for my wife to return to me. Waiting for her to return to me from her lover. My wife who killed my favourite tree.'

'I'm sorry. I can explain.'

'Why did you cut down the tree?'

'It was blocking the sunlight from the flowerbed.'

'No,' his voice sounded rough. 'It wasn't. Why did you kill my semal tree? My semal tree which looked after me all my life? My semal tree which protected me, which cared for me?'

She was shocked. My god, had the tree really been that important? They essayed a mock question-answer session. There was a storm, she ventured. No, not convincing, he shook his head. Municipality gardeners had come in and chopped it down because it was so tall it was obstructing electricity wires, she explained. No, he shook his head again, they wouldn't have done it without permission from me. She looked straight at him. She had to get out of Victoria Villa fast.

He pointed to his chest. 'Clean it,' he ordered.

'Clean what?'

'Clean my puke. Can't you see it's all down my front?'

She stared at his pale, striped face. The vomit had spread around his mouth and up his nose and on his cheeks like gashes of beige.

She got a bucket of water and wiped his pale face and neck. She hadn't noticed how vulnerable his skin was, how slender his neck. Karna's neck was slender too, but so dark that it looked stronger. She helped him take off his shirt and led him to the sofa.

'Vikram,' she whispered as he lay back. 'Vikram, who the hell are you? Are you who you are? Or are you not?'

'I am whatever you want me to be, love-in-a-mist. Just love me this one last time.'

The impending farewell, the sudden quiet of the study after the noise of the party, drew them together. He grabbed her down with him, fumbled at her clothes, snatched away her panties and pushed himself into her with unconscious energy.

'Mia,' he whispered, 'I only want an overdose of you.'

In a few seconds Vivan yawned to life in her womb. She pushed Vik away and pulled on her clothes. She ran out of the study, leaving him asleep on the sofa, threading past the sweating bodies, bolted the door and flung herself on the bed. Her rucksack was already packed. She took Anand's painting down and slid it under the bed. In case Vik found it, god knows what he might do. She looked out of the window into the lawn. The empty space of the semal was full of voices.

At daybreak, leftovers of the party lay asleep in ones and twos on the sofas. The study door was locked. Vik was probably still asleep. She left a note on her pillow:

*'I'll be back to pick up the rest of my things. I don't
know what I'll do afterwards but I won't be coming
back here. Sorry. This should never have happened.
Love, Mia.'*

She shouldered her rucksack and ran down the driveway.
Karna was waiting for her. He had been waiting for her
ever since he had first seen her, ever since he had stepped
out of her father's painting, and had been curious to find
out whether she, of all the people in the world, would walk
with him down the last and deadliest mile.

The garden was lit with a sharp light. Cobwebs of dew
floated above the grass. The guard smiled at her. She
murmured that she was going out for a morning walk. The
veranda arches of Victoria Villa were like slanting eyes as
they watched her leave.

Goodbye, Vik.

Goodbye, Victoria Villa.

Good morning, 2001.

ALQUERIA, GOA

Now the New Year, reviving old desires, recited Justin,
staring at the sea. A year that begins with the Kumbh Mela
would end with a transition, there would be a break in the
continuum, and for him, he felt convinced there would be
release. Some kind of release. Perhaps death from this time
and rebirth into another, without the physical loss of life.
Or perhaps my heart will stop altogether after so many
decades of service to my Sara, my Isis, my Sad-Eyed Lady
of the Lowlands.

The rain in Alqueria was a wondrous creation, he
thought. Sometimes it formed gymnasts over the sea and

somersaulted over the barges like a Nadia Comaneci made
of water. Other times it sluiced through the palms.
Sometimes it became a fairy skirt spreading gently over the
old homes. There were so many different Alquerias. The
sea when it was foamy and celebratory. Pink and white
bougainvillea against the houses. Palms bending towards a
frothy wave like a sprig in a glass of Pina Colada.

A seagull circled over Indi's cottage. The sea shone
away towards the big ships. Barges pulled along slowly,
leaving eddies behind. Water, uncaring of what was
happening on the shore. Slow water, its edges diffusing away
into sunlight. Santa Ana dreamed in the reflection of the
water. Is there, thought, Justin, some ultimate squaring off?
Some way in which scores are settled? Or perhaps scores
are never settled and life just dwindles away into the sun
like the sea. He sat in Indi's locked and barred cottage,
staring at the bow and arrow painted on the wall opposite
her bed. He stared at it for a long time. Then he held his
head in his hands and wiped away tears that wouldn't stop.
He got a pail of water and a rag and began to wash off the
paint. He wiped and scrubbed until the wall was washed
clean and only faint black markings remained. Then he drew
out a crayon from his pocket and drew a giant red heart
where the bow and arrow had been.

He brought his face against the wall and kissed the
heart. 'Forgive me,' he whispered.

The child had once been swinging from a tree, when he
pitched forward and fell on the ground. 'Justin!' he had
cried, 'I is died away.'

'No, sweetheart,' Justin had laughed. 'You isn't died
away. Here you is with your dad, on his lap.'

'Dad?' the child had blinked.

'No!' Justin had shouted, 'Dada doodoo, just fooling.'

He dreamed his son was falling into a swamp but he was paralysed and couldn't help him.

He dreamed his son was being kidnapped by guerillas, spirited away through elephant grass, while his father looked away.

આ

Indi told the boy a story she had heard from north Bengal about the semal.

The semal tree is a strong tree, she told him. It bursts into thick red flowers in season. And because it's so tall, ghosts and goblins come to perch on its crown on nights of the full moon. Many years ago, inside a semal, was a palace made of wood. It belonged to a really ugly witch. She was bald, with a hooked nose and had warts on her chin.

Now the witch had a son who was her pride and joy. She loved him dearly, but he wouldn't take her anywhere because she was so ugly. Nor would he ever bring any friends home because she had no teeth and could barely talk, and she was a bit slow and couldn't cook anything nice. She was just an atrocious old witch. Whenever any children came near, the witch scared them away.

One day, the witch's son came home from school and found the door to the tree locked. He knocked. His mother emerged after a while in crumpled clothes, with leaves in her hair. But this time she no longer looked like an ugly witch – she looked like a beautiful tree nymph. 'Don't I look good?' the tree nymph asked her son.

'Oh, yes,' he smiled back at her. 'How have you become so nice?'

'Because there is a magician inside my house who makes me look very pretty. He knows many magic tricks. So now all I have to do is bring more magicians to our palace and they'll make me look nice. Then you won't be afraid to take me with you to school and you won't be scared of bringing your friends home.'

'What magician?' the boy asked. 'Where is the magician?'

The witch opened the door wide and inside stood a tall man wearing a long cloak who smiled and waved at the boy.

'See, that's the magician. Now, I'll get another magician who'll make me look nice tomorrow also, all right?'

'All right,' said the boy, happy that his mother was no longer an ugly witch. 'Can I come in now?'

'No, no, you can't come in here. You have to go to another tree. From now on you and I will live in separate trees so I can be beautiful. That's the price we'll have to pay, but in return you'll be able to show me to your friends.'

So, everyday the witch would bring home a magician and he would make the witch look nice. When the boy came home from school, he went to his own tree and in the evenings came to visit her, happy that she no longer looked ugly.

'Nice story, right?' Indi said to Vik.

'No,' he closed his eyes. 'Stupid.'

Why?' demanded Indi. 'Why is it stupid? What do you mean, stupid?'

'I mean why did she want to be beautiful, the witch?'

'It's a sort of metaphor for a better life.'

'It's not what I would call a great story,' pronounced Vik after a pause. 'Not even pass. Maybe D grade.'

'What rubbish!' shouted Indi. 'D grade! It's a great story. It's a story from Siliguri. It contains all kinds of metaphors about individual respect and individual freedom. The boy and mother both respected each other's freedom. And by doing so, they were able to improve their lives. Personal liberty is seen as the basis for community improvement.'

'Where did the boy live if the witch lived with the magician?' he interrupted.

'The boy lived in another tree,' said Indi absently. 'Because that helped the witch become better. See, he let the witch have her freedom and in return she loved him.'

'Crap!' Vik cried. 'What about the boy's freedom? Who would have freed him, if the witch was always trying to be free?'

'She was doing it so he could be happy,' explained Indi condescendingly. 'Don't you understand anything at all? It's a story of understanding between two people.'

'It's a pathetic story,' said Vik. 'You can't tell stories like these and expect me to believe them. They're so silly. You can't tell good stories. You're weak at stories.'

'What do you mean?' Indi cried. 'This is folklore with such a sophisticated message. You are such a dumb child. God knows what you'll do in life.'

'It's a bad story,' he said.

'Don't talk to me like that, you moron!' said Indi. 'You idiot! Perhaps I should get you a collection of writing from India so you can learn about all sorts of traditions of story-telling. These tales are part of your heritage, you should learn to appreciate them.'

She stalked off but he paced the floor of his room thinking of alternative endings to his story. There could be many endings and many different characters, but she had told it in such a stupid way. He became angry at her for pissing the story away.

His story would have been neater, richer and not set in a tree but in a proper house with flowers in vases and chandeliers hanging from the ceiling.

She was dirty, he thought.

Icky. Far too curvaceous for her clothes. Her tightly braided plait came undone at the end of the day. Her breasts burst out of her tight, high-necked blouses, as if she was a seal wrapped in bandages. She smelt too – a fishy smell of perfume and sweat. She never shaved her underarms and wiry hair grew out of her sleeveless nightdresses. Her nails were not filed, sometimes they were black with grime. Her feet were dirty, her heels were cracked. Her neck would be beautiful if she washed it. Maybe he should offer to help her wash her neck and while he was washing it, he would punish her for being so impure and for always making him feel he wasn't as clever as she was.

Punish her for seeking so many magicians to make her beautiful when she should have been content to remain a witch.

10

KUMBH MELA, PRAYAG

Mia entered her father's painting. The pilgrim came to the Kumbh Mela. *To my dearest little Maya, with love from Papa.*

At the gigantic festival site thousands paced the walkways and bridges across the Ganga. Some in processions, others alone, chanting and murmuring. Hundreds washed and bathed in the river like insects feeding off an avalanche of honey. Clumps of police in riot gear carrying sticks and wearing helmets stood about in case some mystics got carried away and charged at their devotees with their tridents. Pilgrims placed little offerings on the sand: frankinscence, sugar, and three blades of grass.

God and advertising were everywhere. Lurking in the lavatories and skulking in the dark tents were banners and hot air balloons announcing Pepsi and eternal peace. Kwality's ice cream came wrapped in decorated cones. Down from the mountains, up from the backwaters, out of the forests, walking out from Himalayan temples, from venerable institutions in Benares, from scholarly mathas in the Sahayadri mountains or flying out from Californian ranches, they had come, some clad in diaphanous white, some in

bright colours, some in saffron lungis, some with followers –
to live here for two months and watch the river become a
bridge between life and death.

There were rockers who sought inspiration for new
tunes, wildlife photographers seeking escape from the
traumas of the sanctuary, millionaires hoping to impress
their latest girlfriends, wellness bimbettes from Mumbai
whispering excitedly about the latest hot sadhu, and
industrialists' trophy wives padding after their yoga
instructors. There were priestly orders from the hills of the
north-east, who had handed down prayers by word of mouth,
other sects with miles of written tradition, Vaishnav singers,
Shaivite ascetics, a family of temple guardians from the
western seashore who were also environmentalists, another
temple trust working with local governments to rinse the
Ganga of the detritus of worship.

Opposite the rows of sadhus' camps, skinny, caparisoned
elephants and ragged horses were being readied for the
bath. The Nagas with their dreadlocks, superbly smeared
with ash and wearing long marigold garlands, had been
quarrelling among themselves about which order of priests
would bathe in the Ganga first. One of the more unusual
babas had the final say because his penis was bent around
a sword and there was no knowing what he would do if
enraged.

Lines of tents stretched along the river banks. Hermits
stuffed their faces in sackfuls of marijuana and emerged
groggy-eyed and detached. Entrepreneurial ascetics set up
clay collecting-pots and did brisk business telling fortunes.
Dopey-eyed sadhus with dreadlocks piled on their head
lurched by in dusty taxis.

Mia wandered along the tents to gaze at men and women
of different denominations: rich pandits sitting grandly under

glittering canopies tended by dozens of attendants offering their guru oranges and bananas on brass plates. Vedic intellectuals from Tamil Nadu, levitation artists from Birmingham, lamas who had come walking all the way from Tibet, Harvard Business School graduates who had become monks, and prophets from among the fisherfolk communities on the Andhra coast. Journalists and cameramen raced around. A naked ascetic with his penis bent around a sword was guaranteed to make the gods of the newsroom smile.

She arrived breathless at the appointed place in Sector 10; Karna emerged, dishevelled, from a tent and pulled her in. He looked calmer and happier than she had ever seen him.

'Maya,' his smile was broad. 'You came.'

✿

They spent the night in a tent on the banks of the river. At night, a procession of candles and lanterns moved along the water. A chorus of lamps and chants rose into the sky. Smoke reached out from the woodfires. She sat with Karna and a group of Naga sadhus around a dhuni. One of them, with his head piled with ashen locks, reached out and drank from a steel bucket brimful with transparent liquid. Mia peered into the bucket.

'Don't worry, Madam,' he smiled, 'it's not anything bad. It's only ghee...'

'Oh,' she laughed. 'Sorry.'

'You look confused,' he said.

'No,' she shook her head. 'Interested.'

On the flats by the river, she lay stiffly next to Karna in her sleeping bag. Mithu and Tiger were a million miles away. She had no claims there any more. She had lost everything. She had lost her London marriage. She had lost Vik. All she had was Karna.

'Tomorrow is the holy bath,' he whispered. 'After the bath you'll see what you were meant to see.'

'See what?'

'You'll see.'

By the time she woke, he had gone. It was not yet dawn. She raced along towards the river for her plunge into the water. The sand was grey and wet. The Ganga looked discoloured, rippling like a long, sleeping beast under the clouds. Thousands had gathered and lamps, torches and candles flickered against the faces of the crowds.

There was a rush to find a corner of emptiness on the banks. To fill a swiftly closing vacuum with one's shivering body before other bodies rushed into the flesh-enclosed space, arms upraised, clothes billowing, the muddy river slipping between their toes, dripping underwear running drops down the leg and onto other people's feet. An arm on a shoulder blade, thighs against waist, faces close and smelling of the last meal; the private processes of undressing, there in the open, for all to see.

In the suffocating press of bodies her toes darted out in imaginary circles, trying to create space for the body to expand and take in air. Elbows came up against children and the elderly, crushed flowers and sand squelched underfoot.

The pilgrims came on. Trailing their old and young. Flower-sellers sat along the paths marked out by bamboo barricades. The moon still stormed in the clouds overhead, but the night was patient and suspenseful. Dawn would bring the first communion of pilgrim and water.

Mia felt her heart grow still and become enveloped by silence. Among the walking thousands, a quietness came to her like an answer. She was alone, under the sprouting galaxy. Nothing could be more ordinary or so familiar. This was a spreading realization from the stomach: that the universe was just an arena of vast commonsense. God was natural and ordinary. There were no final arrivals or final departures. Death was nothing but an ordinary turn of the head in another direction. The end or the abyss was spectacularly safe, it was crowded, it was cosy. There was nothing to fear.

Madness drained away, leaving her limp. She was many different people living at the same time. What was there to fear? If one of her existences died out, another would live somewhere else in another space and time. She was an old lady, a young girl, an old man, she was everyone and everyone was her.

And death? Simply walking along a highway and turning down a familiar alley. That was all there was to it.

She was in a protected place.

God was irrelevant here, belief or unbelief didn't matter. What mattered was this, this human crowd, reaching upwards into a greying sky, lifting off into a greater understanding of themselves for a few seconds. This grave, serious crowd, not celebratory, not festive, yet dignified with tragedy and forgiveness, was whatever god was. In the embrace of this crowd, for thousands of years, at this very spot, lay the realization that death was the safest thing on earth.

The sky began to lighten, making the moon look overdressed against its muteness. Mia was like the sky. Observant, thoughtful, Mia, until recently driven mad by circumstance, was a sweep of fast-drying paint.

The sadhus and high priests in their decorated chariots rolled along their designated avenues. The crowd swelled to immense proportions as the first pink shards pierced the sky like bright stuffing oozing from a dull pillow. The scholarly orders had been allotted first place in the order of the bath and portly crowned priests sitting fatly under glittering umbrellas and being fanned by devotees on elephants and cow-drawn carts approached the river. Their followers pranced ahead of them, clearing the way among the pilgrims walked along on either side.

This was their moment, this sheepish moment. The spectacle they had helped to create. The water was meaningless in itself. It was they, the pilgrims, who raised it to godliness. No wonder they looked on at the river with possessive pride.

The pressure of the crowd was overpowering. Everywhere she looked a surging tide of heads and bodies pulsated together. The fog was beginning to skirt cunningly around the boats, profiles and crowns formed in the clouds. Light from sulphur lamps was vanquished by the first rays.

She took a deep breath and began to run. She pushed through the bodies, pushed against a solid wall of people that didn't seem to give an inch. Near her ankles, a child and its mother sat, eating and changing at the same time. A set of heads crushed against her stomach. She pushed with all her might and felt the sand grit against her toes.

Suddenly a small whirlpool of bathers gathered behind her. There was a circling and murmuring and they began to spread out in concentric circles towards the water. She bounced between them like a broken asteroid in the solar system, hurtling from one group of people to the next, and found herself at last on the banks of the river. In a crowd of at least a hundred, she leapt into what felt like a square centimetre of unoccupied water.

The water was freezing. She felt suddenly cold and then began to shiver. She felt crowded in on herself, palms pointing inwards at a gaping open mouth. She felt her legs curl under her in the bejewelled water. She bent into it feeling marigolds in her hair, flecks of incense in the crevices of her neck, a floating nail near her lips.

'Mia!' She heard a familiar voice.

Standing next to her in the water was her stepfather, Tiger, recently shifted to New York.

'Tiger? Tiger! My god, what are you doing here?'

'Hallo darling! Surprised, eh? Now tell me how could I miss the Kumbh Mela? Couldn't miss it for the world! Isn't it fab? Look at you. You look very nice. Thin, but nice. Better to be thin, after marriage, eh?'

'Is Ma here too?'

'Oh, no. Left your mother behind in America. She's scared of crowds. But she wanted me to come, particularly because Vik was so insistent and told us you were going to be here. And because of Anand's painting. So peaceful... ahhhhh.'

'How did you know I was going to be here, Tiger?' she asked again slowly.

'Vik told us. Isn't he here with you? He said he would be. He told us to meet you here.'

'Vik? Vik told you?'

'Yes, sweetheart. He said we would all meet here. He called about a week ago. You see,' Tiger chuckled, 'a couple of months before he met you, before he came to the Belsize Park flat, I had shown him your photograph. You know, just to make sure he would like you. And I told him how sad you had become after your father had died and he seemed to be really taken up with that because he said he hadn't recovered from his father's death, either. He said he knew you were right for him when he heard how you had wept for Anand. Then I took him back to the flat and showed him your dad's painting. Just to make sure he understood you properly. Anand's painting, you know, the one you had up on your wall? You know, the painting which you loved? The Kumbh Mela painting? I took him up to your room and I showed it to him. And he said it was such a coincidence that the Kumbh Mela was just a year away. That's when we made the plan to come here. So, ever since then, he has told me that we would all come and meet here. Cute, eh? Didn't he tell you about the plan, darling?'

Vik had decided to marry her because they had dead fathers in common. He had seen Karna in the painting. And he had become the bearded close-up. No wonder he looked so different from the other Brothers of the Purification Journey. No wonder they were all clean shaven and Vik was the only one with the thick beard and long hair. Moksha Herbals, with access to one of the best make-up range in the world. His make-up room was state-of-the-art. The make-up room with the murals of gods painted on the walls. Good over evil, weren't those the stories he liked best? He knew how to create good drama. He had created the perfect alibi in an outrageous plot. The skin dyed black. The eyes darkened with contact lenses. The beard and hair, so bushy and unruly, added next, taking care to always remain at a distance, never get close. The voice, affected through the back of the throat, made Karna's sound husky and Vik's loud and high-pitched. The portraits of his mother, whose existence had deprived him of his manliness and his sanity. The chemical smell of make-up, of dye, of foundation, of false skin and glue. Dustin Hoffman in *Tootsie* must have smelled similarly when his make-over transmogrified his persona.

Oh, Vik. The holy war against oneself. Wasn't that the true definition of jihad, of the Mahabharata, of the eternal struggle within? The war inside the self?

He hated himself above all.

Why had Karna cut down the semal tree? Because Vik hated it. Why was Vik a party animal? Because Karna was a renunciant. He wanted to be sympathetic, to love, to take care of his blind mother. Instead, he had put on a false beard and white robes to take revenge for being less clever, less beautiful and less accomplished than her. No wonder she had mistaken Karna for Justin.

Vik was Justin's son. His unclaimed, unacknowledged son. Indi had conquered Justin by damning his fatherhood into irrelevance. His trips, once to Berlin, then to London. In London, both Vik and Karna were gone together, that must have been the time of the 'mission'. The party trick about virgin blood, it was a trick that would befit any member of the Purification Journey who detested women. The Pure Love of the Mother Woman was surely the opposite of the egoism of Indi.

Poor Vik. Poor Vik with his insulin pump hoping to please his wife who was obsessed with her father's painting. Poor Vik, gazing quietly at her infatuation with Karna and thinking he was unworthy of pure love. He had always been unworthy of being loved the way he was.

He had once made Victoria Villa pretty for Indi too. She was careless with details of home decoration. But Vik would always make sure that the lawn was well trimmed and the flowers planted in season. He would light a lamp in his grandfather's study. He would hang up a garland of mango leaves above the front door. In between volumes of dusty books, Vik would place a vase of flowers.

He had wanted Mia to be pure. He had treasured her in so many ways. He had treasured her when he was Vik. And he had loved her when he was Karna. He had loved her from opposite sides. He had met her in the city centre on the banks of a lily lake. He had married her with a bow and arrow strapped to his back and played Cupid in bringing her to her lover. He had killed the tree which knew his secret. He had brought her to the Kumbh Mela so that she might understand his sorrow and banish her own madness.

He had nothing to do with the Purification Journey, she saw it all clearly now. He had only identified with the monks and travelled with them briefly because their ideology appealed to him. But he was not part of Sanatkumara's Brotherhood. He had only used them as an alibi, he was a rogue lone agent, no wonder Sanatkumara had no idea who he was and no wonder Karna had stayed away from Pavitra Ashram. It was a plot, an elaborate charade.

She saw him standing far way in the water, next to a pilgrim, surrounded by floating marigolds. She saw him without his disguise, without his false hair, beard or glasses. She saw that his skin was pink. The make-up studio at Moksha Herbals had served him well. That make-up room decorated with gods and demons with the half-man, half-lion dismembering an evil king.

He was looking at her in a mocking, half-smile, as if to say that he had succeeded, after all, in winning her love. That he, the emperor with the soft pale body was also her roaring jungle mystic. He got out of the water and walked up to her.

'Vik,' she whispered. 'Vik...'

'Yes,' he whispered back. 'It's me. Fooled you completely, baby. I told you, you would see something in the Kumbh Mela. This is what your father wanted you to see, Mia / Maya. This is what he wanted you to see. Wanted you to see how wrong a painting can be.'

'I've also been blind, Vik,' she pleaded. 'Don't do it. You don't have to. I'm here. I'll always love you. Don't do it.'

'But,' he beamed at her, 'it's too late now. I'm too far
down the road. Besides, they're waiting for me, you see. I
must go. Wait for me, Mia. Wait for me. Wait for me on
the other side of the river, once the ruffian is dead forever.
You said you would walk the last and deadliest mile with
me, didn't you? Remember, you said you would walk with
me down the last and deadliest mile? I'll be waiting for you
in Paradise.'

'But why, Vik? Let's run away together. Let's go away.
Please, let's go away.'

'No, I have to kill the terrorist, remember? I have to
eliminate him so he doesn't hurt and harm anyone any more.
He is a curse, Maya. He is a curse who has to be finished.'

'Vik, why?'

'All I really wanted,' he shrugged, 'was to love and receive
love, in the best purest form available. That's all I ever
wanted.'

'Wait...'

He smiled and turned away. She pushed blindly through
the crowd towards him. Tiger followed at her heels. But
there were too many people between them. She thought she
saw him dive into the water. She pushed on towards the
banks. If she didn't get to him fast enough, she knew she
would never see him again.

'No, Vik! Please! Come back.'

By the time she struggled through the crowded water
and got to the river bank, Vik had gone.

'Where's that other man?' she shouted to a nearby
pilgrim. 'Where did he go?'

'He's gone,' said the pilgrim.

'Where?'

'Chala gaya bechara,' the pilgrim pointed towards the
gate. 'Away from the river.'

'Tiger!' Mia turned desperate eyes to Tiger. 'I must find him. I must find Vik. He's about to do something terrible.'

'What' – Tiger shook his head confusedly – 'terrible? *What* terrible?'

'Please help me find him,' Mia cried, her eyes liquid and huge with tears.

'Of course, definitely, darling, my god, what is this mess, meri bachchi!' Tiger looked bewildered. 'Just call him from my phone quickly. Quickly.'

'Vik?' asked Mia on his mobile telephone, 'Vik, it's you, isn't it? You are Karna.'

'Yup,' his voice was cheerful. 'Sorry, baby. I'm afraid it is me.'

'Oh god, how could I not have known? How could I not have known! My god, Vik, it's you!'

'Wait for me, Maya. We're going to have a long and happy life together. It won't be on earth but in a place more pure and perfect. You know, when I went to Alqueria, I realized that I saw you everywhere. I was – I am – so enchanted by you. I want to love you in the best possible way. I want to love you in the purest way, not in the impure way of Justin and his woman. The war must be fought. The war with one's worse nature. The constant war within, remember what the Brothers said? The war between good and evil contained in one body?'

'Vik...'

'Being born is like dying, Maya. It is dying, which is like being born. Your father knew that. I know it too.'

'Wait, please wait. Let me talk to you one last time.'

But he had disconnected.

'No, please!' she sobbed out loud. 'Please come back. Please let me see you again.'

Tears came faster down her cheeks than the water of the Ganga. She had to go to back to Victoria Villa and wait for him there. No, she had to go to the ashram and find out what he planned to do. But they wouldn't know anything. What should she do?

Sweat ran off her forehead. She felt feverish and the dust made her eyes water. The walkways and pontoon bridges were throbbing with thousands of soft footfalls. Buntings fluttered in the breeze, strung over the camps and along electric wires. Clusters of loudspeakers bloomed on electric poles, belting out announcements of lost widows and children.

She ran through the Mela, her mind split in many directions. She was looking for her lover. She was looking for her husband. She grew bigger than her father's painting. She tossed Anand aside. Anand had wanted her to visit the Kumbh so she would rid herself of her dependence on him, free herself from her father and realize how partial his vision had been. He had tired of her, had been exhausted by her dependence. To acquire one's own vision was the greatest gift. Not vision that was bottled and canned and purchased for a price. Without one's own true vision one may as well be blind. As blind as the British were about a country they ruled. As blind as Indi was about her son. Anand had removed himself from her life so she would no longer remain blind.

She heard a prayer from one of the pilgrims: *I am the ever-shining unborn, one alone, imperishable, stainless, all-pervading and non-dual – that am I, and I am forever released.*

'What does this mean?' she asked him, clutching his arm. 'What's this prayer?'

'Non-duality,' he replied. 'All in the end is One. Him. The Brahman. In the end there is only One. It is the philosophy of Advaita.'

ALQUERIA, GOA

That night, a man in a white shirt walked calmly up the zigzag in Alqueria. He carried his Smith & Wesson in his hand and strapped to his back was a quiver of arrows. He walked past Indi's abandoned cottage, towards Sharkey's Hotel. Tears gathered in his eyes and trickled into his beard. He was a half-man, inadequate, humiliated by her imposing brilliance. He was the perpetual also-ran, the number two, the ignored one, cast aside, never able to win his father's love.

She was always number one. She was the primary force in the world. Always contemptuous of him. Contemptuous that he wasn't clever enough, contemptuous of his business, his silly little make-up shop, his ridiculous parties. She, Magsaysay award winner and civil servant, had done real work. She had built roads and bridges and carried war widows to safety. She had started schools, she had moved a prime minister. What had he done? Sold lipstick to Bollywood. Sold eyeliner to The Body Shop.

He was only a little decoration. A mere paper flag flying on an impressive edifice constructed by her; flimsy compared to her granite achievement.

Her unseeing presence was suffocating. He had not been able to breathe. Her beauty, the absurdly perfect, sensuous beauty that crushed all opposition; that had turned his father into a spineless worm.

She was so tall, just a few inches shorter than his six feet. She had never soothed his inferiority.

Nor had his father.

Instead, they had both recoiled from his insufficiency, recoiled in revulsion. Preferring to live in their own world, far away from the unchangeable fact of his own mediocrity. The love that they shared was so formidable, so perfect, so majestic, that it was only the ultimate act by him that could defeat it.

A final heroic flourish that would reduce a lifetime's commitment to nothing but a silly teenage crush.

It was late. The police detachment posted at Sharkey's was snoring on the beach. He knew all the hotel fuse-boxes well and set all the wires alight. He had been to Alqueria so many times as Karna. He had snarled up the computer system, flung the dead rats in, put a bullet through Francis Xavier and dressed his mother up in bed with hibiscus flowers in her hair.

The wires began to burn – blue tongues of flames snickering along the walls. He stood back, framed by the fire like a thoughtful Jesus and felt gratified at how easily a fire could begin if it was started right. How obedient a fire was. It did exactly what you wanted it to; it was a mistake to think that a fire was uncontrollable. In fact, a fire required nurturing, guidance and hard work. It pulled itself back constantly and had to be gently pushed along to its full potential. Flames began to snake up towards the rooms and the sleeping guests began to stir with the smell of smoke.

The police were still sound asleep on the beach; snoring off their beer and toddy. He shouted upwards into the sky. Shouted out his creed: the world was becoming value-less, pornographic, the female ego was ruining the planet. His shouts grew louder and louder until the waiters who were sleeping in the kitchen woke up, saw the fire, shook the police awake and telephoned Justin in St Theresa's Hospital.

By now Sharkey's Hotel was roaring with fire. Some of the residents of the upper floor were already charred. Others had begun to jump out from the windows, throwing their children onto the beach. Screams and wails filled the air as villagers came shrieking up and Father Rudy rushed down from Santa Ana still in his pyjamas. Holding Indi's hand, Justin walked slowly forward. Hot black fumes from the kitchen went spiralling up the banyan. Karna's shirt billowed in the breeze.

On his back was his quiver of arrows and a bow strapped across his chest.

'Who are you?' Indi shouted. 'What do you want?'

'Close down this hotel!' Karna shouted. 'This hotel is a crime against the Almighty Presence!'

She had recognized her Phantom Listener a long time ago. Ever since the attack on her in her cottage, she had known, but not admitted to herself because she could not accept it. She knew that he had passed into a realm she had no idea of, that she could not only not see, but not even understand. I know who you are, her heart spoke. I've always known. I'm your enemy. I, in my huge noisy existence, I who will never be pure. You will set up pure enclaves for me, but I will come flying at you with my impure body and laugh at you.

Justin walked towards him. 'Come here,' his voice was calm. 'Come, we can talk. Come.'

'Get out!' Karna screamed. 'The whole place is on fire. Can't you hear the people burn? Don't try to save it or you'll die.'

Justin stared at his dark mirror image. Here was his son whichever way you looked at it. The same height, the same hair, the same beard and the same eyes. In his disguise, (too stated and explicit) he was identical to his father. A childish voice clamoured loud and clear in his inner ear:

Justin! Justin, Indi's lover! Why did you choose her and not me? Why did you love her so much that you had nothing left for me?

'Don't misunderstand me,' shouted Justin in his stomach. 'You belong to a world far bigger than the one you imagine.

I cared and loved you as much as I could, with the leftovers of my selfish love for your mother. But I taught you to look for meaning in the hollows of a silk cotton tree. To me, that was enough.'

'You are corrupting this village!' shouted Karna. 'You should know that there are people who oppose you. That you can't do as you want and get away with it all the time. You have obscene values!'

'It is you who is obscene!' shouted Indi. 'It is you who has corrupted religion and turned his back on god.'

'Shut up!' Karna shouted back.

'Leave us alone!' cried Justin. 'We're not trying to destroy anything. Leave us in peace!'

'You are evil!' Karna shouted again. 'You are violating the laws of the Almighty Presence.'

'Evil?' Indi drew herself up and flung the words at him. 'How dare you, Vikram? Come on now, pull yourself together, you little idiot. Enough is enough.'

Her condescension infuriated him, as it always had. He became enraged that she dared to claim the authority of motherhood. He screamed. The scream was so high-pitched that the abolim flowers in the village courtyards flew into the air.

Once, on a dark night, when Justin had walked the Victoria Villa lawn with Vik on his shoulder, he had pointed towards Orion in the sky. See, he had pointed. That's Orion, the hunter. Orion is brave and strong and that's how you must be.

Karna raced towards the restaurant. Indi blundered towards the sound of his voice, her cane swinging ahead.

'Vikram!' Indi shouted, her voice cracking, 'I know it's you. You killed Francis Xavier! There are people dead,

burned beyond recognition, because of your hate. Listen to
me! Listen to me! We can talk! We can negotiate! I know
it's you! I've known for a long time. Stop now! Stop where
you are!'

'You?' his voice took on its usual politeness when he
addressed her. 'Who are you to talk to me? I don't even
know your name. I never have!'

By now the police were pushing their way towards the
burning hotel. A few guests staggered out, their clothes in
flames, as villagers rushed to wrap their burning bodies in
blankets. Children with sooty faces wandered crying through
the smoke.

'Indi!' shouted Justin. 'Come away from him. Come
away.'

She turned her face towards the strongest smell of fire.
Then threw away her cane and ran, arms outstretched,
towards the smell and the sound of Karna's voice. As she
came blundering at him, he took aim with his revolver but
hesitated for a moment. True to family tradition, where his
mother stood, he saw the Four-Armed-One. In place of
Indi, he saw the same ancestress of death who had visited
every member of his family – including his grandfather
Ashish Kumar – when death was imminent. There she was,
two arms akimbo, two others raised above his head. A
woman with long black hair and his mother's sea-storm
eyes. She crossed and uncrossed her arms. She smiled but
she had come for him. She had come to carry him back to
the ocean. The family curse was upon him.

'How dare you bring me into this world,' he shouted in
his heart, 'and make me wait for you? Make me become
your sidekick, your also-ran because I wasn't as clever as
you, as blind as you or as beautiful as you? But now I'm
ahead of you because my life is a one-way ticket to Paradise.

In Paradise I will reign as a conqueror of death itself. My cause will remain, my crusade against women like you will go down in the annals of history. I will win the last and holiest war by being dead and leaving you to mop up my remains. I will fight in two realms, my spirit will tower over the earth, unforgettably and my cause against you, against your ego will be imbued with a nobility and a magnificence that will endure for centuries.'

He hesitated, transfixed by his vision.

She came lurching towards the direction of his voice with a long scream, lunging at him to try and pull him away from the fire. But it was too late. The revolver flashed and he fell back into the door of the restaurant which had become an open mouth of pure fire.

Sharkey's Hotel was smoking from the roof and walls like an illuminated gas chamber. She heard the gunshot; she felt the warm flare of the flames as they fed on his body. She knew immediately what had happened. As District Magistrate in Siliguri, she had once given shoot-at-sight orders to quell a lynch mob that had gathered around a house. Fugitives had cowered inside, while outside, bloodthirsty faces had bobbed up and down brandishing knives and axes. She remembered clearly the face of the ringleader, his eyes wide open, yet somehow calm, as he strode around with his chest thrust forward as hysterical laughter boiled in his throat, daring the police to fire at him. She had jumped off the jeep – how clearly she had seen the road ahead at that time – and faced him. He had taunted her, daring her to act, even made a lunge for her chest... a skinny boy from his group had suddenly dashed at the policemen waiting behind and thrown a knife into a policeman's belly. Indi had raised her hand in command shouting at him to stop but the ringleader ignored her. He had walked straight into a hail of bullets. He had made no attempt to run, had made no attempt to save himself; he had walked into the line of fire like a bride walking up to the altar, as if summoned at last to receive the prize he had always craved. He had been killed almost immediately, the mob had melted away, leaving her to gaze on the fallen young body, his pockets bulging with ammunition.

Why had he not run, she had wondered later. Why had he thrown his life away, that strapping youth blessed with good looks, an education – indeed with everything that others would have cherished? He had walked to his death in a swagger of bravado, daring others to follow, a final act of masculine potency, a shot perhaps at world conquest. His expression when he died had been one of dull accomplishment, the weary responsibility of a completed task, like a CEO satisfied with his balance sheet.

She had read of the death cults through history that had spurred young men to glorious suicide rather than banal surrender to humdrum circumstance. The kamikaze pilots of Japan, the samurai before them, sanctioned to sacrifice their lives if they had been humiliated or dishonoured. Death was heroic; light as a feather. Honourable manhood rising in a giant wall of steel before the mere bullets of everyday existence.

Perhaps the ringleader's mission had been to die like a hero before a woman, so that his death would tower over her even though his body crumpled at her feet.

She had not regretted the command to open fire. A law and order problem had been confronted and dealt with in the best possible manner. Best was the wrong word. The situation had been dealt with in the only manner that was possible. When a civil servant gives orders for the police to fire, she makes a tryst with death. She knows that sons and brothers will be torn away from their families by her act. But she stands, in that instance, for progress, for rationality, for the reasonable way forward. She must turn her back on death cults and calls to suicide. Because there are rules on which democratic societies are based and those rules must be followed, however glorious or heroic it may be to disobey or to rebel.

Yet, in this case, unlike in the case of the rioters, she had played a part in the creation of the problem. She had been the reason for the problem itself, not, as in Siliguri, the bringer of a solution.

Her son had chosen death as his ultimate weapon against her – against she who had given him life.

She had resented him for feeding off her body. She wished she could have devised some way by which foetuses were able to be self-sufficient, living off some science-created uterus she would have had to have nothing to do with. And after he was born, he had demanded things from her that she simply could not – would not – give, because she had instead demanded the freedom not to be his mother.

She had always envied him his energy; she imagined his limbs as skinny, whiplash, so unlike her own soft curves. After he was born, she felt her breasts become ungainly rocks that dragged her chest down to her navel.

She had tried to outdo her son in lightness. He whistled past her in the garden, sturdy and alert, while she lumbered tiredly behind him, imagining the smelly fluids of childbirth still trickling from her vagina. He seemed to her to be as fresh and as energetic as the incoming tide, always dashing back for a new charge at the beach. After his birth, Indi had starved herself to malnourished thinness and tried to run as fast as him. When he beat her effortlessly in the races they had in the Victoria Villa garden she would go back to her room and stare at the stretch lines around her stomach. The terrible fear of being outdone had created sharp lines around her mouth. Her silky hair coarsened with anxiety.

In the curve of his adolescent cheek, Indi had sensed a frightening resoluteness. She hated his falsetto baby voice and told him so. She hated his thin wrists and told him to cover them up. As he grew into a young boy she told him terrifying ghost stories. His grandmother's ghost still haunted the garden, she told him, so he must never go out to play at night. Some afternoons, he would lie in bed listening to the call of his dead grandmother. One afternoon, he thought he heard a voice that sounded exactly like Indi's throaty tone. 'Come,' the voice called, 'my little son, come.' He had shut his ears. If he answered, he feared she would eat him up.

She detested his diabetes and dealt with it contemptuously, demanding instead that he attend to her own, much more serious, handicap. She would leave bottles of jam open on the table to tempt him into sugar, but he would close the lids tightly and arrange them away neatly. She forced him into adult companionship, laughing and joking about things he didn't understand. She brushed off his wounds which healed only after many weeks, mocking his babyish tones and insisting that he stop being a child.

He grew used to hearing her lovers' light footsteps. Used to hearing soft steps climb up the iron ladder to the roof in the dead of night. And the shadows that slunk out later. Sometimes, before he went to sleep, Indi would sing, 'Sleep my little baby one' but if he tried to snuggle closer, she would brush him off and quickly switch from lullaby to a thumping film song, impatient with his desire for love.

She would walk under the semal tree, thinking of the tasks she would have to accomplish the next day. She wouldn't be able to see that he was lying in bed and gazing at the blue night light watching it turn into the eye of a serpent.

She ran about with him under the shadows of the trees. She played with him on a see-saw. She took photos of him, telling him he was all she had. She pranced about and sang out loud but he terrified her. He reminded her of burnt palms and dead husbands. Of widows who didn't get invited to their sisters' weddings. Of fathers who never forgave their daughters even on their deathbed. Every time he smiled she became determined to defeat him.

Perhaps all mothers are secretly jealous of their sons. Jealous that they are like waves that break on the shore and then dash around again for another charge at the beach. Sons were luckier, superior beings. No suspicion and hostility greeted his skip and jump on the street. No one would look askance if he flung his head in the air and laughed. Everybody would smile along, happy to be caught up in his joy. Sons were lithe jaguars; mothers were blind and slow, they were cow elephants.

They had both sprung from the same Four-Armed-One. Between mother and son, there had always been an equally matched war. She would always come flying at her adversary with her impure heart to defend herself and her chosen task, her own work and the path she believed was good true and moral, the nation-building tasks, the law and order tasks, however lowly or dirty he may call her, however loudly he may call her a whore, she would press ahead.

No Purification Journey would ever defeat Indi.

※

His resolve had been as strong as hers, although it was directed in the opposite direction. Indi had fought for life,

Vik had chosen death as the only achievement that would match his mother. His death would haunt her, would drive Justin to his own, his death would take away her beauty and send Justin weeping to his grave.

※

The fire engines arrived. One of the firemen came panting through the smoke, hoisted Indi onto his shoulders and staggered back towards the beach. Water came bursting through the pipes. Greyness and transparency merged. Liquid pursued vapour. Father Rudy sat Indi down on the beach. Villagers, models, taichi instructors and druggies stood in a trembling semi-circle around Sharkey's, now reduced to a smoking shell.

The firemen found the body and brought it to Indi. She heard Justin behind her, crying as if his heart was being wrenched from his body. She sat with her son's body on the beach, upright, quite calm, as if she was a magistrate listening to public complaints. She ran her hands along what remained of his face. Of course it was him. Of course it was the boy who had once lived with her. She would recognize him anywhere, because she had been aware of him every day of her life. A frightening stranger? Not really. Nothing but that silly child, running around in a costume. He had become a menace, an antisocial element, a criminal the papers would have called him, and she had struck out, as she always had, for the good of the public, whom she had always held as her most important responsibility. He had not known how to cure himself and he would have harmed others if she had not stopped him. It had been her duty to stop him.

'This is a terrible tragedy for us all,' Indi told them in her clear, ringing voice. Her voice was devoid of all sorrow or remorse. Instead it was a voice which was confident, as if it had only been confirmed to her once again, how savage the world was and how lucky she was not to be able to see it. The villagers formed a circle around her and prayed and wept, as Indi announced, 'The madness of the world infected him too much.'

'God help us,' sobbed Father Rudy.

'All the families of the dead will receive whatever assistance   possible,' declared Indi in her civil-servant voice. 'Our country is young and these are the pangs of growth. But he is gone and the threat is nullified, the danger is neutralized.'

She turned to Vik again and drew his charred body onto her lap. She kissed his face, his chest and his legs. She pressed his arms. The first time he wore a vest, I laughed and said he musn't wear them because they made him look more puny. When the hair started to grow on his back and shoulders, it was so blond, like Justin's, all the hair on his body was blond, then slowly it began to turn darker. Then he went off and did some exercises so his shoulders would become broader and his hips narrower just like Justin's. And they did. My last vision of him was of a tall and handsome man. Don't I know every part of him? Didn't I carry him in my body for nine months?

Yes, I know every bit of him but I lost him along the way.

It's funny between mothers and sons, isn't it, sobbed the villagers. How they kiss and cuddle and whisper sweet nothings after death. Who knows why she had hated him so, why he had reminded her of her father, of all men, except the one who had wanted to save her. She was like Aditi, mother of the gods, who buried her son Martanda alive. But Martanda defeated her, he survived and emerged from the earth to taunt her.

The worst type of woman is the one defined by her children. It's the easy way out. To pretend one's achieved something just because one has popped a few pups.

❦

What had she lived for?

She had lived, she realized, not for Justin, but for her country. She had always acted in the common interest. She had been imbued with dreams of the country, been touched by a prime minister whose name she bore, been moved by speeches she read about young civil servants who could change the way things were. As she raged and fumed at her blindness, her work had become her only sanity. Her work and Justin had saved her and kept her thinking always of the unfinished task, the larger purpose, the goal ahead. Even though her world had closed up after that hot afternoon in a hospital when she knew her son had already died, she had lived with the knowledge that, like Othello the moor of Venice, she had done the state some service.

She had existed, she had worked, she had poured herself into the public and her monuments would remain. At every forum to which she had ever been invited, at the Magsaysay Award ceremony, at the seminars she had attended, she had never tired of her plans for the people. She had spoken about the irrelevance of theory, the need only for action and more action, to serve, to build, to defend this country, to embrace its poorest citizen and live up to a dream of bringing welfare and voting rights to those whose lives were no better than dogs and cats. She had been called every name in the book: irascible, intolerant, scandalous. Her cigarettes, her illegitimate child, her shattered family. Yet her work had acquired an incandescence that few others had achieved. Her dedication had inspired; her stern backbone, her inflexible incorruptibility in a service riddled with money-takers, would be remembered. Yes, all this would be remembered, thought Indi, beyond the gory present, the blood and ash of my revenge on the world, beyond the destroyed hotel and the dead body, beyond all this, there would be that small service, my service that would be remembered.

At long last, after a lifetime's struggle, Indi became thankful for her blindness. Her blindness was not a curse, it was a sacred place to which she had undertaken a lifelong pilgrimage. How peaceful was the darkness that blocked out the ugliness of this world. For the first time in her life, she felt relieved that she would never be able to see it anymore. She was relieved and thankful that she couldn't see. She sank into blessed blackness like an exhausted marathon runner sinks into deep sleep.

There had been quite a few casualties in the fire. A handful of guests had been able to jump out of the window and save themselves. They laid the bodies on the beach. Indi sat among them staring expressionlessly into the sea. Justin, no longer able to stand on his feet, sobbed like a child in Father Rudy's arms. Father Rudy said he would take all the ashes and immerse them at the Kumbh Mela so at least their souls would be at peace.

᠅

In the sky, as if in response to the shocking developments on earth, an aeroplane suddenly exploded. South Wind Airways flight SW 448 from Delhi to Goa, became the victim of a suicide bomber's dress rehearsal. One of the passengers pulled a toggle strapped to his chest and the plane broke apart and crashed into the Alqueria bay.

That night Alqueria was surrounded by fire. In the water the crashed plane. On land Sharkey's Hotel in flames. In Alqueria, of all places, where peace had lived for centuries. The rockers froze in mid-smoke. The bells in Santa Ana forgot to ring. And Father Rudy sank to his knees wondering where god was.

The divers from the navy who dived into the sea to search for the dead bodies, found all the dead passengers except one. All the bodies were recovered. Except one.

'We are calling to tell you, Madam' – South Wind Airways told Mia, after tracing her mobile number from the address on Vik's ticket– 'your husband's name is in the passenger manifest, Madam, yes, his name is on the passenger list but we regret to tell you that we are still unable to find his body. It's very puzzling, Madam. Because we've found all the other bodies. Your husband's body is the only one that we are unable to trace. We are still searching. Our records tell us that no boarding card was issued to him, so it is possible he never boarded the plane. Perhaps he never boarded the plane after all?' Of course Vik never boarded the plane. He had never intended to. He had bought a ticket and put his name on the passenger list only to prove that he hadn't been in Alqueria when 'Karna' took his own life. To his business associates, his employees, his buyers and suppliers, Vik would just have gone missing; it would be Karna who would have completed his suicide attack on Sharkey's Hotel.

Perhaps giving birth is indeed dealing out a certain kind of death, thought Father Rudy.

Perhaps the act of creation carries within it the act of destruction.

And only a mother knows this secret.

Deep underwater, the debris of the burnt plane drifted to the seabed. It looked like a convent in the ocean. With nuns floating like underwater weeds.

11

LONDON

The oil-paint-and-turpentine flat was tinged with dawn when Mia came back to London. She opened the door and windows to let in the sun. The cherry tree leant gently against her bedroom and she heard church bells far away.

Time slowed down. She projected herself on the wall where Anand's painting used to be. Time took her backwards into herself. Time jumped up and dragged her forward, towards the next twenty years. She and her child bending together over a lily lake. She and her child thirty years later. She at his school. At his wedding. At the birth of his children.

'Do you want to keep staying on here, Goldie?' Mithu whispered. 'Why back here to this awful place?

'I'll be fine. Don't worry about me, Ma.'

This flat is my festival and every street corner is a pilgrimage and every chance acquaintance on an elevator is a sage. I chased after a mystic and I found that he was none other than my businessman husband. I ran to the holy festival to see things, but the festival only sent me home, giving me the answers to my father's death.

What airy-fairy castles we construct on this mundane earth.

I charged after a sadhu, who, I thought, encapsulated everything fantastic and mystical and found he was none other than a corporate executive in drag. I was like the English colonialists in India, like the orientalists from Edward Said. I indulged my fantasies, without bothering to unmask the single human being under the differences of costume. The ash-smeared, naked priest is an executive on his day off. The snake-charmer with the swaying cobra is simply a travelling salesman providing an ordinary service. The owner of an international business can easily double as a spiritualist.

The Kumbh Mela is not about naked ascetics doing bizarre things with their bodies, but grandmothers and grandsons keeping family traditions alive. That's all there is to it. I was naïve, no different from the others who had visited India in the last two centuries, and whose skin colour was many shades lighter than mine. Memsahibs who had been swept off their feet by enigmatic preachers and mystics, sahibs from London who had mistaken simple poverty for pagan ritual. The Dark Man from the east, playing Aziz to my Adele. My false assumption of two realities, of two Indias, Vik's India and Karna's, of the shallow life of parties and the deeper meaning of life revealed, Vik, the corporate guerilla and Karna – what had she called him – 'touched by an extraordinary current of air', all in the end, one.

I am the ever-shining unborn, one alone...non dual, that am I.

Oneness as an ideal, oneness at the heart of the variety of the Kumbh, all individuals, all opposites, denominations, all faiths, all sects of the world, yet arching over it: the great human canon, belonging to no civilization and belonging to all, the One Being standing alone in the wayside shrines manifested in innumerable folk saints across the globe, in tiny shared spaces of memories and rituals, in churches, in mosques, in synagogues in temples, all streams ending in the great one shared revelation.

I'm the pilgrim of the One. Orient versus Occident, West versus East, all petty wars ending in a final crowded march to the One. The opposition between believers and doubters is nonsense because each exists because of the other. The miracle is that we don't have to choose, we are not compelled to choose, yet we believe we must make that choice between belief and rationality.

Between Papa's way and mine.

Vik tried to keep my dreams alive, tried to give me a reality I could believe in; he created something for my schoolgirl innocence. But he knew that somewhere his energy would give, he wouldn't have the strength to keep it up for too long and faded away exhausted by the daily effort of stoking my romantic yearnings.

He had grown up alone, wandered here and there, becoming many different people. He had met mendicants, businessmen, officers and thugs. He had explored worldviews, learnt about the creation of personas, learnt the secrets of marriage and the techniques of make-up. The Purification Journey had taught him well. He had learnt to speak with genuine belief. Or perhaps he had actually believed in the words. The businessman/prophet with the perfect dialogue for each identity. Emperor Jehangir, always Akbar's weaker son, the effete beautiful son, the luxury-loving cruel son of the great parent. An emperor weakened by sentimentality, shackled by need, while the parent soared like Everest because she had no need for anyone or anything but her own actions.

Furious that he could not pull himself back from the brink, that he slid into evil madness when he could easily

have crawled out of the quicksand and been strong enough
to forgive and grow taller than his memories. Why could he
not have tamed himself? He, so successful, so at ease, his
life so full, could he not have reined in his perversion?
But, perhaps, he too was possessed of the same demon as
Indi, the demon that urges destruction, a demon that lived
in that silk cotton tree. The power, the indelible mark
upon the memory, one's continuation branded onto
another's; the final victory embedded in the act of taking
one's own life.

⚜

How my daughter has changed, thought Mithu. She seems
to have become taller. Her hair has grown long, her
shoulders are broader, her bosom is fuller, her eyes have
lost their confusion.

Mia's gaze had become direct and calm. The nervous,
brittle girl was gone. In her place stood a woman who was
confident about her choices. *The Drama of Depression* was
put away in the bookshelf. She no longer talked of Anand's
death. She gave his Kumbh Mela painting to the Tate Modern
to be stared at by students and tourists, for them to be
taken where it had led her. The painting was a gateway, a
riddle, a clue to opening a secret door. The Kumbh Mela
was not just a celebration of nakedness or a hashish heaven.
It was about failure. About learning to accept failure. The
naked ascetic in all his rejection of politenesses, norms,
correct paths forward through life. The naked sadhu is a
monumental failure. A failure at life. He goes backwards
instead of forwards. He is naked because he doesn't fear
being ridiculed. But there's hope for a world that permits
such failures to celebrate their existence.

There is hope.

'My poor fatherless Goldie!' cried Mithu. 'Newly married and now a widow! A child widow with a child.' Mithu shook her head, 'Who would have thought such a fine young man would turn out to be a horror? And all the while I thought he was a decent businessman from a very upper class family! *Hé bhogoban*...and that mother of his...the blind one, she sounds like a witch!'

'I don't think so,' Mia shook her head. 'I don't think so.'

'Not a witch?' Mithu frowned. 'What then, haan, then what?'

There had been a sparrow's nest in the cherry tree once when she was very young. But one night there was a terrible storm and the chicks had fallen out and died. The mother bird, whom Mia had seen every day, painstakingly building the nest and then brooding over the eggs for weeks, had suddenly disappeared. She never came back. Perhaps the mother bird had just not wanted to grieve. Mia had scooped up the little fuzzy bodies in newspaper and buried them next to the tree. Mia said, almost to herself, 'I guess Indi just concentrated on a single thing at a time.'

'I never heard of such goings-on in my day. Thank god all my family is far away from that horrible land! It's obviously going to the dogs.'

Mithu sped into the kitchen and spent the next two days cooking a multi-course meal for the neighbours and told Tiger that although Mia had at last shed her father fixation, she hoped she wouldn't give birth to the possessed child from *The Exorcist*.

A letter arrived by courier for Mia. It was from Sanatkumara. She realized the reason Sanatkumara hadn't recognized the name Karna that day in London. He hadn't recognized the name because instead of Karna she should have been asking for Vik.

Bless you Sister Mia,

We have learnt of this news and we are all shocked. Shocked beyond belief. Vikram was such a wonderful person. We met him about ten years ago in New Delhi. He came to our ashram and said he had heard of the Purification Journey and wanted to join us because he agreed with our cause, our cause of fighting the Inner War and of fighting to create the Pure Love of the Mother Woman.

He offered us a substantial sum of money and as a charity working for a better world, we thought no ill of accepting his generous offer. He said our aims suited him very well.

His involvement with us was top secret, he was never a formal part of our group. He performed his own actions. Kept going away for what he called his 'mission'. Sister, we never asked any questions. To some extent we were silenced, I must confess, by the funds he made available to us.

Sister Mia, you must believe me when I say that we had no idea of his motives. We are basically a global philanthropic body, nor did we know anything about his family. We tried to ask about his life, but he evaded answers and we let be thinking we would give him time. But in many ways he was strange. Sometimes he threw such tantrums. At other times he was charming, so generous, as I mentioned saying, with money.

When he went away for the last time, saying he was on the last stages of his mission, we didn't know what it was. None of us did. You must believe us. We had no idea of this mission, we thought he was talking about his business. We have wept about those innocent people killed in the fire at Sharkey's Hotel, we have prayed for many nights for Vikram.

What we do know is that he really truly loved you. We met him in London. By then he had put on some funny false beard and hair and told us it was a game he was playing with you. We did not ask questions. But we realized he adored you. He told us that you were the love of his life, you were innocent and trusting, and that you should find a world that didn't ever make you cynical. He fell in love with you the minute he saw your picture in London and when he heard of the sad loss of your father.

After he saw your father's painting, he changed his dress. That is when he acquired that beard from somewhere. Of course, as you know we have our white uniform. But he said for some personal reason he wanted to disguise himself and wear the bow and arrow. He said he had a mission, he was on a path of spiritual awakening, and so we agreed. To some extent we were swayed also by the generosity of his donation, who wouldn't be?

He later confessed that he had dressed himself up into a character from your father's painting! He said you and he were meant to be together because of your dead fathers.

Dead fathers united you.

Sister Mia, how can I express my shock and sorrow? Our ways are totally non-violent and we cannot even conceive of something like this. Some of our Brothers are still in a state of shock.

Do come and visit us at the Pavitra Ashram whenever you want, Sister. You will be blessed by the way of Pure Love and a Pure Way Of Life. Come and help us in the coming war.

The Almighty Presence bless you, Sister,
Sanatkumara.

On September 11, while the world watched television, Vivan
was born. He had his mother's penetrating gaze. He had his
grandfather's blond hair, his father's athletic body and his
grandmother's wraparound, oceanic eyes.

'What a beautiful baby boy!' shouted Tiger. 'And he's
a Virgo!'

'Goldie!' – Mithu's smile next to Tiger's – 'Your little
prince has come.'

The doctors confessed that they had been worried.
For a few seconds during the Caearean section, Mia's blood
pressure had plummeted and she had almost stopped
breathing. But, miraculously, her life had returned as
suddenly as it had ebbed. As she felt herself being pulled
upwards towards the surface of consciousness, Mia knew
that it was Vik whom she had seen in the darkness below
when her breath had almost given out. Vik had been
standing very still wearing Karna's white clothes and hair,
looking at her with serious eyes. I could not understand
myself, his eyes seemed to say, as if in answer to her
question. I hated Karna and I hated Vik. Why was I, the
practitioner of Pure Love, incapable of compassion? I had
the words, the speeches, the beliefs; everything except the
feeling. Why could I not care for and sympathize with a
blind woman, a handicapped victim who needed nothing
but my protection and support? Instead, her blindness was
her power, her weapon against me, her war with the world.
I had to obliterate the demon that would have done her
more harm. Can you and my son still love me, he seemed
to plead. Me, the sinful murderer, me, dead on arrival,
with my brochure of purity, yet too timid, too fearful, to
love?

I can never forgive you for what you did, she answered him, but I can love you for giving me my vision.

In the tumult over the next year, the wars and lost lives, Mia took over the reins of Moksha Herbals. On the long lonely evenings she spent mastering the business, feeling a control and calm she had not felt before, her thoughts would often turn to Indi. They had never met and were completely unalike – she compliant and fearful, Indi defiant and fearsome – yet, how deeply their actions had resonated in each other's lives. Like Karna to Vik, Indi was her polar opposite, her dark self: all pervasive, non-dual. *That am I*, thought Mia, and *I am forever released.*

After a long correspondence with Indi, Mia decided to sell Victoria Villa and use the money to rebuild Sharkey's.

Mia would stay somewhere else during her trips to India, and was glad for the opportunity to travel up and down at least twice a year.

She repaired the oil-paint-and-turpentine flat; papering the walls so that the damp faces disappeared. She spread out bright cushions on the floor and rang up all her old friends, including Sudden. In place of her father's painting, Mia put up a photograph of Vik, neat and normal in his ironed shirt and bright tie, so Vivan would see his father as he would want to be seen.

The city became hers again. People cheered when she went back to the Eagle And Flag and her friends held a welcome home party for her.

The city was hers, even though she had tried to run away. Hyde Park was reassuringly familiar and the tourists in Speaker's Corner she could see were clustering around another group of fervent speakers – only now they were ringed around with police. The city had called her back and pleaded with her to discover its flawed love.

ALQUERIA, GOA

The sun began to set in Alqueria. Set to the tune of a thousand emails darting across the world. The emails had been going around thick and fast. What times we are living through. First the horrible attack on America. Then the equally horrible attack on Afghanistan and now god knows which other country they'll attack next. The events in Alqueria had been equally frightening, said the Sydney Alquerians, who still talked about the Sharkey's Hotel fire and the plane crash.

The Californian Alquerians all sent messages to Indi about Justin and expressed their gratification that Justin was buried in Alqueria.

Justin had not survived the sight of his son's death. Speechless and trembling, he had gone without food and water for days; had defied even Indi when she sat pleading by his bed. He died within a month, carried away to Orion, still holding Indi's hand as he fell back on his pillow vowing he would watch over her from wherever he was. On his gravestone, at Indi's wish, they had chiselled a prancing horse.

Father Rudy whispered a story to his congregation. On nights of the full moon, the ghost of Dom Fernando, a Portuguese nobleman in the fifteenth century, comes to sit by Justin's grave in sympathy, to compare Justin's plight with his own lovesickness for a local beauty named Mogarem. Dom Fernando tells Justin that great empires remain strong because in their interstices exist small relationships of transcendent love.

Indi was unrecognizable. She was scrawny, bent almost double, and her hair had turned completely grey. The aquiline nose and arched eyebrows were smudged with blotches of veins. Her body had shrunk to a raisin-like miniature and her face was furrowed with deep lines. Dressed in a plain grey sari, only a breath of beauty remained in the occasional flash of her sea-squall eyes. She lived in Justin's rooms in St Theresa's Hospital and a day and night nurse took care of her.

I have sunk, pleasantly, into the nastiness of old age. The body and mind decay and become selfish, leaving me to care only about small comforts, so that death, when it comes, will be a release from my perpetually shrinking universe. She read about the World Trade Center attacks, then the tragedies in Afghanistan. Young men pushed towards all manner of unimaginable acts. She read about the leader of the group of suicide terrorists. She would like to meet his mother; they could compare notes on their sons.

She fancifully thought of herself as an Empire in which Vik had been a freedom fighter, a fighter for his liberty against a blind, brutally beautiful Empire that had pushed a young man to his death. She was an unbearably successful force, an excluding, dazzling, cruel and pulverizing presence bearing down on him, creating in him an urge to grow bigger, to tower over her somehow or the other, to protect his honour and his manhood as an escape from her prodigious force.

Alqueria saved Indi from bitterness. Whenever she felt tributaries of tears race down her cheeks, the sea breeze

dried them and carried them off to the distant steamers.
The air filled with song. Songs from the fisherwomen who
sat with their prawns and mussels by the roadside. Music
from the mandolin players on the beach. And music from
the choir of Santa Ana.

Alqueria was not rich. The houses were mossy. The
wooden carvings on the verandas were termite-ridden and
the zigzag was marked with pot-holes. But during feast days
when the village homes were en fete and the face of Santa
Ana was reflected in the sea, Alqueria became the pinnacle
of the world.

At last she accepted her blindness; her lifelong pilgrimage
to darkness had been completed. The pilgrimage had been
a bloody one but had brought her unfailingly to the doorstep
of her destined shrine. People make too much of a fuss
about seeing. See this. See that. See this painting. Take a
photograph. Make a video. Vision is a highly overrated virtue
and much of this world's ugliness is best left unseen. In her
dark temple, Indi found the gods of Alqueria. The fisherfolk
looked nondescript but they weren't. The cosmos slowed
down around them. If they wanted to, they could have pulled
the moon down and dragged it up in their fishing nets. They
could have reached up and pushed away a rogue cloud left
over from the monsoon. All existence ran through the people
of Alqueria because they lived so close to the sea.

When the creature was taken out, she whispered to the
lagoon, taken out of my body, spattered with my blood,
spattered with my peaceful singing companionship, it was
out and gone. I tried to build bridges but by nightfall the
constructions between me and the child disappeared because
he held his nose every time he saw me. I couldn't see him
but I knew he was holding his nose, as if I was the source
of some polluted smell. When the mother mountain produces

a herb, the fisherwomen sang, she lets it go away from her to far-off lands to heal the sick. When the mother ocean produces a pearl, she has no idea whose neck it will eventually adorn. When a mother gives birth, she doesn't know into which undiscovered country her child will lead her.

Indi sat by the lagoon, with her face turned towards the sun, the smell of the ash from Sharkey's still wafting in the overhanging palms.

***

Off the Panjim bus, came two figures, lit by sunlight. A young woman with a little boy in her arms, the sea reflected in the woman's eyes. Indi had no idea they were there but she sensed their footfalls.

A straight-backed woman with a rucksack on her shoulders, a mop of curls framing her face, held the boy close to her and came towards Indi down the zigzag.

A woman and her son.

Indi and Vik.

'Indi,' Father Rudy's voice shouted down the red dust hill from the courtyard of Santa Ana, 'I'm sending one of the nurses down. Hold her hand and come up slowly to the road, dear. Careful, now, careful.'

The bells of Santa Ana began to ring. From the bay came the friendly honk of a barge.

Acknowledgments

Thanks to Bhaskar Ghose and Ranjana Sengupta, stern critics and tireless readers of every draft. Also to Leela Gandhi and Radha Mohan. And to Ravi Singh at Penguin. GS Ghurye's *Indian Sadhus* remains a comprehensive account of the Hindu religious orders.

Sarvepalli Radhakrishnan's *The Principal Upanisads* was invaluable. Thanks to Dilip and Nandini Sardesai for introducing me to Goa; Maria and Alban Couto for giving me the benefit of their insight and wisdom.

Sanjay Hazarika (St Stephen's 1983-1986) wrote a poem that has stayed with me and which I have taken the liberty of quoting. And thanks most of all to Nandita Aggarwal for being friend and editor.

About the author

About the book

Read on

Insights,
Interviews
& More ...

Meet Sagarika Ghose

SAGARIKA GHOSE was born in New Delhi on November 8, 1964. She is an only child. Her father, Bhaskar Ghose, was in the Indian Administrative Service for the Indian civil service; her mother, Chitra, worked in the advertising industry. Sagarika was educated in Loreto House Kolkata, then Loreto Convent, Delhi, and Delhi Public School, Delhi.

She graduated in history with honors from St. Stephen's College in Delhi in 1986 and was awarded a Rhodes Scholarship to Oxford University, England. At Oxford, she read modern history at Magdalen College and received a master of philosophy degree in International Relations from St. Antony's College.

66 Sagarika graduated in history with honors from St. Stephen's College in Delhi in 1986 and was awarded a Rhodes Scholarship to Oxford University, England. 99

She returned to India in 1991 to join the *Times of India* as an assistant editor. At the *Times*, she traveled to Sri Lanka, Bhutan, Nepal, and Pakistan, reporting extensively from the ground as well as writing lead articles on the editorial page.

At this time (1994) she married her Oxford friend and companion Rajdeep Sardesai (son of former Test cricketer Dilip Sardesai), who was also working at the *Times of India* in Mumbai. Rajdeep has since gone on to become India's leading journalist and television anchorman, after moving to television in 1994 and becoming extremely popular for his hard news reportage and political insight.

Sagarika's parents divorced in 1998. Her father remarried the renowned Bharatanatyam dancer Alarmel Valli and now divides his time between Delhi and Chennai. Sagarika's mother lives in New Delhi. Perhaps the biggest tragedy in Sagarika's life occurred at this time. Her beloved idealistic cousin Sanjoy was abducted by militants in India's North East, never to return. Sanjoy's disappearance was a terrible blow to Sagarika's entire family, a wound which is still raw.

After four years at the *Times of India*, Sagarika joined the start-up magazine *Outlook*, where she became a senior special correspondent. At *Outlook*, Sagarika reported on a wide range of topics, from election coverage and ▶

Meet Sagarika Ghose *(continued)*

development stories to accounts of social change and trends in urban culture. She became known for her unusual and witty writing style and a quirky sense of humor.

She was also recognized for her depth of vision and intelligent views. While working for *Outlook*, Rajdeep and Sagarika had two children, a son, Ishan (born February 1995), and a daughter, Tarini (born January 1997). In 1999, Sagarika's first novel, *The Gin Drinkers*, was published by HarperCollins India and by De Gues in the Netherlands. The book received critical acclaim and became a bestseller in India and the Netherlands.

At the end of 2001, Sagarika moved to the *Indian Express* newspaper as senior editor. Once again she reported and traveled on her trademark beat of politics and social change. She reported on elections, religious communities, and social trends. She reported on the first run of the train journey between India and Pakistan, the Samjhauta Express. Her lead editorial articles at the *Indian Express* became very popular and she was awarded the Media Achiever of the Year by the Federation of Indian Chambers and Commerce and Industry award.

In 2002, she was selected by the British Broadcasting Corporation (BBC) to be anchorwoman of the

66 She became known for her unusual and witty writing style and a quirky sense of humor. 99

flagship BBC program *Question Time India*. In 2006, her second novel, *Blind Faith*, was published by HarperCollins India.

In 2005, Rajdeep left his eleven-year-long tenure at New Delhi Television to set up another television company with his partners, named Global Broadcast News (GBN). GBN launched a new news and current affairs channel, named CNN-IBN. Sagarika joined CNN-IBN as a founder employee and as senior editor and anchorwoman.

CNN-IBN is a co-branded relationship between the US network CNN and IBN, the channel owned by GBN. Rajdeep is the channel's editor in chief, and in the short space of two years, CNN-IBN has become the number one news and current affairs channel in India, winning a number of awards and cementing Rajdeep's reputation as India's star journalist. Sagarika's work has been equally well regarded and her flagship show, *Face the Nation*, has won acclaim for its passion and intensity.

Today, Rajdeep and Sagarika live in New Delhi with their children. Sagarika runs the special features news team at CNN-IBN, a team that has won several prestigious awards and been recognized for its original and hard-hitting stories and grassroots reportage. Sagarika has ▶

Meet Sagarika Ghose *(continued)*

become a well-known face on the channel; her writings, in the *Hindustan Times* and on her blog, continue to attract both devoted admirers and fierce critics. ∾

A Conversation with Sagarika Ghose

Are there any specific events or people that have had a special role in informing the content of your novel? If so, how did those experiences affect the ways in which you address gender in your book?

Blind Faith was written in the year 2001, the year of the Maha Kumbh Mela (January) and the 9/11 attack in New York (September). Both events shaped my writing of the novel and I have focused on an emotional and spiritual journey of a woman as well as trying to understand why a young man may be driven to an act of unimaginable violence. In that sense, *Blind Faith* is not a woman's novel; it is as much about a man, Vikram and "Karna," as it is about Mia and Indi. It is about lonely, vulnerable Mia and her pilgrimage to the Kumbh Mela. It is about the dazzling Indi and her pilgrimage to peace. And it is about the pilgrimage of Vik and Karna to their own macabre and violent destiny. It is also about Justin and his pilgrimage to love. The male protagonist in the book, I believe, is just as strong as the woman. The entire book, in fact, rests on relationships. I have tried to build in a metaphysical undertow in the book, as I wrote it after reading Radhakrishnan's *The Principal* ▸

> 66 The male protagonist in the book, I believe, is just as strong as the woman. 99

A Conversation with Sagarika Ghose
(*continued*)

Upanishads as well as the Advaita Philosophy of Sankara. The metaphysical undertow rests on the principle of "nonduality" or advaita. Is truth ultimately nondual?

Have you written yourself into the novel? In other words, have you undergone a similar spiritual journey to that of Mia?

The lead protagonist, Mia, is similar to me in many ways. She, too, is a journalist imprisoned perhaps in the cage of words and images. When her father suddenly dies, she undertakes a journey in her father's footsteps to try and discover what other realities she was missing out on. Perhaps there was something her father had been trying to tell her; perhaps travel, a sense of discovery, a sense of the unknowable had been denied to her all this time. Mia's journey in the book is in many ways similar to a journey that I made when I went to cover the Maha Kumbh Mela for *Outlook* magazine. I approached the Kumbh Mela as a skeptic, as a rationalist, and as a secular nonbeliever. I came away from the Kumbh Mela with a profound sense of the extraordinary and with a palpable sense of the unknowable. I believe this was a gift given to me at that particular time and place and I wanted to share this experience with readers. It sounds corny when I say it like this, all so-called religious experiences have been reduced to such a joke in our so-called modern experience, but through *Blind Faith* I have tried to communicate the "revelation" that I experienced on the banks of the Kumbh Mela. Yes, me, totally cut off from religion, scornful of the beads and baubles of prayer, dismissive of all things to do with faith; for me the Kumbh Mela was a turning point in my relationship with myself and my awareness of a different reality than the one I live in. And this is the "revelation" that I wanted to share, this is the journey of Mia that I wanted to describe in the book.

Do you enjoy exploring masculinity and femininity equally in your characters? What do you gain by probing the topic of gender?

Vikram and Karna are equally powerful protagonists in the book, and it is through this male character that I explore the notion of nonduality. I don't want to give the ending away, but after 9/11, I, like many others, did become fascinated by the mind of the terrorist, the mind of the suicide bomber, and the mind of a young man who believes that there is glory in ▶

66 For me the Kumbh Mela was a turning point in my relationship with myself and my awareness of a different reality than the one I live in. 99

death. Is life on earth mediocre and dull, is it only through death that true manhood can be attained? And what happens when masculinity is threatened by a powerful woman, what happens when the male comes up against a woman or a life force that threatens to overpower him? Is the solution, then, just mutual annihilation? Vik's relationship with Indi is a struggle of mutual egos, poised perhaps for mutual destruction. To be a little fanciful, a bit perhaps like the relationship between America and her enemies!

Indi is such a strong character. What do you think are the main characteristics that comprise her sense of fortitude?

I have cast the character of the beautiful Indi as the enemy of patriarchy. She is blind, she is willful, she is beautiful, and she is not terribly nice. Indi, in my opinion, blazes like a 100-watt bulb among the other characters. I have made Indi a victim as well as an oppressor, I have made her beautiful as well as brutal, and I have made her successful as well as a failure as a mother. Indi rejects motherhood, she forges a professional life for herself, she is loved to death by her lover, Justin, but in the end perhaps invites tragedy by her own "blindness" to others. She is

> 66 I have made Indi a victim as well as an oppressor, I have made her beautiful as well as brutal, and I have made her successful as well as a failure as a mother. 99

not compassionate because she bears a grudge against the world, she is unable to be selfless as society expects women to be, she is incapable of the sweet quiet virtues that women are supposed to have; instead she is brazen and brilliant and selfish, and thus, in the world in which she lives, she is doomed to disaster.

How do you use your characters to explore Hinduism? Are they at all reflections of the state in which you see your faith, or are they just characters who happen to share the same religion as you?

I explore the principle of nonduality through Vikram and Karna, and also through Mia and Indi. Are we all aspects of each other? Are certain characters simply the other halves of other characters that make up the entire nondual consciousness? Once again I know I'm sounding hopelessly corny and like a dharma bum or all those things but I do think that my religion, that Hinduism, has been so terribly bastardized by the West and ruined by the hippies. After *Blind Faith* I have reached a space in my life where I seek a lot of solace from the religion of my ancestors; I can appreciate the symbols it contains and I have realized how desperately Hinduism needs to ►

> " [M]y religion . . . has been so terribly bastardized by the West and ruined by the hippies. "

A Conversation with Sagarika Ghose
(continued)

reform and change itself if it is to
survive as a vital life force. I believe
that unless we reform religion, unless
religion becomes a vital powerful moral
force in people's lives, India will remain
trapped in the stale jargon of Left
elitism and the hideous aberrations
of Hindutva fundamentalism. The
small flutter of the Indian soul will be
extinguished if Hinduism is allowed to
fall into the hands of politicians or be
scorned by rootless cosmopolitans.

*Is there anything that is particularly
important about your novel that Western
readers may not have picked up on?*

I must also mention the place of Goa
in my book. In *Blind Faith* I have
used Goa as a metaphor for religious
coexistence. As you know, I am a
daughter-in-law of Goa. My husband's
family comes from Goa and I go there
regularly. Goa is full of so many
different gods. Gods prance in the
shadow of humans. God is everywhere
and yet it is a deep countryside full
of peace, because Gods exist there in
all their plurality and their variety
and nobody treads on anyone's toes.
Beautiful tranquil Goa, I believe, is one
of the world's ancestors; for lessons in
true secularism and true pluralism, we
must look to Goa. ॐ

Author's Picks
Indian Literature

IF YOU ENJOYED *Blind Faith* and would like to read more great works of Indian literature, consider these titles, recommended by Sagarika Ghose.

1. *Devdas*
   by Sarat Chandra Chatterjee
2. *The Crooked Line* (as well as her short story "Lihaaf-the Quilt") by Ismat Chugtai
3. *Nashtanir* (*The Broken Nest*) and *Ghare Baire* (*The Home and the World*) by Rabindranath Tagore
4. *Cold Meat* by Saadat Hasan Manto
5. *The Second Wife* by Premchand-Nirmala
6. *Midnight's Children* by Salman Rushdie
7. *The Shadow Lines* by Amitav Ghosh
8. *The God of Small Things* by Arundhati Roy
9. *English, August* by Upamanyu Chatterjee
10. *Essence of Camphor* by Naiyer Masud

Web Detective

FOR MORE INFORMATION on the Kumbh
Mela, check out these websites:

http://www.kumbhamela.net/
http://www.divinerevelation.org/
    KumbhMela.html
http://en.wikipedia.org/wiki/
    Kumbh_Mela
http://www.kmp2001.com/

For more information on Goa, India,
check out these websites:

http://www.goainformation.org/html/
http://goacentral.com/
http://www.goacom.com/
http://www.lonelyplanet.com/
    worldguide/destinations/asia/
    india/goa

Don't miss the next
book by your favorite
author. Sign up now for
AuthorTracker by visiting
www.AuthorTracker.com.